# The House Near Fallowfield

# By James Fillmore

i

This novel couldn't have been written without the patient and loving help of my dear wife, Ana. All my thanks and love to my loving friend, my beautiful wife for all your invaluable suggestions and for rescuing me from so many pitfalls. How much we enjoyed working together.

# Table of Contents

# THE HOUSE NEAR FALLOWFIELD

Book cover by @ana.fillmore
©Ana Fillmore

# Chapter One

A big house on the corner. An elaborate garden, full of secret paths and artificial ponds. That is what she always remembered. And behind the house, fields and a hill leading down to the river. She used to play there with her friends. After the war and in the early fifties. And now it was empty. And it belonged to her.

She had never expected to be so alone. Twenty-four years old, a widow after only three years of marriage and now this. She was still living in the rented house she had shared with her husband in Des Moines when she received the call with the news of the car accident. Dead on impact. They were almost sixty and she had been counting on her parents for another ten years at least. Now she had nobody, only the house and a generous pension from her husband's insurance company.

It was December, 1964 and she was in the north of England. What a contrast with Iowa, now full of snow and ice. Green grass. Roses in the front garden. No heating in the house though. She always remembered that. She went in and turned on the little electric fire in her mother's lounge.

The house was just as it had been left. She went into the kitchen, made some tea, took some biscuits and sat again in the freezing living room in front of the little heater.

Not for the first time she regretted not having any siblings, not as playmates now, but to share her grief, her loneliness. She didn't even have to look for a job. House, income, but no family. Did she even have any friends left? She had kept in contact with so few. She never wrote letters.

There was a knock on the door. Two men, one with a camera.

'Oh. Good morning. Mrs. Blakeley?'

'Yes?'

'We're from the Evening News. Heard you'd just arrived in England and we were wondering if we could write a short article about you and your impressions.'

'Well it's not really a good time. I've only just arrived and my parents' funeral is tomorrow morning.'

'A few words about your father, Professor Cooper. He's a national hero, you know.'

'Well I'd hardly say that. Why don't you come in a moment.'

She led them into her mother's lounge. They sat down without taking off their coats.

'Very sorry about your loss, Mrs. Blakeley. Your father was about to retire, wasn't he?'

'I don't know. The truth is I never knew very much about his work. I know he wanted to join the navy when war was declared and he was retained for essential research. He was a scientist and he continued working in the same government laboratory after the war finished. What he did there was also a mystery to us. He never spoke much about his work. If that's why you came I won't be able to help you much. They came to visit about a year ago. Before my husband died. To Iowa.'

After a month working in Virginia, she could have said, but did not. Her father never liked them talking about his work. He used to get nervous.

'Could we take some photographs?'

'No, I've only just arrived. I'd rather not. Haven't had time to tidy up.'

'I meant the garden.'

'The garden? Why?'

'Your parents' garden was famous for its exotic plants. Didn't you know?'

Another family secret, she supposed. She led them out to the side door through the kitchen, where she remained.

They did not come back into the house, but said good bye at the kitchen door, as they hastily made their way to the car parked in the road.

Within short walking distance of the house, there was a shopping district known as the Village. An hour later she was walking around. Little had changed. She went into a pub, ordered a gin and tonic, sat at a table and lit a cigarette.

It was early, only half past twelve and the lunchtime business had only just begun. But, almost immediately, a young man sat down at the same table with a jug of beer.

'Are you American?'

3

'What makes you think that?'

'Well you have an American accent, you're smoking an American cigarette and there's a label on your handbag that says New York. Elementary, my dear Watson.'

'It isn't an American accent. I never fooled anyone in Iowa. They used to think I was German. Until the Beatles, and then they thought I was from Liverpool'

'So, you have come from America?'

'I lived there three years. I came back last night.'

'Like it better here?'

'It's a long story and rather personal.'

She got up.

'Oh, wouldn't you like another drink?'

'No, thanks. I'm meeting someone. Good bye.'

She bought some things in the Village and went back to the house. Made a frugal lunch, turned on the television, as she would have done in Iowa, hoping to see an old sitcom or movie and found nothing but a test card and some music. She finished her sandwich and fell asleep on the sofa.

It was dark and very cold when a noise at the door woke her up. She turned on the light and went into the hall. The evening paper. She opened it. She saw her photo on the second page. Only a brief paragraph. Her name and details of the accident in which her parents had been killed. The photo was old and there wasn't anything about the garden.

She began the days early remembering how as a girl she used to tramp the fields with her friends. She walked down the hill to the river, crossed a bridge and continued to a village on the other side. She wasn't alone. It was a Sunday morning and there were quite a few walkers, many with dogs. The green vegetation and smell of the damp filled her with nostalgia.

Another smell, of burning coal, very pungent, brought back memories of an English childhood. She felt happy and carefree. And then suddenly this turned into alarm.

Someone was following her.

She couldn't say when she had first noticed. The man was some distance away and could not really be perceived as an immediate threat but he stopped when she stopped, walked when she began walking and he never took his eyes off her.

She continued behind a small group of two men, three women and a pair of big dogs which ran to and fro, chasing playfully after each other. She felt safe and quickly reached the village. By now the lunchtime drinkers were in the pubs.

One pub caught her eye. The Old Cock. Obviously from a century gone by, low ceilings, timber beams. You could almost feel the ghosts around you, she thought. She ordered a gin and tonic from the barmaid, sat at a table and lit a cigarette from a packet, taking care to cover the name of the brand with her hand. She would soon have to buy English cigarettes.

She looked up and saw that the man had walked into the pub. Not young, maybe about her father's age, she imagined. Not English looking at all. She fancied he had seen her through the corner of his eye. She watched him as he went up to the bar and ordered a pint of beer. He sat down at a table at the far end of the lounge and lit a cigarette. She realised then that he was carrying a newspaper which he unfolded and began to read.

Was he following her? She decided to find out. Getting up quite quickly, she walked to the door. There was a bench in an alcove, on the outside, where she sat down and remained hidden from anyone leaving the pub.

A moment later he was outside, looking up and down the street. She crouched behind a beam, watching him. He hesitated a moment and then began walking quickly towards the nearest shops.

She went back into the pub. Her drink was still untouched so she sat down again at the table and smoked another cigarette reflecting on the situation.

He had been following her. Of that she was sure. The reason? No idea. Next problem was how to leave and return home without being followed.

There was a pay phone near the bar. She phoned a taxi.

Twenty minutes later she was home.

She was standing in the kitchenette, an expression her mother had always used to describe the tiny room. No refrigerator, only a pantry to keep food cool. In the corner a ridiculously small washing machine with rollers. Her mother had always gone to the launderette in the Village.

She made herself a sandwich and sat down in front of the television by the little electric fire with its decorative orange coals. Sunday afternoon there was a movie on the BBC. Jack Warner in a POW camp. She ate her lunch. Half past three already. It was getting dark.

She realised how much she missed Chuck. How nice it would have been to live in her parents' house with her American pension and her husband. What a fine time they would have had together. She wiped away some tears, felt suddenly tired and fell asleep in front of the television.

The knock on the door woke her up. She had not drawn her mother's curtains over the bay windows and although the room was in darkness anyone looking in would be able to see light from the fire and the flickering TV. She got up, turned on the light, went out into the freezing hall to answer the door.

'Good evening. I saw there was someone home and thought I might introduce myself and see if you needed anything. I'm your next door neighbour. You must be Frances Cooper. But I think we've already met. In the pub, on Friday. You remember? I thought you were American because of your cigarettes. My name's Albert.'

She would hardly have recognized him. He was considerably taller than he had seemed earlier when sitting in the pub, with fair hair, cut in a classic short, back and sides hairstyle. He had a kindly, handsome face and she immediately warmed to him.

She smiled when she spoke to him;

'I used to live here. Before I went to America. I don't remember you. What happened to Mrs. Davis and Uncle Willy? They used to live next door.'

'Oh, she passed away and the old fellow went into a home. About two years ago. That's when I moved in. So. Do you need anything?'

'Would you like a cup of tea? Come into the lounge. It's cold out here.'

The two armchairs were positioned at either side of the fire. Immediately, in front of the grate, was a hearth rug and then the sofa with a small coffee table. He sat down in one of the armchairs. She brought in the tea service and some digestive biscuits she had found, on a small tray.

She sat down in the other chair and poured the tea.

'My husband was from Iowa. We met when I was at university. We married and lived there, for three years. Until he died. Then my parents had this accident. And I decided to come home. I went to the funeral yesterday. And here I am. Freezing in this house. I didn't remember how cold it got.'

'Nice and warm in America?'

'Not in Iowa. It's much colder in winter. But the houses all have central heating. It's only cold if you go outside. In England you can go out for long walks in the country in December. Back there it's all snow and ice. I went out to Fallowfield this morning across the river.'

'Well you didn't walk long you came back in a taxi.'

He paused, realising that the remark had been a mistake. She glanced up at him first with suspicion and then reproachfully.

'I forgot for a moment what it's like to live on this road. My mother sometimes described it as a goldfish bowl.'

'I'm sorry. I shouldn't't've said that.'

'It's OK. I came back in a taxi because I was frightened and didn't want to walk back by myself.'

She recounted her little adventure.

'Quite the Dick Barton, aren't you?'

'Who?' she asked.

'Dick Barton, the detective, on the radio.'

'I wouldn't remember. But I had to find out.'

'And you did very well. Why do you think he was following you?'

'Don't know. But something else has been puzzling me.'

'What?'

'The day I got back, two newspaper men came to interview me.'

'From the city evening newspaper? That's fairly normal. My cousin came back from New York, on holiday, four years ago and they came and took pictures of her and her three children. Good ones. We had them framed.'

'But they only published one photo and it was an old one. From years ago. They didn't use any they took. And they wanted photos of the garden, spouting some rubbish about the famous exotic plants. There are no exotic plants. I looked. Only roses and lots of little ponds and gnomes fishing. My mum loved gnomes.'

'Where did they get the old photo?'

'Oh, my father won a prize a long time ago and we all came out in the paper. They even took one of Mrs. Davis and Uncle Willy.'

'Were they relatives?'

'No,' she replied. 'Just neighbours. He was an old man with a wooden leg. He lost it in the Great War. She always called him Uncle Willy, but I don't really know what their relationship was. I always thought he was a brother.'

'Or a lover?'

She blushed slightly and then added haughtily,

'I don't think so. She was a very respectable woman.'

'Well, I'd better be getting a move on.' he said. 'My mother will be getting my tea.'

'You live with your parents?'

'No, I live alone. My mum lives with her sister, around the corner. My dad was killed in the war.'

'Oh, I'm sorry.'

'I never met him. So it's no skin off my nose. But it's been hard for my mum. I have my tea with her almost every day at this time. Normally egg and chips.'

She opened the door for him.

'Anyway,' he said. 'You know where I am if you need anything. Cheerio.'

Albert left the house, walked down the path to the gate. It was cold out in the street and he could see his breath come out as white smoke as he walked under a lamp post. The night seemed invigorating and he decided to walk into the Village and buy some cigarettes and an evening newspaper.

He had enjoyed speaking to the girl and was now experiencing a fleeting moment of happiness. He wondered how old she was and decided no more than twenty five.

Perhaps a little younger, rather than older.

She had dancing blue eyes, but how they had flashed and turned dark when he mentioned the taxi. Light brown hair, straight and cut short. A beautiful little face, narrow waist. Oh yes, the type of girl who marries an American and goes off to America.

Well, he thought, this one has come back.

He turned the corner at the end of the road and began walking towards the sweet and tobacconist's, which also served as a newsagent's.

The night was dark and part of the road unlit. He heard footsteps moving towards him. For just a moment he was back in the army, his senses alert.

An elderly gentleman passed him and then a young couple. Lamp posts again illuminated the pavement. He relaxed, wandered into the shop and waited his turn behind another customer.


'I didn't know you had a dog.'

Once again she was ambling along the country path down to the bridge leading to Fallowfield. Albert was coming in the opposite direction with an enormous German Shepherd.

'I'd be pretty lonely without Marlen. But she has to go out three times a day, which is a bit of a bind. Any new adventures, mysterious men visiting you?'

Thinking he was making fun of her, she drew herself up slightly.

'Not at all. A very uneventful life. Maybe I'll get a dog for a friend too. Or better a cat. I've always had cats. Had a beautiful one in Iowa which I had to leave behind.'

She stopped speaking and said, almost whispering.

'Don't look now. But he's right behind you. Maybe he's been following you too'

Albert was standing with his back to the man, whilst she stood looking in the opposite direction, right at him.

Suddenly, he was almost on top of them.

He spoke to Albert.

'Excuse me, sir. I wonder if I could trouble you for a light?'

Albert turned round and the man took, out of his pocket, a crumpled packet of Woodbines and put one in his mouth. Albert, a little startled, handed the man a box of Swan Vestas. The man, somewhat shorter than Albert, lit his cigarette and returned the matches.

'Much obliged, sir.'

His accent was definitely foreign, she thought. At least sixty, greying black hair, wavy on top and short at the back and the sides. Clean-shaven, decidedly not handsome, but at the same time with an unusual face, a hooked nose and penetrating eyes. He was wearing a long, expensive looking, brown coat.

'Beautiful morning for a walk, isn't it?' he said.

His eyes rested on her, as he inhaled the smoke from his cigarette, which he held in his very white, bony fingers.

12

'Yes. It is. Lovely day.'

She blurted the words out, wondering how to make him talk, tell her everything, find out why he had been following her.

It was Albert who asked him, bluntly.

'Never seen you here before. Are you a stranger to these parts?'

'Yes. Visiting friends in Fallowfield. Thanks for your help. Good morning.'

And he was gone.

'You see, he was following me again.'

'I don't think so, if anything he was following me.'

'No, look even now, he's walking towards Fallowfield. He was walking behind me.'

They both looked on as the man made his way over the bridge, crossing the river to the town.

'Frances,' he said.

'Everyone calls me Frankie.'

'Well, Frankie. Can I invite you to have morning coffee in the Village? Walk back with me. I'll leave Marlen at my mother's house and we'll go to a coffee shop, I know.'

'If you aren't busy.'

'You mean, why aren't I at work right now? I'm a writer and I work at home. I can call myself that because two of my books have been published and I'm working on a third. And I am working. I seek inspiration on my morning walks with Marlen. I think I may have found it. Or at least, I've found you. And you shall inspire me. Let's go!'

On the way, he explained that he had been apprenticed to a printer when he was fifteen. He did his National Service in Malaya and started his first novel soon after being demobbed, completing it at the same time as he finished his apprenticeship.

A modest success, it gave him sufficient capital to purchase a house and begin work on a second book. This, in turn, opened the way to a third novel, on which he was working at the moment.

At first, his mother and his aunt, who had brought him up together, had not approved of his life choices and his joyful rejection of the printing trade. But they soon discovered that the books had brought a prosperity the family had never expected.

'What kind of books do you write?'

They were sitting at a table in a smart, modern coffee shop on the main thoroughfare between the Village and Fallowfield. Their order had just been taken. As there were few customers that morning, they were almost alone.

'The first one was a kind of detective novel. And the second one was too, really.'

'A whodunnit?'

'No, not exactly. More a thriller. Quite a lot of action. I was trained in special services when I was in Malaya. Unarmed combat, guerrilla warfare,

I wanted to write about my experiences. But yes, they were both really detective novels.'

'And the third?'

'Well, I haven't exactly started, yet. I'm looking for inspiration.'

She looked at him. He was somewhat older than she was. Early thirties she might have said. Old enough to remember the radio detectives on whom he seemed so keen. By the time she was old enough for detectives, they had a television. And she had always disliked mysteries.


The following weekend she was in good spirits. She had met an old school friend in the Village that week and they had arranged to go out together on Saturday night, just the two girls together. Her friend had also been married to an American, a pilot in the Air Force from Kentucky. Now divorced, with two children, she was living with her mother and working at the American Consulate in town.

'It's a well-paid job. They need people who've worked in the States and know the ropes. I'm sure I could get you on there if you're interested.'

The bus stop into town was only a five-minute walk from her mother's house. Her friend, Beryl, was already at the stop, waiting for her, when she arrived. As always, she was impeccably dressed, face beautifully made up. Flaming red hair piled up high on her head.

'You want to go to the Orchid, don't you? I always liked dancing in Mecca ballrooms. That's where I met Ray. He was on weekend leave from the base in Karlsruhe.'

15

'Where's that?'

'In Germany. Near the Black Forest.'

'What did he do there?'

'He was working with the FBI. I'm not supposed to tell you. In fact, I'm not supposed to know. But I was married to the man. You'll never guess what they were investigating.'

'What?'

'Aliens! Little green men. Flying saucers. You know how paranoid the Americans are. Thought there was some alien technology that the Communists were going to get. Apparently, before the war, there'd been some kind of crash. There were rumours, about a flying saucer. Yanks'll believe anything. Two FBI agents even quizzed me at the airport before I left. They wanted to know if I knew anything. Of course I didn't let on. Anyway, keep it under your hat. Especially if you want to work in the consulate. They really believe that stuff, you know. God, I'll never go to America again.'

'Why do you work in the consulate if you feel like that?'

'The same reason all the English girls work there. They don't pay US salaries anywhere else in the city. And they really do want English people who've worked in the States. And even if they haven't worked there they say they have. You want to get in there, kiddo.'

The bus came. They went upstairs for a smoke. The bus was full. Young people, all going into town on a Saturday night. They got off in the town centre and made their way to the dancehall. Frankie suddenly felt the same excitement she used to experience when she went out as a young girl. She realised she had forgotten about Chuck for the moment and did not even feel guilty about it.

The night awaited her.

# Chapter Two

The sun, streaming through the bedroom window, woke her. At first she thought she was in Iowa and then, not for the first time, wondered what she was doing back in England. Beryl's continual moaning about life in the States, the night before, had slightly spoiled her night out.

Two men had invited them to dance and then spent the evening buying them drinks. Beryl told them all about Kentucky, did several imitations of the accent and once again mentioned the FBI had interrogated her in New York before letting her leave the US, this time omitting to explain the reason why, thus adding more mystery.

Using the need to catch the last bus as an excuse, they left early feeling rather drunk, although Beryl left her phone number with one of the men. Frankie, of course, didn't have a number as her parents had never had a phone.

The heavy door knocker was banging as she was coming down the stairs. Through the opaque glass door she could make out the figure of a man. She was sure it was Albert and for some reason did not want to see him. At least not now, in her pyjamas, with a hangover and a guilty conscience. Guilty conscience? Why? The man was no more than a friend, not really even that. Still, she sat on the stairs and waited for him to go away.

The knocking went on for some time. Longer than she had expected. After it finished, she remained seated for a very long time. Tired from the night before, she decided she rather enjoyed just sitting there.

She went into the kitchenette to put the kettle on and start breakfast. She looked up and saw Albert's knuckles rapping on the kitchen window. He had come up the side path.

'I knew you must be in,' he said, when she opened the kitchen door.

'I saw the curtains were still drawn in the lounge. Did you go out late last night?'

Once again, she remembered her mother complaining about living in a goldfish bowl.

'Where did you go?'

What she wanted to say was, mind your own business. An English girl she knew in Des Moines, who had lived in both the north and the south of England, once told her what northerners call being friendly, southerners call being nosy. She smiled.

'Had a lovely evening, with an old school friend in town. Spent the whole night chatting about old times.'

'Where did you go?'

'Oh, here and there. Nowhere special.'

'I wanted to know if you wanted to go out for a drink at lunchtime and then dinner at our house, at least my mum's. She's making roast beef.'

Oh no, she thought. He's taking me to meet his mother. Well, if I show up looking like the morning after the night before, that will probably finish it off.

'That sounds very nice. Thank you very much.'

She gave him what she hoped was a warm smile.

Sunday dinner had been planned for two o'clock, which gave them ample time for a couple of drinks in the pub and to buy a bottle of cider at the off licence on the way home. He explained they always drank cider at Sunday lunch.

Frankie from being hungover was now beginning to feel quite splendid. She hardly drank in America. Sunday lunch with her in-laws had also been with cider although what they drank was non-alcoholic, more a kind of apple juice. And there were not any proper pubs in Des Moines, only bars and nice girls did not go into bars in Iowa.

Yes, maybe that was why she had come home, not to drink, of course, she thought, but because she liked the life better. And the food. Rather roast beef, Yorkshire pudding, roast potatoes than the inevitable roast ham, boiled potatoes and sour cream on everything.


'And what do you prefer now, America or England?'

Albert's Auntie Flo was a short, plump lady. Rather jolly with a flat north Lancashire accent, she exuded warmth and good humour, thought Frankie.

Albert's mother was quite different. A sober, straight-laced woman of very few words. In fact, thought Frankie, she had not said more than two words since they sat down. It was Auntie Flo who had managed the conversation. Frankie had little interest in speaking at all, which was just as well as the plump, little aunt completely monopolized the conversation, asking questions and then answering them herself. No one seemed to notice, least of all Frankie, who was seeing everything through a light alcoholic haze.

21

'And then he came back from Karlsruhe. Very poorly he was, poor lad.'

Frankie, suddenly, sobered up.

'I'm sorry, Auntie Flo. I didn't hear you. Who came back from Karlsruhe? It's in Germany, isn't it? Near the Black Forest.'

'Yes, but I've been telling you. Bill of course. He was poorly when he came back. And then they found him. In a hotel room. In Sheffield. Stabbed twice, my poor love. And that was in 1949. Why was he in Sheffield? They would never tell me. But it must have been important because they gave me an enormous pension and that was to shut me up. But no man born can shut me up, I can tell you. He told me something about the Black Forest and the goings-on there. I'll tell everybody one day when I have a mind to it. But I don't know if the world's ready for it yet.'

Auntie Flo rapidly changed the subject.

'Anyway does anyone want a cup of tea? The film's beginning now on the BBC. Albert RN. Smashing one. About escaping from a prison camp in Germany. Vera and I saw it twice at the cinema when it came out ten years ago. Jack Warner's in it.'

Without waiting for an answer she turned the television on.

They watched until the religious programmes began about half past six.

Albert wanted to leave, having made plans to see friends that evening and he wanted Frankie to accompany him. It was dark when they left the house.

'Karlsruhe. I remember now. I've heard about that place before.'

She was sitting next to Albert on the top deck of a bus.

'When I was in Iowa I worked for a woman as her personal assistant. A kind of secretary that manages all her personal affairs. She was German from the Black Forest. She was always receiving letters from Karlsruhe.'

'Did you answer her letters for her, too?'

'Not the ones in German, of course. I don't know any German.'

'How did you come to be working for a German woman?'

'Well I married Chuck at the end of my first year at university. We continued living in England until he graduated but I still hadn't finished my degree when we left for Des Moines. I thought I'd study there, but with one thing and another, it wasn't as easy as I had been told. Then I got a job with this woman and spent my time looking after her affairs.'

'Yes, but how did you meet her? Did you answer an ad in the paper? Did you go to an agency?'

'No, I met her at a Lutheran Church lunch. My mother-in-law wanted us to become more involved in her church. Of course, Chuck had no interest and I have never been religious, but I didn't have much else to do when I got to Des Moines, so once a week at least, I used to go with her to her church dos. That's really how Americans seem to socialise. This German woman had lived in Iowa most of her life. Her husband had been very wealthy and had left her a fortune. She needed an assistant to manage her house and wouldn't take no for an answer. Very insistent and offered me a good salary for doing, really, not very much. But I couldn't leave the house during working hours, even though I had nothing to do. "Just watch TV", she used to say. "But you have to open the door and answer the phone".'

23

'What did you study at university?'

'History of Art. But there wasn't anything artistic about that job.'

'You could go back to university now and finish the course.'

'Yes, I suppose so.'

'Did you mind working for a German? After all we've been through?'

'Mrs. Petersen was Jewish. She went to Iowa long before the war. But I met lots of Germans in America and in England too. Life goes on. Anyway I'm not as old as you. I hardly remember the Blitz.'

He offered her a cigarette and lit it for her. They sat smoking in silence each lost in their own thoughts.

Frankie remembered Mrs. Petersen, always heavily made up, bulging slightly out of corseted clothes and her bracelets and rings all made of gold. In the morning, before going out to lunch, she used to talk to Frankie about her life and her late husband.

She made no secret of marrying for money; in fact, she seemed to flaunt it, as much as she liked to flaunt her wealth. I married for love. Fool that I was. She used to say. When my first husband passed away I set my sights higher and got myself a rich husband. And now look at me. She would laugh loudly, showing off her beautiful teeth.

He interrupted her thoughts, suddenly.

'How did you meet a Jewish woman at a Protestant church lunch?'

'Her husband had been Lutheran and she converted when she married. They let her sing in the choir. She was a very practical woman. And so rich that she had no difficulty making friends.'

24

The pub was on the corner where the bus stopped. The night was cold and they hurried into the lounge bar. Several people waved to Albert.

The five friends, including two women, all older than Frankie, had been drinking and talking for some time and showed little interest in the newcomers. She quickly realised that they were all writers of some sort. Albert bought her a gin and tonic and she accepted a cigarette from someone.

The youngest of them introduced himself as Bernard. A lad in his late twenties, with black hair in a Beatle style cut. He grinned at her.

'Albert says you're from America.'

'Well, not exactly. I lived in Iowa for a few years. My late husband was an American.'

'You sound American.'

'Not to an American. Where are you from?'

'France. From Picardy. Amiens.'

'You don't sound French.'

'That's because I was brought up in Kent. In Canterbury. Until I was seven. My accent is a little strange.'

'And what do you do now?'

'I write for a French newspaper. In French. About England. I live in London, but sometimes I come up north. I am also writing a book. About a German secret weapon before the war. But for that no one pays me.'

Bernard got her another drink. She finished it quickly and someone bought her another. Luckily, being Sunday, the pub closed at ten and within minutes they had caught the bus home. It stopped on the corner, outside her house and Albert looked at her.

'Aren't you going to ask me in for a cup of tea?'

'Albert, I'm really knackered. I'm going straight to bed. Thanks for everything.'

She turned her back, walked straight to the front door, walked in and closed it behind her. She reached for the light switch and something heavy came down on the back of her head. How drunk I must be, was the last she remembered.

# Chapter Three

Light was streaming in. Someone was banging the heavy door knocker. Her head was throbbing. She opened her eyes. She was lying in the entrance hall of the house. I did not even make it to bed, she thought. Oh, what a hangover. Then she saw she had been bleeding. She made an enormous effort and sat up. Another act of will saw her on her feet. She opened the door.

'Hello, what happened to you?'

Bernard grinned at her but his face quickly showed alarm.

'Did you fall?'

'I don't know. I must have been very drunk.'

He came in. She turned round and suddenly screamed.

Sprawled between the dining room and the kitchenette was a man's body. Bernard quickly went over to it.

'Is he all right? He's not dead, is he?'

'He seems to be breathing. My goodness me. It's Albert. Someone's hit him on the head. Did they hit you too? You're covered in blood but Albert isn't. Look. He seems to be waking up.'

Bernard went into the little kitchen to make a pot of tea. Albert sat up and then stood up. Both he and Frankie went into the lounge and sat down on the couch whilst Bernard poured them their tea and Albert went over the events of the previous night. Something had aroused his suspicions and he went round the side of the house and entered through the kitchen door. The intruder zapped him from behind and left him just as unconscious as Frankie.

Why was the intruder in the house? As far as Frankie could see nothing had been disturbed. It would take a long time to confirm that nothing had been stolen but at first glance it would appear that she had arrived earlier than expected and he had had insufficient time to find whatever he wanted.

Frankie went upstairs. She examined herself in the mirror and decided that although she had been bleeding her wounds did not need stitches. She ran a bath, washed her hair, changed, and came down a new woman.

Albert had left, presumably to lick his own wounds. Bernard was still sitting in the lounge.

'How did you know where I lived?'

'You told me last night when we agreed to go out together this morning.'

'Go out? Where?'

'To Fallowfield. Don't you remember? There was something I wanted to show you, or better said that you wanted to see.'

Bernard's little sports car pulled into the main road and they roared off. It was, she thought, the first time she had seen a convertible since her arrival in England.

'Where are we going?'

He glanced at her, grinning.

'Don't you really remember anything? I explained it all last night.'

'You told me you were writing a book. About a German secret weapon.'

'That's right. And you asked me where it was. And I told you I would show you. And that's where we're going.'

'Didn't Albert want to come?'

'Albert doesn't know anything about it. Nobody does. Only me. And now you.'

He grinned again.

A large sign announced Fallowfield Market. He pulled up outside what looked like an enormous warehouse. They walked in and found themselves surrounded by crowds of people, stalls, shouting and a pungent smell of raw meat.

She began speaking and found her companion was not with her. She looked around and fancied she saw him in front of a stall, a few yards away. As she made her way in his direction, she found her interest was suddenly taken by a door on the far side of the building. She began walking towards it. She moved very quickly and on arrival found it opened easily.

Almost directly in front of the door was the entrance to an enclosed field. She climbed over the stile and glided over the path to another stile. Still walking along a path, but this time through a field, not dissimilar to the cornfields of Iowa. She continued walking and found herself in a meadow and not far before her, a wood. She stopped and looked down. A flat, circular, metallic object, maybe two feet in diameter lay at her feet. She was not sure what it was but whatever it might be, she knew that this is what she had been looking for. The reason why she had come.

She looked up, startled. Bernard was standing next to her, grinning at her.

'Where did you come from? Were you following me?'

'I've been waiting for you, Frankie.'

'Waiting? Why did you think I would come here?'

'Well, you tell me. Why did you come?'

Frankie looked at him. Black hair. A foreign, dark complexion, sensual face. Slight build. Casual, but expensive clothes. Last night had not been the first time she had seen him. She remembered him now, from the mourners at her parents' funeral.

The funeral, of course. Her second day in England. A car had come to collect her at ten o'clock.

The short religious ceremony and eulogies took place in a complex located on the other side of the city. Then the cemetery. An austere meal in an expensive hotel. She remembered interminable condolences from people she had never met. Very anonymous, well organized, but nothing to do with her. Then a car back home and it had been over.

But Bernard had been there. In the crowd. Why had she not realised before? Because he had never spoken to her?

'You were at the funeral. Why?'

He grinned again.

'There is an Italian restaurant not far from Fallowfield. The owner is French and the food is quite good. We'll have some lunch and you can tell me all about it.'

'No,' she said. 'You will tell me.'

'Of course.'

They walked towards a bend. He had apparently moved the car, which was parked in front of them. They got in and without speaking to each other, sped to their destination.

Mancini was the name of the restaurant. In a wooded area, just outside the town, stood what at first appeared to be a continental style house, which gave onto a discreet car park. Here, they left the car and made their way up the steps. The glass doors were all open and the aroma of pizza and herbs almost overwhelmed her.

The French owner seemed to be waiting for them in the entrance and effusively greeted them in French. Bernard responded with equal enthusiasm, also in French, and introduced his companion.

Unusual for England, thought Frankie, with its austere reserve but something with which she was well acquainted in Iowa, especially when accompanying her wealthy employer.

They were shown to a table. There were several people already seated, but the dining room was far from full. Jean Pierre brought them a drink, which he called an apéritif, along with a plate of green olives.

'A French, Italian restaurant. Unusual.'

'Jean Pierre was in England studying when Paris was invaded. He joined the British army. He was wounded, while fighting with Monty against Rommel, in North Africa. Spent two years in Italy, convalescing and learning to cook.'

A waiter uncorked a bottle of red wine and poured them each a small glass. Once again she began to feel quite euphoric. The lunch, an exotic salad, followed by Osso Buco and a dessert of chocolate and clotted cream was nothing like the food in the Italian restaurants of Iowa. By the time they finished, she realised she had drunk more than half the bottle of wine and still wanted more.

They chatted over lunch about Italy, France, Iowa and when the Germans invaded Paris. There was something else she wanted to talk about, but she found that she was not able to remember.

Then she said,

'Do you think Albert's all right? I really should get back. That was a nasty bang on the head. Maybe we should have called the police. And taken him to hospital. I don't know how I ran off like that.'

Bernard grinned at her.

'Yes. Let's be getting back. Look, it's beginning to get dark already.'

'It gets dark so early in winter in England. I didn't remember that when I lived in America.'

'Well, it's nearly Christmas. These are the shortest days of the year. By the way, what are you doing on Christmas Day?'

'Nothing at all. I have no family here.'

'Neither have I. But my friends have invited me to Christmas lunch in a village, not too far away from here. Would you like to come with me? They told me to bring a friend. And I think we are now friends. Wouldn't you say?'

She opened her eyes. Not sure how long she had been asleep, she looked up at her mother's clock on the mantelpiece over the fireplace. Half past seven. It was very dark outside and the room was cold.

She stood up, turned on the little electric fire and then the television. She drew the curtains. On one channel, a police drama and, on the other side, some kind of soap opera. She stayed with the second option as it had commercial breaks. She went into the kitchenette to make an instant coffee and reflect on the day.

She had been attacked by a burglar. And so had Albert. Really they had not attached any importance to that. And something had happened at the market. But, for some reason, she was not able to remember. A very long, exotic lunch, lots of wine. Her drinking was getting out of hand. And affecting her memory, it seemed.

And Bernard had invited her out for Christmas. And she really liked him. Or did she? For some reason, he did not seem trustworthy, whilst Albert did. But Albert was very staid. Mature. More like the elder brother she had never had.

When she got back a cowboy film had begun. An hour later she went to bed and, in spite of the coffee, slept like a log.

# Chapter Four

The house was very cold when she woke up the following morning. A fog had settled outside. She opened the door to get the milk off the doorstep and a wall of polluted smog made it impossible to see more than a few inches in front of her.

She ate her breakfast in the lounge, in front of the little electric fire and found a music programme on the radio. Music While You Work, the presenter announced. It went on for some time, but before it ended, she had a visit from the police.

Albert had reported the break-in. The policeman, a tall young man, very efficient, noted all her replies to his numerous questions in a little notebook. He inspected the back door and advised her to keep it bolted in future.

There had been other break-ins in the area and they imagined that it was the same culprit. If she found anything missing she promised to report it.

The policeman disappeared into the fog and Albert emerged out of it.

'I know you were very concerned after I was attacked trying to rescue you. But there is no need to worry, thank you very much. I went to see the doctor, talked to the police. Couldn't find you anywhere, which was somewhat worrying, as you had been covered in blood the last time I saw you. Thought you might have been kidnapped but no, you were being driven over the English countryside, in a sports car, by a Frenchman.'

'Well, good morning to you, too, Albert. Nice to see you, as always. I'm glad you're feeling better. Neither of us seems any the worse for our experiences. The police officer you sent round tells me that a number of neighbouring houses have been broken into recently, so apparently I am in no danger of being kidnapped. Yes, I did have a nice day out, thank you very much, and as you are my neighbour, not my husband, brother, boyfriend or really anything other than a friend I made a little over a week ago, I hardly see the necessity to give explanations of my travels in any type of vehicle, nor do I see what the nationality of the driver has to do with you. Now if you have nothing else to add, perhaps we could bring this interview to a close.'

Albert looked somewhat nonplussed and stood for a few moments, without saying anything. For a moment, she thought he was going to leave without further ado. However, he smiled and began speaking in an apologetic vein.

'Look, I don't want to pry into your personal life. It's just that I was worried about you. I'm sorry to snap at you and be sarcastic. If we are friends, you could give me a cup of tea.'

'All right, come in. I'll put the kettle on.'

When she had poured the tea, he looked at her meekly. But it was she who broke the silence.

'I'm glad you came. Really, I am. I feel that somehow I'm involved in something and I don't know what it is. But something is going on around me.'

'Why do you say that? Because of that man you thought was following you? Have you seen him again?'

'No. But yesterday, when I went to Fallowfield Market with Bernard, something happened.'

'What?'

'I don't know. I can't remember. I got to the market and lost Bernard. I thought I saw him and then I wandered out into some fields and suddenly we were driving off to a weird Italian restaurant which was really French. But something had happened to me. I wanted to talk to him about it but every time I began he started grinning and I would forget. And then I felt a little drunk....'

Albert laughed.

'You do seem to like knocking it back. What were you drinking?'

'Oh, lots of things. The owner gave us something really strong and then some kind of red wine, probably Italian. Did you know that Bernard is writing a book about a German secret weapon?'

'No, he's never mentioned it. He works for a French newspaper. But I don't know him very well. He used to go out with a friend of one of the girls you met the other night. But you seemed to get on very well with him.'

He looked up at her with what she thought were sad eyes.

She tensed and spoke with great dignity.

'I tend to get on well with most people.'

He abruptly changed the subject.

'Have you any plans for Christmas? On Christmas Day, we always go to Auntie Flo's mother-in-law's bungalow. I can't get out of it; it's not something I would wish on anyone so I can't invite you. But I've tickets to the Orchid, the Mecca ballroom, for their Christmas Eve party. It's with a group. Mostly Irish friends, so they may make us go to church at midnight. But it'll be fun.'

The fog lasted all day and into the next and she did not go out for some time. When she woke up next morning she was not even sure of the day. Deciding it must be Wednesday, she galloped down the stairs to make her tea and breakfast.

Almost immediately there was a knock on the door. Who might this be? Albert, who would never take no for an answer and nip to the kitchen window? The postman? No, much too late at half past eight. She was still in her dressing gown, wanted to fry up her sausages and bacon. The visitor knocked a second time. She opened the door.

It was Auntie Flo.

'Hello love. I saw the curtains were still drawn, so I knew you must be in. Did I wake you? I know young people like to sleep, but I'm always up and about at six. But, yes, I will have a cup of tea although I've already had several this morning already. This is your lounge, isn't it? Well, we'll just open the curtains, shall we? Oh it's lovely. No, don't put the fire on for me, I won't take my hat and coat off. Just let me sit down here for a moment. I'll let you go and make the tea, while I get my breath back.'

Frankie did as she was told and came back with a tray of tea and digestive biscuits. Without unbuttoning her coat, her visitor attacked the biscuits with vigour.

'Our Albert tells me you're alone for Christmas. We're all going to my mother-in-law's on Christmas Day. She used to live round here, but a few years ago, she bought one of those bungalows in Timperley. I think that's what I want, too. No stairs you see. My mother-in-law has always been a very practical woman. Anyway, she wants to invite you to Christmas lunch. We'll have turkey and sprouts and Christmas pudding. I told her all about you and how things are with you and our Albert.'

Frankie still had not been able to utter a word.

'Oh. How very kind. That is really so nice of all of you. I am somewhat overwhelmed. But I am spending the day with some friends of my parents, so I won't be able to accept. But another day I would like to meet your mother-in-law. She sounds like a very kind person.'

'Well, she certainly wants to meet you. I'll have another cup of tea, if I can. You see, my Bill knew your father and we always thought he knew why Bill was in Sheffield that night. But if he knew anything he never let on. I think I know, but until someone tells me the truth, it stays inside me. Do you know anything?'

'My father would never talk about his work.'

'Yes, but Bill always said you were the key. Oh, there, now I've said more than I wanted to. Look, I'm going home. I know you'll be going dancing with our Albert on Thursday evening, so maybe I'll see you before you go.

39

Our Albert says he thinks you know something and if you tell me, perhaps I'll tell you what I know. If something doesn't happen to me first, like my poor Bill. Be careful, love, there are dark forces here.'

She left.

The fog had lifted a little when she walked to the shops in the early afternoon. However, by three o'clock it was almost dark, the freezing fog was getting thicker and the smell of coal permeated everything. She found her front door, more by instinct, and went into the house.

The post was delivered twice a day over Christmas and there was a letter waiting for her. She opened it. It was from Beryl. Inviting her to a New Year's Eve party at the Mecca ballroom in town. This, she thought, was becoming just a little monotonous. She had left her phone number so that Frankie could give her a ring the following week.

She had settled down to a cup of tea and was watching the television, when there was a knock on the door. At first she thought about ignoring it but realised that although there was nobody she wanted to see, the lights and noise from the house confirmed that she was indeed home. And, whoever it was, would persist until she had opened the door.

'Good evening. My name is Daniel Bessel. You, I imagine are Mrs. Frances Blakeley. I believe we have already met. If you remember, you and your friend were kind enough to lend me a box of matches, I think about a week ago, on the path to Fallowfield. How are you Mrs. Blakeley?'

Frankie began to feel slightly faint. She could hear her heart pounding in her head. Think fast. Under no circumstances was he to be allowed into the house.

'Good evening,' she replied. 'I'm not sure I do remember you. How can I help you?'

'May I come in?'

'I'm afraid that's not possible at the moment. What can I help you with?'

'Mrs. Blakeley, I represent a client who is willing to pay a very large sum to recuperate some artifacts, which he believes were in your father's possession.'

'What artifacts would those be?'

'Flat, metallic, circular discs. There are a number of them. Money, my client has told me, is no object. He wants to recuperate them.'

'Recuperate. You mean, they belonged to him and he lost them?'

'That is correct.'

'Who is your client?'

'That madam, I am not at liberty to divulge.'

'And why do you think I have these discs?'

'I don't know. But my client believes that you, Mrs. Blakeley, are the key to the whole operation.'

'Well,' she said. 'I really know nothing about this. I've been out of the country for years. I never knew anything about my father's work and I don't believe I am the key here to anything. So if there is nothing else, perhaps we could bring this interview to a close.'

'Well, here is my business card, in case you remember anything. My client is able to make you a very rich woman. Good night.'

He turned and walked off into the black fog. Frankie closed the door and bolted it.

In the corner of the lounge was her father's cocktail cabinet. Up until now she had ignored it, but she turned and opened it. There were several bottles, she chose bourbon, poured a glass and sat down on the sofa. She drained the glass and, still shaking, poured another.

After the third glass she went into the kitchen to check the door. It was still bolted. She turned off the lights and went to bed, sleeping fitfully if somewhat drunkenly, until the morning.

## Chapter Five

When she woke up the fog had lifted and her bedroom was full of sunshine. She felt much braver than the night before. She went into the bathroom and spent some time getting ready to go out.

Downstairs, in the dining room, there was an enormous, elaborate coal burning fireplace. Above the mantelpiece, a large frameless mirror. She stood next to the dining table and looked at herself.

She knew very well that she was an attractive young woman. Light brown hair, straight and cut short, blue eyes. She was not wearing makeup and was dressed to walk in the country. Albert was probably walking his dog and she wanted to talk to him.

She made her way across the field, down the path to the river when she saw him and his dog trudging homeward up the hill.

'Hello Albert. Happy Christmas Eve.'

He had seen her from a distance and had been waving to her.

'Where are you going? To Fallowfield?'

'No, I was looking for you actually. Your Auntie Flo very kindly invited me to Christmas dinner.'

'I know. But you have a previous engagement, she told me.'

'She told me that you thought I knew something.'

'Well, I suppose you know a lot of things.'

'She meant about the metallic discs.'

He put his arm around his dog and, without looking at her, began to tickle the under part of its neck. He picked up a stick and threw it. Immediately Marlen ran to fetch it, brought it back, and waited for him to throw it again.

'Metallic discs? Did she say that?'

'No, she didn't. Daniel Bessel came to see me last night and offered me a large sum of money to recuperate the discs.'

The dog came back with the stick and he threw it once again.

'Who is Daniel Bessel?' he asked.

'I thought you might tell me.'

'I don't know him. Should I know him?'

'He came to the door last night. The man who was following me the other day.'

She recounted the events of the previous evening.

'A little bit cloak and dagger, all this. And what has my auntie got to do with it?'

'She said the same thing. I was the key to the operation. Her husband had told her. And then she said that you thought I knew something.'

'I never said anything of the sort. I bet she told you we were courting, too.'

'Yes, more or less.'

'Well, there you are. Pay no attention to Auntie Flo. She's been living in a cloud since her husband died. More important is this Bessel character.'

'You know nothing about the discs or why I should know where they are?'

The dog brought the stick back, rolled over, expecting to be tickled. Without looking at her, he caressed the animal and once again threw the stick.

'I was nine years old when the war finished. My father never came back. I never met him. Uncle Bill came back, but we never saw him very much. He was always in Sheffield and London and Germany. And then, when I was about thirteen, he was killed. The police said it was robbery, but Auntie Flo said it was because of his work. My mother used to work nights at the hospital and I often used to spend the evenings with my auntie. After the radio programmes finished we used to chat, normally about what we'd been listening to. One night, there was a documentary about the German pilotless plane. Afterwards, we were chatting about it when she began to cry about how her husband had been killed because of what he knew about German secret weapons. She said she was going to show me something, but I must promise never to tell anyone. She went to the bookcase, found an old book, and took out a photo which she kept in it. Of a metallic disc. I wasn't very impressed but I never told anyone about it. Until now, that is.'

'Was that the only time?'

'She insisted that she'd been told not to say anything about it. Then she often used to ramble on about it, but would never say anything specific. Just insinuations. But we never pressed her or if we did ask, she would just clam up, or worse get upset.'

'Well, someone's interested in these discs. And why do they think I have them? Do they think I have them in the house? Is that why I had a burglar that night?'

The dog came back and laid the stick on the ground in front of him. Albert picked it up again and threw it, quite far this time.

Marlen ran after it.

'Did your father have any secret hiding places in the house?'

'If he did, he never told me about them. I never knew anything about his work. It was always very hush hush. I sometimes asked my mother about what he did and she just said essential war work for the government. When I pointed out that the war had ended she would say that now it was the Cold War and even more essential. They came to visit us in Iowa but I always thought that was a pretext, because first they spent some weeks in Virginia. And they never talked about that either. My mother telephoned one day and the next morning the two of them arrived at my door. Their driver was a military man who deposited them and their luggage on our doorstep. Two weeks later he came to collect them. My English friends also received visits from their relatives. But they had to meet them at the airport.'

'Well, if your mum and dad were in the country on government business.'

'Something else. On two evenings, they were invited out to dinner and I know that on one of these occasions at least, my boss Mrs. Petersen was present.'

'Is that important?'

'Well it made me think that my working for her was more than just a coincidence. She had been so insistent, she paid so well, and really I did very little.'

The dog came back again.

'Let's go for a Christmas coffee, Frankie. I have to think about all this.'

There were no free tables at the coffee shop. Groups of people full of festive spirit, chatter and laughter filled the little café.

There were two free stools behind a kind of bar at the window and they sat there. Outside shoppers hurried past, well wrapped up, but still enjoying the midday sunshine.

Frankie, once again, thought about her old boss. Then in her early fifties, she had been in Des Moines since arriving with her husband in 1934. Her husband, some years older than she, a doctor, had really been more prosperous than she made out. However, he died shortly after their arrival.

Within six months she was married again, this time to a rich financier. Much older than she was, he died just before the end of the war, leaving her a widow for the second time.

They had little time to talk over their coffee. Almost at once, they were joined by two of Albert's friends who wished them a Happy Christmas. The two young men were brothers and lived nearby, so they walked home with them as they chatted happily about their plans for the holiday weekend.

Opening her front door, she found the postman had left three Christmas cards. One was from Albert, his mother and Auntie Flo. Another from

Bernard reminding her of their date on Christmas Day. The third post, marked from London, was from Mrs. Petersen.

She was in England for Christmas and would be up north the following week. Staying at the Northern, she said. They could have English tea together. What a strange coincidence, Frankie thought. Well, something else to tell Albert this evening.

She went into the lounge and stood in the bay window looking out at the street. It was already getting dark and she could see the Christmas trees illuminated in so many of the windows in the other houses. When she lived with her parents they used to have a tree at Christmas. Perhaps she should have put one up. A little silly for a lone woman. The words made her choke. All alone at Christmas. No husband, no parents. And yet everyone seemed to want something from her.

Well, she thought with determination, she was not that vulnerable.

And she had at least one ally. Albert, she knew, really liked her. And he was not as old as she thought he was. About twenty-eight she worked out from what he had told her. That was a year younger than Chuck.

Although Chuck had always looked very young. In Des Moines they used to ask him for ID when buying liquor. How that used to annoy him. A boyish face. Her handsome American beau.

Now she knew why people cried at Christmas.

She wandered into her mother's dining room and looked at herself in the mirror. No false modesty here. She knew she was, what her husband had called, a looker. And she must use this to her advantage.

For some reason that she could not fathom she perceived that she was in danger. Someone had tried to get into the house. She had been offered money for objects about which she knew nothing.

And then there was Bernard. Once again she was going out with him. Was he friend or foe? And what did Mrs. Petersen want? Her presence in the North of England could hardly be fortuitous.

A sudden noise made her start.

The dining room bay windows at the back of the house gave onto the garden and from there, on a clear day, one could see all the way down the hill to the river and then the little bridge and the path which led to Fallowfield.

Now it was dark. But Frankie thought she could see something moving in the garden.

And then a cry of pain and a crash as one of the gnomes fell to the ground. She opened a window. The cold night air mixed with the smell of coal came rushing in.

'Who's there? I warn you, I am armed and will shoot if you don't answer. I'll count three.'

She saw a dark form jump over the wall at the back of the garden. Whoever it was had made his escape. She closed the window. It was too dark for her go out and investigate now.

She looked again at the mirror and drew herself up. No crying, she thought. Christmas was only one day.

And she was going to get to the bottom of this mystery. No one was going to get the better of her.

Making sure the doors were bolted, she went upstairs to prepare for her night out.


'I imagine the last thing he expected was to be shot at. You showed great presence of mind.'

Albert might have laughed when she recounted her latest experience. However a second intruder, in such a short period of time, made them reflect on the seriousness of the situation.

'If we call the police again, don't tell them you threatened to shoot him. This isn't America.'

'I haven't any guns in the house.'

'They might think you have and use it as a pretext to search the house.'

'A pretext? What do you mean?'

'I don't know. I'm beginning to see plots everywhere.'

They made their way into the enormous dancehall, filled to capacity with revellers. Sitting at a table were a number of young men and women who enthusiastically welcomed them. There was a group on a stage playing a slow dance melody and one of the boys asked her to dance. After that another lad asked her. Soon she noticed the stage revolved and another group appeared, playing faster music from the top twenty. She found herself dancing with Albert.

'Enjoying yourself?'

'Oh, yes. Thank you very much for inviting me. Your friends are all very nice. I expected to see Bernard here.'

'He's not really a friend of mine,' said Albert. 'I hardly know him. Only, that he's a French journalist.'

'I wish you knew him better. He's taking me to lunch tomorrow with some friends. I'm beginning to regret that I accepted his invitation.'

'When did he invite you?'

'We talked about it some time ago but I got a card from him confirming it.'

'Why are you worried?'

'Like you, I'm beginning to see plots everywhere. Something happened to me in Fallowfield Market. I don't know what. But I think he does know.'

'Why don't you ask him about the discs? Tell him about that weird man. See how he reacts. Let's have a drink.'

Everything finished between eleven and twelve. As Albert had predicted his friends wanted to go to midnight mass but he and Frankie caught the bus back. He accompanied her into the house, turned on the lights, checked the doors and windows, and bid her good night.

# Chapter Six

'You know in France we don't really celebrate Christmas Day,' said Bernard. 'The big celebration is the night before, Christmas Eve.'

'Oh, like in Norway. My mother-in-law was from a Norwegian family and they used to celebrate Christmas Eve. Then, she said, she married an Englishman and had to celebrate on the 25th.'

'Your father-in law was English?'

'No, it was just their way of identifying their origins. His ancestors had come from England. In the seventeenth century. He was an authentic WASP.'

'What do you mean by that?'

'White, Anglo Saxon, Protestant.'

'Oh, I'm a White, Latin Roman Catholic but that doesn't spell anything'

He grinned at her. It was cold in the convertible and although it was a sunny day, the sun did not warm them, as it would have done in Iowa. It just hung in the sky like some cold neon illumination.

The countryside everywhere radiated a deep green. From the decorated houses to the landscape, she was very conscious of being in England on Christmas Day.

It was an hour's drive to, wherever they were going. Then, suddenly, he pulled into the car park of a small restaurant. Nothing foreign about this place. Mock Tudor style. She caught sight of a sign as they were walking in, Ye Olde... something or other.

It was very warm inside. There was a fireplace in the corner of the restaurant. Two or three trestle tables, where places had been set, flanked by long benches.  It all looked like a medieval scene from an old movie.

A large number of people, all standing, chatting, laughing, and drinking wine. No beer at all. As she came closer to the jovial groups, she heard they were speaking French.

Bernard was greeted effusively and he introduced Frankie. She was kissed on both cheeks by, she was sure, every person in the room. Then a glass of wine was thrust into her hand and people began chatting to her. Apparently they were mostly journalists although not everyone, as she had previously thought, was French. Most certainly foreign, all of them.

In the background she could hear foreign pop music. She recognized some French songs, one or two Italian ones. Nothing English or American.

The lunch was old fashioned, English, Christmas fare. Turkey and then Christmas pudding.

Lots of French wine followed by champagne. As always Frankie began to feel perfectly splendid and the mysteries surrounding her life fell into insignificance.

At some point coffee was served and she was offered a brandy. With an act of will she rejected the spirits but she did accept a second cup of coffee.

Feeling a little more in control she wandered over to Bernard. He had been chatting to a young man, who had been introduced to her as a Mexican journalist.

'Did you enjoy the lunch? Very traditional, I thought.'

'Oh, yes. Thank you for bringing me here. I've met some very interesting people. I expected to see your friend Daniel Bessel here this afternoon.'

She watched his face, but he just grinned back at her.

'Who would that be? The name doesn't ring a bell.'

'Doesn't it? He said he knew you.'

'No, what does he look like?'

She looked at him closely.

'He offered me money for the metallic discs.'

He continued grinning at her.

'Oh. What did you say?'

'I said I would think about it.'

'Where are they?'

He blurted out quickly and then stopped.

For a moment his grin had disappeared. And then just as quickly, he began smiling again.

'What discs are these?'

'Well, he seems to think I'm the key to the whole operation. What do you think?'

'I think you're full of Christmas spirit. I'm not sure what you're on about, but you're trying to pull my leg here. Look, there's another friend of mine, over there. He's Russian. I'll introduce you to him.'

She did not drink any more that afternoon. An hour later, they were back in the convertible and Bernard was driving her home in the dark.

'You still didn't tell me about your mysterious Mr. Bessel. How did you meet him? What does he look like?'

For no reason that Frankie could justify, she did not want to tell Bernard any more at the moment.

'Oh it isn't important. I think I was a little bit dizzy with the wine. I never used to drink so much in America. I seem to be drinking all the time here. In Iowa I used to drink Kool Aid.'

'What's that?'

'A soft drink they make. You buy flavoured powder in a packet. Mix it with sugar, ice and water in a pitcher and serve it as a kind of non-alcoholic punch. American Protestants don't approve of alcohol and tobacco. Lutherans don't even dance.'

'WASPS. Like you said.'

He pulled up outside her house.

'I will go in with you and we'll put the lights on.'

They went into the empty house. He entered the kitchen and checked the bolts. She was standing just behind him. He stumbled. Whether this was engineered or not, she did not know, but suddenly they were face to face and she felt his sensual mouth next to hers. He kissed her quickly and passionately and she found herself doing the same.

She pushed him away. She had been prepared for this, she thought, and knew what to say.

'No, please. I'm not ready for this. I'm still grieving for my husband.'

She began to cry softly.

'Don't worry.'

He said something to her in French. He kissed her again, this time on the cheek, and left the house.

She smiled and bolted the door behind him.


She awoke with a deep feeling of satisfaction. Christmas was over and she had celebrated it, in spite of having no family.

She went downstairs for breakfast, but stopped first in the dining room and looked out the window at her parents' garden.

Exactly as she had imagined a gnome had crashed, broken to the ground, although not without first having inflicted some kind of injury with its pointed cap.

She went out into the garden to have a look. It was quite chilly in the early morning and fog had come across the hill from the river below. A smell of coal permeated everything. She looked down at the broken gnome. Under the pieces she found a packet of Gaulloise sans filtre and a key ring and several keys. The key ring with a little plaque. A saint, perhaps. She did not know. She picked the things up and walked into the house.

There were several groups of walkers out that Boxing Day morning as she wandered down the green hill to the river. She did not cross over the bridge, but sat down on a fallen tree watching the water flow past.

Different birds flew overhead. What a difference from the Upper Midwest of North America with something like twelve inches of snow.

She was glad to be back home. Even if everything did smell of coal.

She turned and found Albert's German Shepherd next to her. She stood up as the dog began to kiss her face and instead gave it her hands to lick.

She looked round and saw Albert close by.

'Marlen seems to have taken a liking to you. You're out very early. Did you have a nice Christmas?'

'Yes. We went to a kind of party of foreign journalists in a medieval type restaurant in the country. Very interesting people.'

'Did you ask Bernard about the discs?'

'Oh yes, but he wasn't letting on, if he knew anything. I think he does know something. He just stood there with that enigmatic French smile. Only once did he seem to slip when I suggested I might know where the discs were. But he got over it so quickly that I was left wondering.'

She went on to tell him what she had found in the garden.

'Does Bernard smoke French fags?'

'I don't think he smokes at all. He never accepted any of my cigarettes. I've never seen him smoke. And that creepy guy smoked Woodbines.'

'Maybe he smokes Gaulloise too. It can't be easy to buy French ciggies round here. He'd have to bring them from France. I'd like to see the key ring.'

'Wouldn't a character in one of your detective stories just figure out what happened? Can't you put the clues together?'

He laughed.

'In my books I know who did it at the very beginning. The clues are just there to confuse the reader. I'm not a detective.'


'Look, it seems to be some kind of saint.'

She handed the key ring to Albert.

'Yes. It's St. Anthony of Padua. People pray to him when they've lost things.'

'Why?

'So that he'll find lost things for them. My Irish friends do that all the time.'

'And they believe that?'

'Of course they do. If you believe something it normally works. Or at least you convince yourself it does.'

'We'll see if it works for our burglar. He seems to have lost some keys.'

'More importantly. Our burglar smokes French cigarettes. He's probably Catholic and maybe superstitious. Must be a foreigner, might have been abroad recently. Let's study the keys.'

They were sitting in the Crown, a pub in the Village. Albert was sipping a pint of bitter whilst Frankie played with her tomato juice and Worcestershire sauce.

'None of the three keys seem foreign. They could all be for locks round here.'

'Something else I don't think I've told you Albert.'

She gave him the card she received from Mrs. Petersen. Albert looked at the envelope and read the card.

'She's in London,' he said. 'She'll be up north next week. She must be coming especially to see you. Otherwise she would have stayed in the south. Only Beatle fans would come up here and then they'd go to Liverpool. And certainly not in winter. Was she very fond of you?'

'The daughter she never had? I'd never thought of it like that. We used to chat a lot in the morning. Before she'd go out to lunch at eleven thirty. She talked about her life in Germany before the Nazis.'

'Where did she live?'

'In the Black Forest. Freiburg in Bavaria. I've seen pictures of it. Very beautiful.'

She took a sip of her juice.

'When Chuck died in February, I decided to give up the job. I spent a long time moping around the house and thinking about my future. I thought at first that I would stay in the States. Perhaps move to the East or West Coast, possibly New York or Boston. I was just getting things together when I learned of my parents' accident. I wasn't nearly as devastated as when Chuck died. In fact, it sometimes upsets me to remember how well I took the news. It was then that I decided to leave the US and come back to England. At least for the present. I am a permanent resident and can go back when I want. Until 1972 that is.'

'We always go back to the Black Forest, don't we? You know what happened there, don't you?'

'No, not really. I know there was an American military base not far away in Karlsruhe. Your Auntie Flo talked about it. Mrs. Petersen was always getting letters from there. And my friend Beryl began talking about it the other night.'

'Your friend Beryl? Who's that?'

'An old school friend I saw last week. She lived a time in the States before she divorced. She was even quizzed by the FBI at the airport before she left. She works at the American Consulate now.'

Albert began speaking again.

'I read some books, quite a long time ago about UFOs. There was a piece about Roswell which you might know about.'

'No I don't know. Where is it?'

'I'm not sure if it's in New Mexico or Arizona. But the important thing was, a flying saucer crashed there in 1947. The newspapers were full of it for about one day until the army or FBI arrived, changed the whole story,

61

and said it was only a weather balloon. They even said that the alien bodies they had found were only stuffed dummies. The sheriff was made to change his story.'

'Or maybe that was the real story,' laughed Frankie. 'Less dramatic but more credible.'

'Before that, there had been another crash. In Freiburg, in 1936. Obviously the FBI couldn't get involved and the Gestapo took charge of everything. The alien technology they found was used to start the German war machine. When the Yanks arrived in 1945 they took everything back to the States.'

Frankie shrugged and shook her head.

'Well that had nothing to do with my boss. She left Germany in 1934. And she and her husband were Jewish. So, this has nothing to do with them. And I don't believe there was any kind of Martian crash.'

'I'm not a detective, only a writer, but I do know you've got to put all the clues in the pot.'

He suddenly changed the subject.

'Oh, I didn't tell you. You're invited to lunch. It's roast lamb and mint sauce because it's Boxing Day. Oh, and we eat Yorkshire pudding with lamb because Auntie Flo likes it. Come on. I have to buy the cider.'

## Chapter Seven

The garden was made up of a maze of little paved paths which surrounded small artificial ponds, each with one or two painted, plaster gnomes; normally one fishing whilst the other looked on. There were a couple of flowerbeds and some grassy, bushy areas with miniature windmills and tiny houses, but there was no real lawn at all.

On the left was a long picket fence, with a line of five fruit trees next to it. With the exception of an old, solitary apple tree at the bottom of the garden, these were the only trees.

All leafless and lifeless in winter.

Frankie picked up the pieces of the broken gnome and threw them away. She swept the paths and even dusted off the gnomes with a damp cloth.

There must have been at least five ponds. Not very deep nor very big, but each one teeming with fish and plant life. The little flowerbeds were still full of roses. She remembered her mother had really loved the garden.

At the bottom of the garden there was a wall. Next to the wall, on an elevated area, was a kind of park bench. Here under an apple tree, the family used to sit and look down the green hill at the river, the bridge, and the path to Fallowfield.

This is where she sat now, watching, as groups of people ambled up and down the slope.

Lost in thought, she remembered the first spring she was in Iowa. She had insisted that they plant a rose bush in their back yard. She managed to get one beautiful rose bud. That autumn the bush had to be buried to protect it from the severe winter's snow. Next year, they dug it up again and she was rewarded with another rose bud.

She looked at her mother's roses, still blooming at the end of December.

It was mid-morning and she began to make plans for the day. Something she had pending was to phone Beryl and confirm their date for New Year. She was not really looking forward to it.

Another party in the same dance hall with more or less the same kind of people. Listening to Beryl's incessant complaints about her life in America.

However, for the moment, Beryl was her only girl friend and she might even be able to get some information out of her.

An hour later she was on her way to the American Steak House, a restaurant in the Village where she knew she could have lunch alone without attracting attention and have a chat in one of the telephone booths in the entrance.

She entered the dark panelled lounge. In the far corner, a white piano. A jazz pianist was playing.

She asked for a table for one and sat down. She noticed there were several people eating alone. Most of them would be foreign office staff and executives from a nearby multinational company.

A waiter came along to see if she wanted to drink wine. She ordered a Coke and asked to use the telephone. The waiter accompanied her to a booth.

Beryl was in good spirits. She had spent the holiday with her parents, siblings and their families, and her children had had the best Christmas of their lives, she said. Of course, that is what they always said, she laughed.

They arranged to meet Thursday night. New Year's Day was not a holiday, of course, but as the American Consulate was closed, she was off work on the first of January.

Once again, she told Frankie there was a job waiting for her when she wanted.

Her Coke was already there when she returned to her table. She ordered a T-bone American style steak with french fries (yes, they called them that) and cole slaw. Beryl would not have approved and calling chips, french fries would have made her bristle but for Frankie, being American was now part of her.

She ordered pecan pie with whipped cream for dessert. All in all, it was turning into a rather expensive lunch, but she was enjoying her splurge.

Next time, she would bring Albert and treat him. He had treated her so many times it would be nice to return his kindness. He was a nice guy and she did enjoy his company.

She asked for the bill.

'The bill has been taken care of. Mr. Gallagher said it was his treat.'

For a moment she was speechless.

The waiter pointed to two men now standing some distance away and on the point of leaving the premises.

One of them, a short, fat, balding, middle aged man, whom she thought looked Irish, and another individual.

She looked again. The other man was Daniel Bessel. The two of them left the restaurant.

'I don't think I know the gentleman.'

'His name is Chris Gallagher and he's a regular client here. A very generous man. He seemed to know you. Said you were a friend of his daughter's. How would you like your coffee? He paid for that, too.'


Frankie was sitting on the top deck of a bus moving slowly towards the city centre. Going into town to do some shopping and walk around would help clear her mind. As she puffed on the second cigarette since she sat down, she reflected that whatever her course of action, she was always left in a quandary.

66

She got off the bus and went into a bank on the corner of the road and made a withdrawal. She then began wandering into shops looking at clothes. She knew that she really had no desire to buy anything, but shopping with money in her handbag always lifted her spirits.

She passed a cinema where a matinee programme was just about to start. She paid the entrance fee, went in, sat down, and smoked at least five cigarettes through a double feature of 1950s comedies and a Pathe newsreel.

When she left the cinema, it was dark. She wandered to the bus stop in a daze. She had had enough of England and this town. She would go back to the States, maybe Boston or even San Francisco.

The bus came almost immediately. It was nearly full and there was standing room only on the lower deck. She held on to a railing and the bus moved off.

'Hello love.'

Frankie looked down and saw Auntie Flo, sitting on the long seat between two other plump ladies, all three with their shopping on their laps.

'Hello, Auntie Flo. How are you?'

'Where have you been, love? Our Albert was out looking for you. First, he went to your house. Then, he took his dog out for a walk on the hill. He didn't say anything, but I saw him from the bedroom window. He looked really disappointed that you weren't at home.'

Frankie really was lost for words. This kind of conversation, in front of everyone on the bus, embarrassed her.

'I went into town to do a bit of shopping. In the end I didn't buy anything.'

'No, you did well. The sales don't start until next week. Don't buy anything yet. It's New Year's Eve tomorrow. I expect you'll be going dancing again with our Albert, won't you? He said you had a very nice time together last week. Are you going to the same place?'

'Oh, I don't know,' she answered.

The bus stopped and several people got off. She saw an empty place behind the driver. She quickly sat down, somewhat relieved. The bus moved off, very slowly, through the rush hour traffic.

Twenty minutes later, they were off the bus and ambling home.

'Would you like a hand with some of those parcels?' asked Frankie.

'Oh, thank you. If you could take some of these bags for me, love? Oh, it's lucky you were on the bus; I would never have been able to carry all this. Such a long way from our house to the bus stop. Well, as I said, our Albert was out looking for you. He seems to be quite sweet on you. You've got to treat him right; he's had bad luck with the lasses. He went out with a lass, a student from down south. She was so posh when she started speaking. But she let him down. Our Albert said she had another fellow. A draughtsman. I don't think she thought our Albert's profession was reliable enough. Writing books and what not.'

'Auntie Flo. Do you know Daniel Bessel?'

'Bessel. There were some Bessels who used to live near Timperley. She was a nurse and her husband was a doctor. Jewish family. Practising. He used to wear this funny hat on Saturdays because for them it's Sunday. But his name wasn't Daniel, I think. Can't remember what it was. We always used to call him Dr. Bessel. Her name was Dorothy. Nice lass. They're both gone now, though. So many have gone. Like my Bill.'

'And Chris Gallagher?'

'Christopher Gallagher? Scottish bloke? From Glasgow? He's done well for himself. He owns a big hotel not that far from here. Near Fallowfield, but out in the country. Luxury place where people play golf. Bought it about eight years ago. My sister's daughter used to know him. She lived in one of his flats when she first got married.'

'I didn't know Albert had a sister.'

'No, my other sister. Our Lydia. She's gone too, I'm afraid. But she had two daughters. Doreen married a GI about 10 years ago and went to live in New York. Not the city. The state. She lives in a little town. Our Doreen came back about two years ago. When her mother died. So sad. She'd come two years before and we all asked, when are you coming back Doreen, and she said, in two years perhaps. Well, she did. Oh, life makes you weep sometimes. Oh, look, here we are. Well, come in for a cup of tea, love. Our Albert might be in for his tea. You stay for tea, too. I've got some fresh sausage rolls in from Lewis's.'

She walked into the dining room. This was at least her third visit but somehow she felt she had never looked at it before. It suddenly appeared very warm and cosy.

Albert was sitting at the dining room table, watching a news programme, on the TV in the corner of the room. There was a roaring coal fire in the fireplace.

On the mantelpiece, over the fireplace, there were framed photos of children, some of them of Albert and others of young men whom she supposed were the late husbands of the two sisters. Above the mantelpiece, hung a large, frameless mirror, not unlike the one that hung in her mother's dining room. To the left, there was a sideboard where someone had placed the cutlery and crockery for the next meal.

Two or three pictures of landscapes hung from picture rails. The striped orange curtains were drawn. They contrasted with the pale green striped wallpaper.

She thought she had better go into the kitchen to help Auntie Flo, but she was quickly shooed out. She went back into the dining room and sat down at the table, with her back to an old fashioned radio.

Albert's mother was nowhere to be seen, but Auntie Flo rapidly placed servings for three plates of sausage rolls, bread and butter, boiled eggs and cold tongue. Although Frankie had had a large lunch, she realised she was hungry again and ate with an unexpected appetite.

Cakes were served. She poured out second cups of tea for Albert and herself whilst Auntie Flo went to the kitchen to get more hot water.

They had all been sitting in silence watching the news programme. Auntie Flo went out again, Albert turned off the television.

'Have you heard any more from that woman in America? The one who wrote to you from London?'

'No, I haven't. But something else happened to me today.'

'Something else? With Auntie Flo? On the bus?'

'No.'

She told him the whole story. From entering the restaurant, the telephone conversation with her friend, the meal and how it had all been paid for by the two men. Albert listened with great attention.

'They wanted to make some kind of contact, didn't they? I mean why did this Gallagher pay for your lunch? And then run off? He must be the mysterious client your Bessel was talking about that night.'

'Do you know anything about him, Albert?'

'Actually, I do. Quite a lot, actually. I don't know if I know enough here to shed more light on the matter. But my cousin knew him and she told me all about him the last time she was in England. But I don't think anyone else knows, and certainly not Auntie Flo.'

The door opened as if on cue. Auntie Flo waddled in wearing her hat and coat.

'Albert, I'm going out for a bit. Mrs. Hambleton phoned and needs a little help. See you later, if you're still here. If not, good night, pets.'

It was early evening. They left the house on foot and made their way to the Crown, which was the nearest pub.

Albert began talking about his cousin as they walked.

'My cousin Doreen had a reputation in the family as being a bit wild. At home they used to say she was spoilt. She's actually very nice and we've always been good friends. She lives in a town near Buffalo, New York. I don't remember what her husband does but he went to college when he finished his national service. He was in the US Air Force over here. There

71

used to be a big base and the city was always full of Yanks at the weekend. Doreen's only a couple of years older than me, but she really belonged to another generation. Things changed a lot after she left England.'

'Anyway,' continued Albert, 'she left home when she was seventeen and shared a flat in town. It was quite a scandal in the family. Wouldn't even tell them where she was living. Imagine that! Anyway she wasn't there five minutes when the place caught fire. I kid you not. Her mum and dad didn't know anything about it but it left her and her flatmate with legal problems and nowhere to live.'

'Was it their fault?' asked Frankie.

'Well, the landlady seemed to think so, and she threatened to take them to court. Anyway her boyfriend, Stephen, now her husband, his best pal, another Yank on the base, was a bit of a spiv.'

'A spiv?'

'He sold stuff on the black market. These lads on the base could buy spirits and fags cheaply and then sell them at a profit. I say booze and cigarettes but there were blokes selling tyres, food, spare parts, parachute jackets, watches, anything they could get their hands on. Now, his contact in the town was a Scottish spiv called Chris Gallagher. Or better said, he was from Glasgow, from an Irish immigrant family.'

'That's why he has an Irish name. Auntie Flo said he was Scottish.'

'Oh. You spoke to her about it, did you?'

'I only asked if she knew him. All she could tell me, was that your cousin had lived in one of his flats and he had a big hotel.'

'Yes. It's called the Highland Village Hotel. The name's nothing to do with him. It was called that before he bought it.'

They wandered into the pub. It was nearly empty. They sat at a table. Albert went to get the drinks. Frankie opened her bag and took out some money.

'Let me get these, Albert. You're always treating me.'

'When you come out with me, I pay. You are my guest.'

'Don't be so silly. I'm beginning to feel a little bit like a kept woman here.'

The barmaid returned with the drinks and she pressed the money into her hands.

'I couldn't even pay for my own lunch.' said Frankie. 'And I had been thinking it would be nice to treat you to dinner there, one evening. Now I don't ever want to return.'

'We'll go there for dinner as soon as we can. We don't have to be scared of anything. Least of all, of people who want to pay for our dinner.'

They sat down. Albert continued with his tale.

'Anyway. Gallagher immediately got them another flat. And a lawyer. Never charged them anything. Not for the flat or the lawyer. And they never heard from the irate landlady again.'

'And they didn't have to pay rent?'

'They weren't there very long. Doreen was going to get married and she returned home to recover respectability, now she had a formal boyfriend, and the flatmate went to Canada. This'd be about 1952, which was 12 years ago. She got married soon afterwards.'

'This Gallagher must've had a lot of money,' said Frankie.

'Well, he started out, I don't know, with used cars after the war. Never did National Service or anything banal like that. These spivs always found a way of avoiding that. Then the government began talking about slum clearance. So he went round buying up slummy houses. He'd buy the property for a pittance. Continue charging the tenants rent and, if the government wanted to knock it down, claim compensation. He even went into the demolition business and got paid for knocking down his own houses. Anyway he still owns houses all over the place.'

'And how does this tie in with your cousin?' she asked.

'Gallagher let them live in one of his apartments rent free. Lots of married GIs lived on base in American type houses. But that was expensive and Doreen wanted to save money as Stephen was going to go to college on the GI bill. The US government would pay tuition fees but not living expenses. And they were already expecting a baby.'

'Well that was nice of him.'

'Doreen told me, when they first went to see the flat, they couldn't find the building, so they went into the local police station to ask directions. The two policemen on duty knew immediately where it was and who the owner was. They treated them with kid gloves and one of them personally went with them. Doreen said they were in his pay.'

'I don't believe that. Not in England,' said Frankie.

'Soon afterwards, Gallagher asked her if Stephen could get him some things from the base. As a favour. He came out with a long detailed list of things he wanted, mainly American cigarettes, cigars and spirits from the base.'

'What did she say?' she asked.

'She told Stephen to bring the stuff. He kicked up a fuss at first.'

'I imagine he would. Americans tend to be very honest.'

'Well,' said Albert. 'Some of them. His pal wasn't very honest, was he?'

'No, I suppose not,' said Frankie.

'Anyway,' Albert continued, 'they started bringing in things from the base and selling them to this bloke at a profit. Stephen was always worried the military police would come to his house; find all this stuff and court martial him. Gallagher laughed when Doreen told him. The MPs couldn't enter premises belonging to an Englishman without a warrant from an English judge and accompanied by an English policeman. And the police were in his pay.'

'Do you think that's true?' asked Frankie.

'Well, that's what he said.'

Albert went on.

'Doreen really coined it in before she left England. When they got to New York State they were able to buy a house and live comfortably until Stephen graduated. No one could figure out how they managed to live so well. And she wasn't telling anyone.'

'And how did you know then?' asked Frankie.

'Well, when she came back two years ago for her mother's funeral, we went for a drink one night and she told me all about it. But she told me to keep it under my hat. Especially not to tell my mum or my auntie. She'd been to visit Gallagher's daughter and was a bit impressed by what she had told her.'

'Oh, so he does have a daughter,' said Frankie. 'In the restaurant, he told them she was a friend of mine.'

'Well, they became friendly because they lived in the same apartment building before Doreen went to New York.'

Frankie sighed and said,

'I was thinking of going back to America. And leaving all this behind. It's just becoming too much for me. No one will bother me if I go back.'

Albert looked at her and shook his head.

'The story hasn't finished. Just so you understand what we're dealing with here.'

'Gallagher,' he continued, 'was keen on having his son-in-law work in one of his businesses. But he didn't want to. The reasons I don't know. Perhaps he didn't like the criminal aspect. That would be my reason. So he tried to get on in local companies. Every time he went for an interview he'd get the job with no problem at all. It seems Gallagher would make a phone call and whoever it was would take on his son-in-law as a favour.'

'And he complained about that?'

'Well,' said Albert. 'He wanted to make it on his own, I suppose.'

'None of this surprises me, though,' replied Frankie. 'I think Mrs. Petersen had that kind of influence in Des Moines.'

76

'Well, he and his wife decided to move out with their kids to Canada. They'd made friends with a Canadian who was going back to Ontario and he talked them into it. That'd be about four years ago.'

'What happened?' she asked.

'Oh, he got himself in a mess. His Canadian pal turned out to be not so nice, introduced him to loan sharks. People who lend money at very high interest and then beat you up if you don't pay.'

'Why'd he do that?'

'Well,' said Albert. 'I asked Doreen the same question. She said that he thought he was going to make a lot of money very quickly and be able to pay it back.'

'And of course, it didn't work out like that?'

'Well,' said Albert. 'Probably he paid for his lack of experience in a new country and thought that he could trust the people who were trying to con him. He was getting roughed up by two thugs because he couldn't pay back the loans. His wife was getting nasty phone calls when he was out. They were terrified.'

'Sounds awful. Why didn't they just come home?'

Frankie shook her head in disbelief.

Albert continued.

'Well they had him over a barrel. I'm not sure exactly how it worked but he would have to present some kind of certificate showing he was free from debt. Otherwise he wasn't allowed to leave the country.'

'And your cousin told you this? Are they still in Canada?'

'No, the daughter telephoned her father. The same day someone came to collect her and the kids, put them on a plane to England. The two nasty types just vanished and were never heard from again. The next step was to hide the husband until they could get him out. Gallagher had him taken to a hotel on Lake Erie. There he was put on a boat which eventually reached Liverpool. When Doreen arrived for the funeral, they'd just come back and were living in one of Gallagher's houses. Her husband was working at the hotel.'

'How did Gallagher manage all that?' she asked.

'Well, there you are. You may think you're far away in San Francisco but believe me if they want something from you they'll find you. We have to get to the bottom of this mystery. Treating you to lunch was a warning.'

'A warning? Is he personally violent?'

'Well he's achieved a lot of respectability what with the hotel and things.'

'I mean am I in physical danger from him?' Frankie insisted.

'Well he's from Glasgow. He pulled himself up out of the mire. He deals with other spivs and criminals. He pays off policemen. He certainly had those two in Canada sorted out. He's no spring chicken now, but I've seen enough films to know that gangsters usually have lads working for them who aren't averse to knocking people about.'

'Well, he was very nice to your cousin.'

'She thought so. But really he was just establishing a contact and using it. These people work on a system of you scratch my back and I'll scratch yours. Another pint of bitter?'

78

'No, I'll have a tomato juice and Worcestershire sauce, please.'

When he came back to the table, she looked at him and said,

'Don't look now Albert, but I think that man Bessel is in the pub. He came in just as you stood up and is sitting in the corner by the fireplace. I'm sure he's seen us.'

Albert got up and turned round, went straight up to Bessel who was, just as Frankie had said, sitting at a table. There was no drink in front of him. He looked up at Albert, nodded, got up and walked out the door.

Albert came back, sat down, looking a little smug, thought Frankie.

'How did you get rid of him?'

'How indeed? Told him I had a gun in my pocket and gave him three seconds to get out.'

'Really'

'No, of course not. I said, tell your boss I want to talk to him about the discs. Sooner or later he was going to have to talk to me anyway. Ring and make an appointment. But not to come round bothering you again or he would have me to deal with. He nodded and left. Didn't even have time to buy a drink.

'Yes,' she said. 'I saw he left very quickly. What are you planning to do?'

'We'll go and talk to them. If Doreen could talk to him, so can we. Somehow or other, we'll get to the bottom of this.'

## Chapter Eight

The next morning Albert came round early.

'Are you making tea? I've got some news for you.'

They sat in the lounge in front of the little electric fire. Frankie poured out the tea and Albert began:

'My agent or rather my agent's secretary telephoned me this morning. I have an unlisted number and all telephone calls which aren't personal go directly to my literary agent who hands on important messages. Mr. Gallagher has received my message and will be in contact in due course.'

'And when will that be?' she asked.

'Well, tomorrow's New Year's Day. Maybe he won't phone until Monday, 4th January.'

'Well I have news, too. Look. It arrived this morning.'

She gave him a greeting card.

'Happy New Year. With best wishes, Ruth Petersen.'

He turned it over and saw there was something written on the back.

'We must have English tea together this weekend. Ring me sometime and we'll make a date. I'll be in the Highland Village Hotel all week. So looking forward to seeing you, liebchen.'

He read it again out loud.

'Liebchen?'

'Yes, she often used to call me that. It's like Auntie Flo calling me love or pet. It means dear in German.'

'Yes, I know what it means although I don't speak much German. Ich liebe dich is about as much as I remember now. I had an Austrian girlfriend some years ago.'

'Oh, Auntie Flo didn't mention that one.'

'Oh, what did she mention?'

'A very posh girl, from the south. In fact, she told the whole bus about it.'

'Oh, no.'

'No,' continued Frankie, 'she told me, after we got off the bus. But she told me the girl let you down.'

'Let them down, she meant. They were both always match making. But I think they didn't like Helga because she was German.'

'I thought you said Austrian.'

'For them she spoke German and they never forgave her that.'

'Well, I don't speak German.'

What's on her lung is on her tongue, her mother used to say. Think before you speak, she thought.

Albert's face lit up in a smile.

'Oh, they love you. They think you're American. They even like your accent from Iowa.'

She reddened a little.

'I haven't got an accent from Iowa, or anywhere else in the States.'

'They think so. Auntie Flo thinks you sound so sophisticated. But not posh and stuck up, like a girl from the south.'

She drew herself up.

'Well, be that as it may, what do we do about Mrs. Petersen? Do I call her up? And when?'

'Let's leave it for the moment,' replied Albert. 'You only got the card an hour ago. Why don't we go to the American Steak House for lunch. You said you wanted to treat me and the truth is, I've thought of nothing else since then. Come on. We'll take the car.'

Although it was early, the restaurant was already full and they had to wait for a table. The jazz pianist was today accompanied by a female vocalist.

Frankie was relieved not to recognise any of the staff from the previous day. Perhaps they regularly changed shifts, she thought.

This time, at least, she was able to pay the rather steep bill and leave a tip with no hindrance.

They were out of the restaurant before half past one and Albert had an idea.

'Why don't we drive over to Fallowfield Market?'

'What for?'

'Something happened to you there. We could investigate a little.'

'I don't know what there is to investigate,' she answered.

'Let's go anyway. It's something to do and it's a nice drive.'

'It'll be dark soon.'

'We've got until three at least, maybe half past three. In half an hour we're there.'

Half an hour later, they were parked outside the large structure which housed the market. They entered.

The place reeked of raw meat. Frankie once again felt a little dizzy. She looked towards the far wall and saw a door. She walked towards it. She opened it and found a fenced field with a stile.

She climbed the stile, walked across the field, to another stile at the other end. Then, a path through a kind of cornfield, finally to a meadow with a wood on the other side.

She looked down and saw a metallic circular object, maybe two feet in diameter.

'What's that?'

She suddenly realised she was not alone. She had completely forgotten about Albert. In fact she had forgotten everything.

'I don't know. I don't know why I came here. Is this one of the discs? Can we take it with us?'

'I don't know what it is,' said Albert. 'It could even be an unexploded bomb of some sort. I would be very careful about trying to dig it up. But, how did you find it?'

'It seemed to attract me, call to me. I can't explain. Nothing else seemed important.'

'So,' said Albert. 'You are the key to the whole operation. That's what they said. I think we should talk to our friend Bernard. He seems to know something about this, too.'

They walked back to the car, got in and Albert started the engine.

'Did you see it the other day when you were here?'

'See what?'

'The disc.'

'I told you and everybody else I don't know anything about any discs.' she replied.

'But the disc we saw at the market?'

'What disc? Albert, what are you talking about?'

'You don't remember, do you?'

'Remember what?'

'Never mind.' he said. 'What time are you meeting your friend Beryl?


She met Beryl at the bus stop near her mother's house. They got on the bus almost immediately and managed to find two seats upstairs.

'Couldn't face half an hour on this bus without a smoke.' said Beryl.

She took out her cigarettes and offered one to Frankie.

'Another long weekend ahead of us. Oh, but your whole life has become a bit of a weekend, hasn't it. What do you do with yourself, now?'

'Well, today I went to lunch with a friend. To the American Steak House in School Lane. I remember Chuck used to like it. Said it was the only place where you could get real American food.'

'Who wants it? I never want to see another McDonald's hamburger the rest of my life. If they ever come here, I'll emigrate. Who'd you go with?'

'Albert, my next door neighbour.'

'You didn't tell me you were courting. And with the boy next door. What's he like?'

'He's just a friend. But he's been very good to me since I got here. And his mum and auntie live close by. I don't know what I would have done without them. We've gone out together to a few places and his mum has invited me to Sunday dinner a few times.'

'So, they've taken you on like one of the family. What does he do?'

'He's a novelist. He's already had two books published and is working on a third. But, as I said, he's just a friend. They are all friends, all three of them. I haven't got any family left, so they've been very kind to me.'

'What kind of books does he write?' asked Beryl. 'Have you read them? Oh, I'd love to read a book by someone I knew.'

'I don't like reading very much. I was dreading that he might make me read one of his books and then ask me about it.'

'And he hasn't?'

'No, not once.'

They got off the bus and made their way into the crowded dance hall. Beryl had a table reserved and after checking in their coats and handbags, they both sat down.

Almost immediately, a man came up to the table and greeted Frankie in French. It was Bernard.

'Oh, hello Bernard. Happy New Year. This is my friend, Beryl.'

Beryl smiled enigmatically, her bright green eyes dancing merrily.

'Oh, are you French?'

'Yes,' Bernard replied. 'I am. Why?'

'Oh, because I thought you were speaking French, just now.'

'Oh, I always speak a little in French with Frankie. It's a little intimacy we share. I am with some friends, but later perhaps, we can dance a little.'

He left and disappeared into the crowd.

'And now a Frenchman,' laughed Beryl. 'You have been busy, haven't you?'

'He very kindly took me to a Christmas party on Christmas Day. He's a French journalist and I met other French journalists at the party.'

'And where did you meet this little bundle of Gallic charm?'

'In a pub about two weeks ago. He was in a group of Albert's friends. He told me he was writing a book, too.'

'Another book? What about?'

'A German secret weapon, I think.'

'Not about the aliens?' asked Beryl.

'I wouldn't know. Why don't you ask him, when he comes back.'

The two friends continued chatting over a drink. Bernard came back, accompanied by another man, and suggested dancing a little. Beryl, without further ado, grabbed Bernard and marched him off to the dance floor, leaving Frankie with his companion, a slim man with abundant black hair, combed back and kept in place with something like Brylcreem.

He smiled politely and she saw he had a long, fine moustache above his lip.

He led her to the dance floor.

'I think I met you on Christmas Day, at the party in that old English pub. You don't remember me. My name is Salvador. I'm from Spain.'

'I'm not sure. I met a lot of people that day. And from so many places. Are you a journalist, too?'

'I'm afraid so,' he replied. 'I work for ABC in Madrid. I live in London actually. I'm only here for Christmas.'

'Visiting relatives?'

'Not exactly. I have no relatives in England. I learned to speak English in America. My father was a university professor there for some years. But the family returned to Spain in the late forties and my father started work in a Spanish university. I was bilingual and when I finished my military service I studied journalism and landed a post here in England.'

'Yes, you speak with an American accent. I would have taken you for American.'

The band had stopped playing and Beryl and Bernard were already sitting at the table drinking and smoking. Beryl was speaking to Bernard in French. She turned to Frankie.

'I'm smoking Gaulloise. Bernard's given me one of his French cigarettes. I didn't remember how strong they are. And they have no filter. My mouth is full of tobacco.'

Frankie looked at Bernard.

'I didn't know you smoked.'

He grinned at her and shrugged.

'All Frenchmen smoke. They start you off in school. In French schools you are allowed to smoke at fourteen. And everybody does. It's true, that I don't smoke, except when I want to. Some people have to smoke all the time. But I can take it or leave it. Do you want a French cigarette? I warn you, they are very strong.'

She declined his offer. Something else to tell Albert.

She looked again at Beryl, who was doing her impersonation of a Kentucky accent and telling Bernard how she had been interviewed by the FBI before leaving the US. Bernard was listening with great attention. He had tilted his sensual face towards her, his eyes on the ground, wearing a small intent frown, as if he could not bear to miss a word.

Beryl was exultant in her stories about the FBI interspersed with phrases in French.

They were soon joined by other members of Bernard's group. She recollected many from the party on Christmas Day. Some of them came to greet her again, almost as if they were old friends.

1964 disappeared at the stroke of midnight. An hour later the premises had closed and she, Beryl, and Salvador were all being driven home in Bernard's convertible.

She was dropped off first and Bernard, without saying anything, entered the house with her to check the doors.

'Let's go out next week.' he said. 'I'll send you a card or come by.'

Frankie had had a long day. She got into bed and everything seemed to go dark around her.

# Chapter Nine

It was January 1st, 1965. Frankie opened her eyes. A new year ahead of her.

As she came down the stairs, someone, almost immediately identified as Albert, knocked on the door.

'Hello Albert. Happy New Year. It's still very early. I didn't go to bed until two o'clock.'

'I spent the evening with my mother and my aunt. Auntie Flo even had a bottle of champagne for us to drink at midnight.'

'Oh, you could have come out with us. I didn't know that you had no plans.'

'No, I wanted to spend the night with them. We almost always spend New Year's Eve together watching telly and drinking cider. It's a family tradition. That's why I didn't want to invite you. Not really that much fun. We have things to talk about. Why don't you get dressed, come next door and I'll make you breakfast.'

Albert's house and Frankie's mother's house were a pair of semi-detached houses with a connecting wall. Frankie had been in the other house many times when Mrs. Davis lived there. One house was simply the mirror image of the other.

She was somewhat surprised to find that Albert had completely renovated the house. Gone was the enormous hall which had been joined to the lounge in order to form a much larger room at the front of the house. A small kitchen had been built in the corner and was surrounded by a bar which acted as a room divider.

No fireplace at all, just a small dining area, with a round table and chairs, and then next to the bay window, the living area, a long modern sofa, an easy chair and the TV set. At the back of the house, in another room, where the kitchenette and part of the dining room that gave onto the garden had been, was his office, where presumably he wrote his books.

'So nice and warm in here,' said Frankie. 'Can I take my coat off?'

'Yes, it's the central heating. I had everything changed when I bought it.'

'So clean and tidy. Not like my house.'

'A lady comes to clean. But it's not difficult to keep tidy if you're all alone and I don't cook very much.'

'What about the garden? Do you have a gardener too?'

'No,' he replied. 'I really enjoy gardening. It helps me unwind, when I've been working.'

Frankie ate a hearty breakfast of sausages, bacon and eggs, washed down with sweet tea.

As they ate, Frankie related the events of the night before.

When she finished speaking, Albert said;

'I'm sure Bernard knows a great deal about all of this. Now there is something I have to tell you and it may upset you.'

'What?'

'Do you remember yesterday, when we went to Fallowfield Market?'

'Yes.'

'Do you remember going out the back door?'

'No. We went in very quickly, I remember the smell put me off and we left as quickly as we could and got back into the car.'

'You don't remember going through the fields?' he asked.

'No, I don't remember doing anything like that. Why? What are you trying to tell me?'

'Listen to me,' replied Albert. 'The moment we entered the market you went into a kind of trance. You ignored me, but very determinedly went out the back door, along a path, through a couple of fields, until we arrived in an area where you looked down at what seemed to be a metallic circle or disc about two maybe three feet in diameter, buried in the ground. You looked at it and we spoke about it. But the moment we moved away from it, you had forgotten all about it.'

'I don't remember anything like that.'

'And I think the same thing happened the day you were with Bernard.' said Albert.

'Well if you know where the discs are, why don't we go and get them?'

'I don't know what this is,' he said. 'But if we start tampering with something like that it might explode in our faces. And obviously Bernard thought the same. And I think he knew it was there. That's why he brought you.'

'Yes,' she answered, 'he told me the night before that he had something to show me. But would this be the disc Daniel Bessel spoke about, or is it something else? You told me about a photograph you had seen. Is it the same thing? Is that what Auntie Flo showed you?'

'It was an old black and white photo. It could be the same thing. But maybe a different size.'

'Do they know about this thing buried out there? And if they do, why are they bothering me? Why don't they just go and get it.'

'I don't know.' said Albert. 'I want to go and look at it again. There was another road nearby. Perhaps if we went that way you might avoid going into a trance.'

'Do you remember where it was, Albert? I mean, could you find it, without going through the market?'

'Oh yes, no problem at all.'

There was another road behind the building that housed Fallowfield Market. It led between a kind of corn field and a meadow with a wood on the far side. Albert stopped the car at the end of the path. They got out of the car and walked along the path to the place where he remembered they had found the disc. The freshly dug earth revealed that indeed something maybe two feet in diameter had been partially buried, but it was, obviously, no longer there. Albert seemed a little disappointed.

'Well, maybe that is the end of our mystery. At least for us. And clearly, it was not an unexploded bomb.'

'It was here?' she asked.

'Oh, there is no doubt about it. Don't you remember anything at all?'

'I remember getting into the car right here with Bernard. But I don't remember seeing anything. Do you think Bernard has it?'

'He must have.' said Albert. 'Let's go home!'

They were very quiet driving back. Frankie still could not understand how it was that she did not remember the disc or how she had found it. But, more confusing, was how she knew where it was. And if she could find it then, could she find it again?

Albert broke the silence.

'If we knew where Bernard lives, or where he's keeping this disc, perhaps you have a special ability to locate it again.'

'Yes,' she replied. 'I was thinking the same thing. Do you know where he lives?'

As Albert pulled into the lane where they lived he caught sight of Bernard's convertible parked in the road.

'You have a visitor it seems, Frankie. Why don't you get out at the corner now, before he sees the car and go and see what he wants.'

Frankie did as she was told and walked along the pavement towards her house. Albert drove back towards the main road.

She opened the gate of the front garden and almost ran into Bernard. He grinned at her.

'Well, you most certainly get up early on New Year's Day. In France everyone gets up very late. Of course, here it is not a holiday. In France, it is. We go out all night, not until only midnight.'

'Oh, I didn't get to bed until two o'clock. Did you all get home all right?'

'Oh, yes,' replied Bernard. 'I drove Salvador Jimenez and your friend, what was her name? I can't quite remember.'

'Beryl.'

'Oh, yes, Beryl, very chatty and such funny accents she imitated. I drove them both home and then went straight home to bed.'

'Beryl was very interested in the book you are writing. About the German secret weapon.'

'Yes, she said so. Frankie, I wanted to invite you out for lunch. That is, if you have no previous commitment.'

'Yes I'd love to. Where did you want to go?'

'Why don't you choose a place?' said Bernard. 'Somewhere nice.'

They walked into the panelled dining room of the American Steak House and asked for a table for two. Although there were more people than there would be on a normal weekday, it was not crowded as it had been the day before. The drinks waiter came, and after ordering a Coke, she asked to use the telephone.

Albert had given her a card with his agent's number and then written his personal number on the other side. He did not answer at home and so she called the agency number. She left a message that she was in the American Steak House with their mutual friend.

When she came back, Bernard was drinking a glass of red wine and looking at the menu.

'Everything all right?'

'Yes, I had to call a friend. We had arranged to meet later and I had forgotten all about it. And I haven't a telephone at home.'

'Oh, I'm sorry if I interrupted something.'

'Oh, no,' replied Frankie. 'It wasn't important. And I'd much prefer to be here.'

She gave him what she hoped was an encouraging smile.

'I used to come here with my husband. He said this was the only restaurant in England with real American food. And he always liked the music.'

'You miss your husband very much, don't you?'

He looked at her from the other side of the table, half closing his eyes and smiling slightly.

'Yes,' she replied. 'I'm afraid I do.'

'I, too, once lost a dear friend. And I know how you feel.'

She looked across the table at him. Of course, this was all well-rehearsed. She thought of Albert. And his straightforward honesty and concern for her. Not to mention the differences with Bernard; his slight build and those ridiculous eyes. What would her mother have called them? French bedroom eyes. More importantly. What did Bernard want from her? Was it just romance? She did not think so.

The food arrived. Frankie spoke.

'I've been meaning to ask you something. Do you remember that day we went to Fallowfield Market?'

Bernard started.

'Oh yes.'

'I was a little confused that day, but now I remember everything very well. We looked down at a kind of round, metal structure about two feet in diameter. Do you remember?'

'Yes,' he replied. 'I do.'

'You told me, before, that you had something to show me. Was that what you wanted me to see?'

'Yes it was. You see, I'm writing a book about a secret weapon the Germans tried to develop during the war. I thought you might know something about it.'

'Why?'

'Because your father worked on a project in Sheffield in which they tried to understand the technology used in this weapon.'

'How did you know who my father was?' she asked.

'The moment I saw you in the pub I recognized you. I have photos of you and your parents. And others. The old man who lived next door and William Morrison who was stabbed to death in Sheffield. I have been studying all this for a long time. But I can't get to the bottom of the mystery. What are these discs? Where do they come from? And what did the Germans develop and what have the British and Americans done with them?'

The waiter came by and he asked for a second glass of wine.

'You weren't going to tell me any of this, were you?'

'No, I wasn't. This is my book and I have no intention of leaking it to anybody. I have spent a long time researching it. But if you know about these discs, we can at least pool our information.'

The waiter returned to take their orders for dessert. Bernard ordered pecan pie, as she recommended.

'How did you know the disc was outside Fallowfield Market? Because you did know before I found it for you, didn't you?'

'Oh, yes,' he replied. 'But I wanted to know if you could find it. And you could. And not only that, but afterwards you forgot all about it. But now you've remembered and that changes all my theories.'

'But, how did you know it was there?'

He looked at her very seriously. He seemed no longer interested in flirting with her.

'Because I put it there.'

She gasped.

'You put it there?'

'Yes, of course.'

'Where did you get it?' she asked.

'I made it. I put it together some time ago. It is a copy of the metal discs in the photographs I have.'

'I don't believe you. If this is only a copy, why did it have this strange effect on me? And you must know. You put it there intentionally and then took me there to see what I would do.'

'Yes,' replied Bernard. 'And you did exactly as I expected. You went out of the market to the spot where it was.'

'Why?'

'Well you tell me. How did you know it was there?'

'I don't know,' said Frankie. 'I can't remember. I went again with Albert and we found it again and I forgot again. Albert told me what had happened, and then the next day, we went back by another road to the same place, and you had already taken it.'

He looked at her startled.

'It's not there?'

'No,' she said. 'We thought you had taken it.'

'No. I haven't touched it.'

He shrugged.

'I don't suppose it really matters that much.'

'Why did you leave it there?'

'Oh I didn't have time to dig it up again. I had so many things to do and I've been in France all week. I just got back yesterday afternoon. And as I said it is valueless. It's only a cheap copy. Anyone could have taken it. I can easily make another one.'

The waiter passed and Bernard asked for the bill.

'It's getting very late, Frankie. I won't say it's been a lovely lunch, although the restaurant and the company couldn't have been nicer. But it has been a most informative lunch. You are not on the phone yet, are you? I'm going to leave you my business card with my phone number if you need anything.'

He left and paid the bill on his way out.

Frankie sat listening to the piano music for a while, then gathered her possessions and wandered towards the exit. As she was leaving, she passed the phone booths and went into one.

First, she phoned Beryl. Beryl's mother answered the phone. Beryl was out, not at work because she was not working today, but at a business meeting. She could hear the children playing in the background and their grandmother sounded a little weary.

She then rang Albert. He answered immediately and offered to pick her up outside the restaurant. She went outside to wait for him.

## Chapter Ten

'I didn't know what to do when you went off with Bernard,' said Albert. 'If I should follow you or wait by the telephone. In the end I followed you and saw that you'd taken him to your favourite restaurant. So I went home and waited by the phone.'

'I didn't know where to go when he asked me to suggest a place. Then I thought your spiv and his henchman might be there and it would be interesting to see his reaction. They weren't there, but he did tell me about the disc. He knew the disc was there when he took me there.'

'And how did he know?' asked Albert.

'Because he had put it there himself. He says it isn't a real disc, just something he ran up himself, copying the old photos from material he had collected for his book.'

Albert pulled up at the side of the road. He looked at her. His normal ruddy complexion had paled considerably.

'I'm sorry. He made it himself and put it there? Why did he do that?'

'As I understand it, he did it for me. To see how I would react and to see if I would find it.'

'How did you find it?' he asked. 'Why did you go into a trance?'

'I don't know. He scurried away before I could get any more out of him. But he left me his business card and phone numbers. Oh, and more importantly. He claims he has nothing to do with the disappearance of the disc. He left it there because he didn't have time to dig it up again. And he has no idea who took it.'

'Let's go back to the place and look again. See if we can find any clues.'

Once again they pulled up outside the building which housed the market.

'I'll go in this way,' said Frankie. 'Why don't you drive around to the other side like we did yesterday. That way we can get through this more quickly.'

She went into the market and again was faced with the reek of fresh meat. She looked again at the door on the far side, opened it and walked through the fields. Looking down, she saw where the disc had been buried. She crossed the road and walked across a meadow to a wood. In the wood there was a kind of small house.

She opened the door.

'Frankie.'

She looked up at Albert.

'I didn't see you.' she said.

'No, I followed you. You looked down at the hole and then you crossed the road and brought us to this little house.'

She looked at the structure. A little stone cottage, hidden by trees. Albert opened the door. One room, in which tramps had slept, perhaps some time ago, and a kitchen. Very obviously abandoned, many years ago. Dirty, white walls.

'You were in a trance again, weren't you? Why did you come here?'

'I suppose because I was alone,' said Frankie. 'I don't know. Oh, let's go! It's getting dark.'

They got into the car and began driving home.

'So why did you cross the road and go to the wood?'

She looked at him.

'You know I don't remember anything. I entered the market; there was this awful smell and next thing I am in the car. Did you find any clues? Perhaps a packet of French cigarettes?'

'No,' said Albert. 'But we have established that the trance has nothing to do with Bernard's disc.'

'Well, if Bernard made it then it can hardly be the cause of my trance.'

'If Bernard is telling the truth about this.'

'I'm pretty sure he is.'

It was dark by the time they got home.

Albert went to his mother's home for his tea and Frankie went and sat in her mother's lounge. She turned on the little electric fire and sat down on the couch covering herself with a knitted, coloured blanket.

Frankie turned on the light. It was about eight o'clock. She drew the curtains and went into the kitchen to prepare something to eat. Albert knocked on the window. She opened the side door and he came in.

'I phoned my agent's secretary. Gallagher has given us an appointment for Monday afternoon. Afternoon tea at his hotel. I have all the details about where to go and everything. I told the secretary to accept. I hope that's all right with you.'

'Fine,' replied Frankie. 'But we're going to have to talk to Bernard first. Does he know anything about these people? We're going to have to go well prepared.'

'I don't really know Bernard. He was never a friend of mine. Over the years I've got to know quite a few writers and journalists and he's been at a lot of parties I've attended, but I've only really spoken to him once or twice. Anyway, I think he really lives in London and only comes up here every once in a while.'

He looked at her.

'Have you got him as a kind of boyfriend?'

She was taken aback and flushed slightly. Then she stiffened.

'Certainly not. What gave you that idea?'

'Well he takes you out in his convertible. You go to restaurants together.'

'I go out in your car too. We go to restaurants together. And to pubs. And to have coffee. I've even met your mother a few times.'

He moved closer to her.

'So that makes me a kind of boyfriend, doesn't it?'

'Kind of,' she said. 'Well, yes, you are very sweet to me. And I do like you, quite a lot, actually.'

She stretched up and kissed him on the cheek and took his hand and squeezed it.

'But, I'm still a grieving widow and I don't want a boyfriend for the moment.'

She looked at him

'You do understand, don't you? I'm still very sad, inside.'

He looked back at her with what she thought was a mournful expression.

'Let's concentrate on our mystery for the moment,' he said.

'The question is,' he went on, 'do you want me to call Bernard or are you going to do it? And shall we see him together or do you want to speak to him alone? My impression is that he's a slippery customer and he avoids answering your questions.'

Frankie shook her head and said;

'I don't know if we should involve Bernard in this at all. First, we ought to get this Gallagher character to talk. Tell us what he wants and maybe give us some idea of what he knows. Up until now, the only thing we know about Bernard, is he's writing a book about it. I'm sure he would just want to use us to get information. He might not have any connection with these two blokes.'

Albert stood for a time thinking. At last he said;

'You, know it might be better if I went alone. As your representative. See what they have to say. This would leave you in reserve and open the door to further meetings.'

Frankie did not seem to hear him and said;

'Something we should do is go back to the house near Fallowfield. Find out what it is. But we must go in the morning and not just before it gets dark. And we seriously have to look for clues. Can we go tomorrow morning?'

'I was hoping you'd say that. Yes, we'll get up early and drive out there tomorrow. But, what do you say, to my going alone to see Gallagher?'

Frankie hesitated, frowned and then said,

'Shall we take a rain check on that one?'

'What's that?'

'An American expression. Postpone taking a decision. I'm not sure what I want to do.'

'All right. We'll talk about it over the weekend. There's no hurry.'

## Chapter Eleven

It was a crisp, very cold, windy morning. Everything was covered in frost. A lifeless sun shone out of the pale blue sky, never warming, purely cosmetic. Well, at least it was not raining, and it was neither cloudy nor grey.

Albert parked the car on the far side of the road, next to the meadow which gave onto the wood.

They got out of the car and he led the way to the wood. The ground was hard and they could hear the frozen vegetation crunch under their feet.

Frankie realised she was no longer aware of her surroundings but wished to continue walking alone. She wandered rapidly towards the little house, opened the door and walked in. There was only one room which gave onto what had been a kitchen. She entered. Almost immediately behind her there was a door which she opened. Here, there was a kind of pantry. And on the floor, by her feet, a circular metallic disc about two feet in diameter.

Albert came up behind her.

'Well this is a turn up for the books. Is this a real one or a copy? Did Bernard leave this one too?'

He bent down and touched it, gingerly. It was not even partially buried, but simply placed on the floor. It was made of some kind of silver coloured metal. He tried moving it. It was quite heavy, but he would be able to carry it back to the car if he decided to.

'What do you think, Albert? Is this real or not?'

'I don't know what a real one looks like. Let's take this home with us.'

He picked it up and walked to the front of the cottage. Cautiously, he looked out the door. They seemed to be quite alone. He carried the disc out to the car. Frankie walked behind him. He opened the boot, placed the disc inside, closed it and then both of them got into the car and they drove off.

She looked at Albert as he drove. His ruddy complexion was deeper than ever as if he had made some effort of strength. He was a strong, rugged looking guy, so she felt quite alarmed to see him still breathing heavily.

'Are you all right? You look very tired.'

'Well. It was quite heavy. I was able to carry it, but after a few minutes it began to weigh a ton.'

She realised that, once again, she had forgotten everything. For a moment she felt a deep sense of emptiness and despair, as if she personally had failed herself and her companion. She decided not to say anything. Sooner or later, he would explain. They carried on, lost in their own thoughts.

The white frost had reminded her of the snow in Iowa. Goodness, how cold it would be now. She laughed to herself. Well at least she was avoiding the cold weather. If she went back to America she would definitely go and live somewhere warmer.

And what about her life in England? Was she falling in love with Albert, she wondered. The night before, she had wanted to throw herself around him, but instead told him she was a grieving widow.

Well, she thought, she did not want to appear cheap. Immediately, she remembered Beryl. Something had happened the night Bernard took her home, she was sure. And that was also behind how she was beginning to feel about Bernard. Could he even be trusted? Had he told her the truth, or was his story just a pack of lies?

They were home again. Albert got out of the car and opened his garage door. The garage seemed to communicate with the house. This was quite different from the arrangement in her parents' house. Her parents had never had a garage at all.

'Did you have the garage built when you renovated the house?'

'Yes,' he replied. 'But I don't use it very often. I usually park in the road.' He closed the garage door behind them.

'In Des Moines, we had a remote control for the garage door.'

'Yes, well, this isn't Des Moines, I'm afraid. Here it's just British elbow grease.'

He opened the boot. She choked in surprise.

'Where did you get that Albert?'

He laughed.

'I imagined that you didn't remember, but I didn't want to go through all that in the car. We found it in the house. Or rather you found it. Now our question is, is it the same one we saw half buried the other day, or is it another one? And is it real, or something Bernard put together? And what do we do with it?'

'Shall we take it into the house, or should we leave it here in the garage?' she asked. 'Would it be dangerous?'

'I don't think I want it in the house. There are some sheds at the back of the garden. One of them is empty. I think I'll leave it there. I don't think it's going to explode or anything like that, but you never know if it might give off something poisonous. Open the door, will you. I'll carry it out to the shed.'

Later, they were sitting in Albert's living room, drinking tea.

'Frankie, what might be a good idea is if you telephone that American woman you worked for in Iowa. See if she wants to have lunch with you tomorrow. Or dinner this evening. You could invite her to that restaurant where you take everyone. You haven't been there for a while. And I could go too. And sit at another table and watch her. How do you feel about that?'

'Good idea. I'll phone her now.'

Mrs. Petersen answered almost immediately and was delighted to talk to Frankie. How she had missed her. Yes, she would love to go to an American restaurant. She didn't like the food in England and the coffee was awful. They arranged to meet for dinner at eight.

Frankie phoned the Steak House and made a reservation for a table for two. A few minutes later, Albert made another reservation, for himself.

Frankie went home for lunch and Albert went to his mother's.


Mrs. Petersen was already sitting at a table, when Frankie arrived in the panelled dining room, which had become so familiar to her in the last few days.

She was drinking a soda and poring over the menu. Frankie spoke and the American woman stood up and hugged her effusively.

She had not changed. Not a tall woman, she was heavily corseted in her tight fitting clothes. Rings on her fingers, earrings, bracelets and necklaces. When she smiled, which she did as often as possible, she revealed pearly white teeth. Thick, curly red hair. Mid fifties, thought Frankie, who had seen her passport and knew her date of birth.

Frankie ordered a Coke from the drinks waiter. Luckily, she thought, they seem to have different people working here every day. This was the fourth time she had come, in as many days.

Just then, she looked up and saw that Albert was being led to a table for one, not far away from where she was sitting.

Her former employer chatted about how she had enjoyed seeing the sights in London, travelling to Stratford-upon-Avon and visiting Brighton.

Everyone had told her to see the north of England and she had plans to visit York, and then go on to Edinburgh which she typically mispronounced.

The main courses arrived and Mrs. Petersen fell on the food enthusiastically. Again she mentioned that she didn't like English food. She had been warned before she came but she had not realised how awful it was. This restaurant was a real treat for her.

'What I don't understand, my dear, is why you are in England. Have you no plans to return to the States?'

'Well, I've been thinking about it. But I have a house here, my money goes much further. But I do miss America. I was thinking of getting a job in the consulate here and working a while. A friend of mine works there and says if you have work experience in the US it's very easy to get a job there.'

'Oh, if you need credentials I can do that. If you want to work there, or anywhere else. You let me know. I'll fix it.'

She expected no less. She tried to look casual when she asked her next question.

'I thought you were going to stay at the Northern. It's a very plush hotel.'

'I was,' replied Mrs. Petersen. 'But I remembered that my late husband had a very dear friend in these parts. He has a darling hotel in the country with a most wonderful golf course. And you know how much I love golf. Here in England you can play all year round. I've been having such a swell time, liebchen. Christopher is so nice to me.'

She looked at Frankie and smiled, showing her neat white teeth.

'But I think you know Christopher. He told me you are a friend of his daughter's.'

'You know, Mrs. Petersen, I have lost contact with so many old friends. Right now I have only one. I ran into her in the Village. And her father died many years ago.'

'More reason for you to go back to America. There are so many opportunities there. England is very quaint but everything is so small and old fashioned. They only have two TV channels here and they turn them off during the day. And you know, I now have colour TV in America. Your money may go further here, but what can you buy with it?'

Mrs. Peterson had thrown out a bait, she thought. I ignored it and so has she.

Frankie stood up.

'I'm going to the restroom for a moment.'

She glanced at Albert sitting at another table. He looked at her and winked. She got up, walked to the ladies room. She went inside and then came out.

Albert was waiting for her.

'What did she say?'

'Gallagher and she have talked about me. She says I know his daughter. I didn't take the bait so she changed the subject.'

'Did she mention anything about the discs?'

'No, not at all. But I'm sure she knows everything. Albert, what do I do?'

She was beginning to feel panic. She had to go back and quickly. But she was sweating slightly and she could hear the pounding of her own heart.

'Just go back. I'll go up to your table casually and you introduce me.'

'All right.'

She went back and sat down. Mrs. Petersen gave her another enormous smile.

'I'm going to order another coffee. Shall I order one for you?'

'Oh, yes, please.'

The waiter came by and took the order. Suddenly, Albert appeared.

'Oh hello, Frances. How are you?'

'Albert. How nice to see you. Mrs. Petersen, this is my neighbour and very good friend. Albert, this is Ruth Petersen, a friend from Des Moines, Iowa. I used to work for her there. I think I've told you about her.'

Albert smiled in the direction of the American woman.

'How do you do? Albert Tucker.'

They shook hands. Mrs. Peterson invited him to sit down and join them in a cup of coffee.

'What do you do, Mr. Tucker?' she asked.

'Really, I'm a novelist. I write detective stories.'

'Under your own name? Or do you have a pen name like Mark Twain.'

'I have never used a nom de plume. The books are signed Albert Tucker.'

'So if I am not wrong you are the author of "Four and Twenty Blackbirds" and "Life Makes You Weep".'

'Guilty as charged.'

'But you've only written two as far as I know. Will there be another?'

'I'm working on it. But it's a slow process. I know Mickey Spillane is famous for being able to run up a book in an evening's work but it takes me much longer.'

116

'Your books are much better if you let me say so. They're worth waiting for. Raymond Chandler only wrote about seven novels in his whole life. I would compare you to him rather than Mr. Spillane.'

'You're very kind.'

Frankie asked for the bill. Mrs. Petersen picked it up when it arrived.

'This is my treat. We must meet again for English Tea. I don't care for English food but I do like the cream cakes. There is a darling little old English tea shop downtown that Christopher Gallagher took me to. We must take tea there next week.'

'Christopher Gallagher?' asked Albert.

'Yes, do you know him?'

She looked at him curiously.

'Not personally. But he is an old friend of my cousin and her husband who happens to be an American, too. They live in New York State. Near Buffalo. And I have a business meeting with him next week. He lives in the Highland Village Hotel near Fallowfield.'

'Yes, that's where I'm staying. Well I must be shoving off now. I would like to invite both of you to tea next week. It's been so nice seeing you again, liebchen. And meeting you Mr. Tucker has been an honour.'

'The honour is all mine.'

Albert smiled and gave her his business card.

'Thank you very much.'

She wandered off leaving the two at the table.

They did not speak at first.

117

Finally Frankie said;

'Well we didn't really get anything out of her at all.'

'Yes, but she didn't get much out of you, either.'

'I didn't realise that you were so well known. Or so pompous. The honour is all mine. My word.'

'I once went to a book signing ceremony in London. The writer was one of my heroes and I said, rather gushingly, what an honour it was to meet him. Then of course I felt a little sycophantic. He saved the situation replying, "The honour is all mine". I appropriated the phrase. As writers tend to do. She loved it.'

'Oh, Americans eat up that kind of thing. I think that you being a writer of books which she had read, rather cramped her style. Whatever she was planning to ask me, was left unsaid. What annoys me, is that I wasn't able to get any information out of her.'

'What did she tell you?'

As accurately as she could, Frankie repeated their conversation.

'Well,' said Albert. 'We know that Gallagher was a friend of her husband.'

'No we don't. Just because she said that doesn't mean it's true. They might have met only recently. She wasn't going to stay at his hotel. She said she was going to stay at the Northern in town which is the poshest hotel outside of London and most certainly much posher than whatever Gallagher's hotel is like.'

'Something else. Gallagher now knows that we know quite a lot about him'

'No, that doesn't necessarily follow. Your cousin told you about him after many years, but she hasn't told anyone else, has she? She didn't tell your mother or Auntie Flo, did she?'

'Aye, that's true.'

'Albert, we're back to square one, except for one thing.'

'What's that?'

'We've got one of the discs.'

## Chapter Twelve

Sunday morning, bright and early they were in Albert's garden. Nothing like his neighbour's labyrinth of paths, dotted with ponds and gnomes, his was a large area of very green grass. Here and there stood deciduous trees, probably all bearing fruit in the summer, but now without leaves.

At the bottom of the garden, there was a picket fence and next to it, long flower beds full of rose bushes. Some blossoms still remained in spite of the recent frosts.

From the bottom of the garden one could look down the hill to the river, the pedestrian bridge which crossed it and, on the other side, the footpath to Fallowfield.

In the far corner were three garden sheds.

The shed which was closest to them housed the disc. Albert took out his keys and pushed one into the Yale lock and turned it. The door opened revealing the contents of the little wooden hut. The disc was on the floor of the shed.

Albert picked it up and placed it on the grass in the sunlight. They bent down and examined it.

'It's like an enormous silver lifesaver,' said Frankie.

'What's that?' asked Albert.

'Oh, I meant like a polo mint. It's completely round and with a big hole in the middle. There's nothing written on it. No markings. Can you turn it over?'

He turned it over, but they found nothing on the other side.

'Something else, Albert. I'm getting no vibes off it, that is if I was supposed to. It's just a big round silver disc.'

She knocked on it with her knuckles.

'It doesn't sound solid. I'd say it was hollow. Maybe it contains messages or something. Is there any way of opening it?'

Albert ran his hands around the side. He touched what seemed to be a button and pushed.

The disc made a sudden movement. Albert felt sudden alarm.

'It's not going to explode, is it?' he said. 'We should move away.'

They got up and moved very quickly towards the house. The disc seemed to jump and then opened in two, leaving two hollow halves on the ground. They moved closer to the object. It was completely empty.

Frankie walked up to it. The inside was not silver at all but seemed to be made of a dark material. Albert looked at it. They both thought it might be lead which would explain why although it was hollow it seemed to be rather heavy. What was it for?

'Albert, this is some kind of recipient to carry things. And there is something I could tell you here. One thing I learned from watching Superman on TV in America. Lead prevents things being detected by X-rays.'

Albert laughed.

'Everyone knows that Superman can't use his X-ray vision to see anything in a lead lined box. You don't have to live in Iowa to know that.'

'Well, it certainly doesn't look like a secret weapon, does it? It's just a kind of heavy box.'

'So, what were they investigating in Sheffield?' asked Frankie. 'Why are those men so interested in it? Why did I go into a trance at the market? And how did this disc find its way to the house near Fallowfield?'

A shout from the garden next door startled them. Frankie looked up. It seemed to be coming from her garden.

'Don't hide. I can see you. Frankie, Albert.'

Bernard could be seen quite clearly behind the picket fence and the leafless fruit trees. He was standing in the garden.

Frankie went over to the fence.

'What are you doing there?'

'I came over to see how you're getting on. You didn't open the door to me, so I tried knocking on the kitchen window. Then I came into the garden. What are you doing?'

'Oh, just a little gardening. Go round to the front and I'll let you in and we'll have a cup of tea. I'm finished here anyway.'

Bernard disappeared back to the front of the house. Albert accompanied her into the house. He looked at her before he opened the front door.

'I don't know if we shouldn't try and get more information out of him. But my gut feeling is for the moment, not to tell him anything. At least until I've talked to this bloke in the hotel tomorrow. Don't let on about the disc we found. Not for the moment. Luckily, I don't think he was able to see it from so far away.'

She made her way back to her own front door. She found Bernard waiting outside. He grinned when he saw her.

'So, now you're gardening in midwinter.'

'Oh, there were one or two things Albert wanted to get done and I was helping him. He's got a real garden with grass, not like my silly paved maze full of gnomes and fish. If I stay here, I think I'll change it all.'

'Oh, yes,' replied Bernard. 'Those gnomes are dangerous.'

She looked at him.

'Why do you say that?'

'I hurt myself and almost ripped my trousers on a gnome's peaked cap just a moment ago. Almost lost my keys and a wallet. They fell out as I stumbled over it.'

'Someone lost their cigarettes and keys here the other night,' said Frankie. 'An intruder we thought. We found a broken gnome, a packet of cigarettes and a key ring with a Catholic saint on it.'

'Well it wouldn't have been my key ring. I stopped praying to saints a long time ago. And I don't smoke.'

'Yes, you do. I saw you smoking the other night.'

'I don't really smoke. Only if I go out and have cigarettes on me. I play a lot of tennis and smoking doesn't help you if you play sports.'

She went into the kitchen and put the kettle on. There was a knock on the door. Bernard opened it.

Still in the kitchenette Frankie heard voices in a foreign language. Clearly not French. She thought Italian or perhaps Spanish.

She hurried to the door.

'Who is it?' she asked.

'It's my friend, Salvador. I asked him in for a cup of tea, too. I hope that's all right.'

Salvador was standing by the door, still open behind him. His jet black hair slicked back, a little black line of a moustache over his upper lip. A heavy overcoat, worn as if it were a cape, hung from his shoulders.

'Good morning, Frankie. I had a message for Bernard and as I knew he had come to visit you I came over looking for him.'

The gate in the front garden creaked open and the two men turned around. Albert was coming up the garden path and stood on the doorstep. How

Albert gave the impression of towering over the other two men. He seemed to dwarf them, thought Frankie. If it came to a struggle.

'Oh, Albert. How nice,' cooed Frankie.

'Now that we're all together we can have a nice little morning tea party. Go into the lounge all three of you. I'll bring the tea and biscuits. Does anyone prefer lemon with their tea?'

'Salvador Jimenez, London correspondent for ABC, Madrid.'

Salvador stretched out his hand to Albert and shook it.

'Albert Tucker, pleased to meet you.'

Frankie came in with a tray.

She placed it on the low table next to the sofa, turned on the little electric fire. The two journalists sat on the couch whilst Albert sat on an armchair next to the electric fire. Neither of the journalists took his coat off and Albert was still wearing the heavy sweater he had been wearing in the garden. Frankie poured out the tea and offered round a plate of digestive biscuits.

No one spoke for a moment. Frankie broke the silence.

'Salvador was telling me he was brought up in the States. His father taught in a university there. Then they went back to Spain after the war.'

Albert looked at him.

'After the Spanish war or World War II?'

'Well, it really was in 1947. Nothing to do with either war. My parents were homesick for Spain and he was offered a professorship in Madrid. I was thirteen and really had no say in the matter. Spain was quite a culture

126

shock for me. I left a world of hamburgers and baseball for a life of soccer and potato omelette sandwiches. But I was always foreign in America. And then in Madrid my friends thought of me as a Yankee which at least was posher than my status in the States. I think that's why I like living in London. Here I can be whatever I want.'

'My uncle was in Spain,' said Albert. 'With the anarchists. Fighting against Franco. Many think that the Spanish war was the rehearsal for the Second World War.'

Albert's ruddy complexion seemed a little darker than usual, thought Frankie.

Salvador looked at him.

'Many foreigners went to fight. At the same time many Spaniards left the country. My parents were worried about protecting their children. We lived in Madrid. My grandparents were murdered by extremists and my father grabbed the chance to get out. In England when war broke out everyone had the same common enemy, but in Spain, no matter what side you were on, the enemy was all around you.'

Albert looked at Bernard.

'Tell me Bernard. How are you getting on with your book?'

Bernard, who had been about to take a sip of his tea, nearly spilt it.

'My book?'

'Yes, your book about a German secret weapon. Have you finished it yet?'

'Oh, the German secret weapon. I'm actually writing two books about the war. The European war,' he added, looking at Salvador.

'I didn't know that,' replied Albert.

Frankie thought Albert seemed to snarl his next comment;

'I only know about the book about the metal discs.'

'The metal discs?' said Bernard.

He took another sip of his tea. Frankie thought he was beginning to look uncomfortable.

'Don't just repeat everything, I say. I'm curious. Have you finished it yet? You investigated my uncle, his murder, Frankie's father, the old man who used to live in my house. What conclusions have you drawn? You left a homemade disc near the market and then dug it up. You put it in a little cottage in the wood by the meadow. You know we have it now, although I don't know how, and you've come for it, haven't you?'

Albert's face now had taken a red hue which Frankie had not seen before.

'And you've brought your little Fascist friend to help you.'

'Albert, be careful,' said Frankie. 'He's got a gun.'

Salvador had suddenly produced a pistol which he was pointing at Albert. They all three stood up.

'The only thing we want, buster, is the disc. If you tell us where it is Bernard will go and get it and nobody will get hurt. Otherwise you and the broad, (is that the expression you use in those cheap novels you write?) are going to be as historic as the Spanish Republic.'

For a moment Salvador was smiling. Bernard, although not grinning, was looking much more confident. Albert swiftly moved towards Salvador, grabbed his arm and at the same time clipped him hard in the face with his fist. He kicked Bernard in the groin. They both fell to the floor and lay there motionless. Albert remained on his feet holding the revolver.

Salvador's nose was bleeding profusely and Bernard was unconscious.

Albert was nearly speechless with rage.

'There is nothing cheap about my novels. Get up.'

Salvador got up slowly and sat down on the sofa again. He had lost all dignity and looked as if he were about to cry.

Frankie felt a sudden deep emptiness.

Bernard, who had been her friend, taken her out on Christmas Day, had shown her such a nice time and even tried to seduce her and probably had seduced Beryl. My goodness, she thought, I had even thought of getting seduced myself.

And the other man who had seemed so nice on New Year's Eve. And now what were they to do? Call the police? They could hardly shoot them in her mother's lounge.

Bernard opened his eyes and began to moan softly. Then he looked around the room and sized up the situation.

He stood up and sat down next to his friend.

'Well, well, well,' said Albert. 'What are we going to do with you two? I think you had better start talking. One of you very quickly. Which one is it going to be? You know the wonderful thing about a pistol is that you don't have to kill anyone. In my last novel, which may not be within your price range Salvador, they threatened to shoot the victim in the ankles. Those little bones take a long time to heal. Sometimes they never do. What would that make you? Un tullido? (If that's the word you use in your censored articles printed in Madrid.) From correspondent in a posh Spanish newspaper to selling fags from a wheelchair in the street in Madrid. Tell us what you know.'

'I don't know anything. Bernard asked for help getting back his disc. You took it from the cottage.'

Albert looked at him.

'Turn out your pockets.'

Salvador took out a set of house keys and another of car keys. A small purse of coins, a wallet, a box of Swan Vestas, a packet of cigarettes.

Albert looked at the keys. The car keys were from a Jaguar.

'You drive a Jag?' asked Albert.

'No, I don't. It's a Vauxhall Victor. A friend gave me the key ring.'

'And the medal on the house keys. That's St. Anthony of Padua, isn't it?'

'Yes. I'm a Roman Catholic. Antonio is my father's name, and his father's name and my brother's name.'

'Would you mind if I smoked?' he asked.

Albert looked at the packet. Gaulloise sans filtre.

'You smoke French cigarettes?'

'No, I smoke Spanish cigarettes. Black tobacco. I can't buy Spanish in London but I can buy French. They're very similar.'

'But the night I met you, you were smoking American cigarettes,' interrupted Frankie.

'I've only been able to buy French cigarettes in London. That night I bought what I could from the cigarette girl.'

Albert looked at him.

'The night you broke the gnome in the garden. What were you looking for?'

'I was trying to find a way into the house. So that we could enter and leave without using the doors and without leaving any trace of having been in the house.'

'You had been in the house before, hadn't you? When you zapped both me and Frankie on the head?'

'That wasn't me. I have never been in this house before.'

Salvador pushed a Gaulloise into his mouth and lit it. The room filled with its pungent odour.

Albert looked at him

'If it wasn't you, do you know who it was?'

Salvador shook his head. Albert looked over at Bernard.

'What about you?'

'The attack on the two of you that night had nothing to do with us. Look I was just trying to get material for the book,' said Bernard.

'You took Frankie to the market. Why?'

'Salvador believed that Frankie has the information hidden inside her. Her father left clues somewhere and he thought that it was in the cottage in the wood. When she gets near the clues her father left, something happens to her and she moves towards them like in a trance. We don't know why but we had to find out.'

'Why did you place the disc on the path?'

'We wanted to find out how much she knew. The disc was a bait. She knew nothing so we moved it. But we were suddenly disturbed and so left it in the cottage thinking to come back the next day. We couldn't come back immediately and when we did it was gone. You had taken it.'

Albert looked at Bernard before asking the next question.

'Where did you get the disc? Don't tell me you made it because I don't believe that. This isn't something put together with tin foil and cardboard.'

Salvador looked at him.

'I brought it from Spain. It belongs to my family. After the European war several political refugees from the defeated German government came across the Pyrenees to Spain on their way to South America. They were helped by Spanish secret agents.'

'They were called the Nazi ratlines,' put in Albert.

'Yes, I think so. One night in 1946, I think, one such German had got so far as my family home in Madrid. Against all advice, he went out one night, I don't know why, to paint the town red, I suppose. He never came back. We don't know if he was recognized or what. However, his belongings remained in our house and the disc was among them. When Bernard and I began our collaboration I decided to bring the disc to London. Has it anything to do with the famous Haunebu disc? I have no idea. But it was useful for photographs and to fool you and Frankie.'

132

Albert looked at him.

'All right, but that doesn't explain why you have come here ready to shoot us if we didn't give it back to you.'

Bernard began speaking.

'A few days ago a man came to visit me and asked me if I had the discs. He said his employer was willing to pay a large sum of money for them. I denied that I had the discs but stated I might be able to get them. He said he would be in contact. We then went back to the cottage and found you had taken it.'

'Was this man Daniel Bessel?' asked Frankie. 'Tall, thin, hooked nose about sixty?'

'No,' answered Bernard. 'He was quite young. More like twenty three, twenty four. Short hair, blonde, sounded Scottish.'

'Look,' said Salvador. 'I'm sorry about what happened here. We are just writing a book. Things got out of hand; we just wanted our disc back. I was never going to shoot you.'

'Where did you get your gun?' asked Albert.

'I brought it from Spain. In pieces. I put it together once I got to London. In my profession it has been useful more than once.'

Albert looked at Frankie.

'Have you any more questions? Do you think they're telling the truth?'

'I don't know what to think. But we can't sit here all day.'

'I'll accompany you two, to the gate. You get into your cars and leave and don't come back. I'm not going to beat you up now, but if I ever see you in this street again, or anywhere else for that matter I'll give you the hiding of your lives.'

The four of them walked to the gate. The two men, very solemnly, got into their respective cars, in silence, and without looking back at their hosts, drove away.

When the road was empty and the sound of the engines had faded away, Frankie turned to her companion.

'I need to drink something. If you want to come in, I'll look and see what my father had in his cocktail cabinet.'

'Come back to my house, Frankie. I don't want to look at that lounge for a while. Come home and have a drink with me.'

Ten minutes later, she was sitting at the bar in his living room and he was putting ice into glasses. He opened a bottle of gin.

'Albert. How did you manage to get the gun away from him so quickly?'

'I told you. I was in a special group in Malaya that was trained in unarmed combat. I was taught to disarm people much more dangerous.'

He looked at her and said.

'Normally, you have to be very careful with people who might have seen active service. They know all kinds of tricks. My uncle Bill told me that when I was just a nipper. And he was right.'

'I don't know what I would have done without you.'

'I knew what Bernard wanted as soon as I saw him in the garden,' said Albert. 'I was watching from the house and when I saw that Spanish bloke, I knew they were planning trouble.'

'You should have brought your dog. That would have imposed respect from the beginning. Where is your dog, by the way? I haven't seen her all day, now I come to think of it.'

'Marlen is at my mother's house. She sleeps there sometimes. She belongs to both of us and we share her.'

'Albert. Do you think it's true that they were offered money for the discs?'

'Why do you say that?' he asked.

'Because I told Bernard about Daniel Bessel on Christmas Day. And now he comes out with a similar story. Maybe he just copied my story.'

'Well, we'll find out tomorrow.'

He looked at his watch.

'It's Sunday and it's roast beef and Yorkshire pudding for dinner. I have to go to the off- licence to buy cider. You're invited, of course. Why don't you come? It'll take your mind off all this nastiness.'

## Chapter Thirteen

They drove through a pair of open gates, up the drive, past landscaped gardens to the imposing Victorian mansion which was the Highland Village Hotel.

A small car park in front of the hotel, where they left the car, and then made their way up the steps into the foyer.

Frankie was wearing a smart, black suit with skirt and matching jacket. Something in which she would have been comfortable going to work or, as she imagined this to be, a business meeting.

Albert was dressed more casually, wearing the heavy fisherman's type sweater of the day before and brown corduroy trousers. A ruddy complexion and fair, undulating hair.

There was a seriousness in his face which she hoped would impress her hosts.

Almost immediately they were shown up to what she imagined were the owner's private quarters.

A spacious, high-ceilinged room with a low table in the centre and long couches at either side. At one end, there was a large desk and armchairs under a picture window. At the other end, what looked like a kitchen with a bar, not unlike the one in Albert's house.

The carpet, under their feet, was light in colour and thick. The walls were covered with gold striped paper. The picture rails painted gold, but no pictures to be seen at all. Although it was a cloudy day, the room filled with light from windows on both sides of the room. Gold coloured curtains hung on either side of each window.

The employee invited them to sit down on the sofa and left them alone.

'They may be listening. Better not speak,' whispered Frankie.

Then she added in a much louder voice;

'Oh, Albert what a lovely room. This really is a nice hotel. And they have a golf course.'

Albert stifled a laugh.

'Shall we sit down? I don't know how long we'll be waiting here.'

They sat down and the door opened almost immediately.

On hearing the door, they turned, stood up again and looked round.

The man who walked towards them with surprising speed was short and thickset, podgy rather than fat, thought Frankie. He was bald on top but with abundant, untidy, curly, red hair on the sides and at the back. Fiftyish, she thought. He wore glasses and a dark business suit, which fit him rather badly. His black shoes had obviously cost him a great deal of money.

'Good afternoon. I am Christopher Gallagher.'

His Glaswegian accent marked him immediately. Although his enunciation was obviously well practised, there was an immediate air of toughness about him.

He looked at Frankie.

'You must be Mrs. Blakeley. How do you do?'

He stretched out his hand and Frankie shook it.

'And your companion is Albert Tucker. I think I spoke to your secretary the other day. A pleasure to meet you.'

They shook hands.

He gestured to the sofas and they sat down, Frankie and Albert on one side of the low table and Gallagher on the other. He smiled without opening his mouth.

'I have ordered tea for three. Oh, here it is.'

The door opened and a waitress came in with a trolley.

'Just leave it here, lassie, next to the coffee table. OK, you can go now. We're not to be disturbed, do you hear?'

'Yes, Mr. Gallagher.'

He stood up. And began pouring tea and passing out plates of tiny cucumber sandwiches and cakes. A competent host, they were served within minutes.

'Now, you know why we are all here. The other day Mr. Bessel offered to buy from you some discs, which he believed were in your possession. You denied all knowledge of these discs. Now, you say, you want to negotiate.

139

Well, I am always willing to negotiate. So, I would like to hear what suggestions you have to make.'

Frankie looked at him coldly.

'Well, first things first, Mr. Gallagher. Before we start with anything, I would like to know exactly how much money here you had in mind. Because, after all, this is all about money, isn't it? Since returning to this country, some four weeks ago, I have now been accosted several times by numerous people, at least one of whom worked for you. I have been followed and seriously assaulted and my property has been trespassed upon, more than once. And before we go any further I want to know that I am going to make a sizable profit out of this. Because, really, I am now a single person and the most important person in my life.'

'A woman of spirit,' he laughed, although without any suggestion of mirth. 'Well, lassie. I always admire a person who puts their cards on the table. You want money and lots of it because you're looking out for your own interests. Aren't we all? Let's be honest from the start. How much money, you ask. Well that depends on what you have, and how many of them, doesn't it?'

'How many would you expect me to have?'

'How many have you got?'

Frankie looked at him, without smiling.

Gallagher shook his head.

'No, that will not do. We can't negotiate like this. You won't tell me what you know, but you expect me to tell everything.'

Albert began speaking.

'Well what we would like to know is why you want the discs. Is it for yourself or have you another buyer? Because we have had other offers.'

'Have you? And what have they offered you and who are they?'

Albert looked at him very seriously.

'I think here we are all in the same boat. If you tell us something, perhaps we will tell you.'

Gallagher stood up.

'When the allies arrived in Wewelsburg Castle in Germany in 1945, they discovered three discs in secret chambers under the castle. At first no one would explain where they had come from, but little by little, it was revealed that they had been found in the wreckage of a flying saucer which had crashed in the Black Forest in 1936.'

He went on speaking.

'The SS, under the orders of Himmler, had brought the discs to his castle. There, they had remained during the war. Other artifacts such as the Haunebu disc machine were taken to other venues. The Germans, were trying a process of reverse technology, it was said. Trying to find out how the machine worked so as to be able to use it as part of their war machine.'

'However these three discs were quite different. Himmler believed they had magical qualities and used them in some of his black magic ceremonies. Some said that they were anti matter machines.'

'Whatever they were,' Gallagher continued, 'they suddenly disappeared from Wewelsburg Castle. Although they had been under heavy guard.'

Frankie looked at him.

'How do you know this?'

'I know,' said Gallagher. 'Because I was in the castle. I was in the army and I formed part of the guard, the night they disappeared.'

'And why do you think my father had anything to do with this?' Frankie asked him.

'Because I know he took them and brought them to England.'

'How do you know?'

'Let's just say, I know. As I also know that you are the key to everything. Look, I'll put my cards on the table. I am prepared to pay you twenty- five thousand pounds for the three discs. You ask me no more questions, I give no more answers and I ask no more questions of you.'

Frankie shrugged.

'You know twenty- five thousand pounds is a lot of money. However, yours is not the first offer I have received, so as you must understand, I will have to roll it over in my mind.'

She stood up.

'We'll be in contact, Mr. Gallagher.'

Gallagher showed no emotion but smiled again without opening his mouth.

'I think you'll find that no one will better my offer, Mrs. Blakeley.'

The door opened and a young man in his early twenties entered the room. Tall, very blond, short hair. Gallagher spoke to him.

'My guests are leaving. Show them out, laddie.'

'Aye, I'll do that all right.'

Morningside, thought Frankie. She had had a Scottish roommate at university who spoke with this accent from a district in Edinburgh.

Once in the car Albert began to speak.

'I didn't imagine we'd get so much out of him. He seemed so taciturn at first. I won't tell you unless you tell me and then how he opened up. You did very well Frankie. You bluffed your way through that very well.'

'Well, she said. 'It wasn't a bluff. We do have one disc, don't we?'

'You mean that old junk of Bernard's? I don't even know if I believe any of that story about it travelling across the Pyrenees to Madrid'.

'So difficult to know what's true, what's made up,' said Frankie. 'Who your friends are.'

'I'm your friend Frankie. Don't forget it!'

'I didn't mean you. I meant the rest of them.'

'Well, Doreen told me that Gallagher had avoided National Service during the war.'

'Maybe she was wrong, or maybe he lied to her.'

'Or maybe he's lying to us,' said Albert. 'And the Scottish boy? That bloke must've been the one who got in contact with Bernard.'

'And why does he want the discs? Twenty-five thousand pounds is a lot of money. Just to do black magic with them. Albert, we always finish up worse than when we started.'

'That's not true. Your father probably had the discs. And you probably know where they are.'

'I don't know.'

'Frankie, you think you don't know. If it weren't dark now we could go back to the little house and look for clues. As it is we'll go home and work all this out.'


Frankie was sitting in Albert's living room drinking coffee and watching TV. Albert had gone to his mother's house to fetch Marlen.

A noise, in what had been the kitchen and now formed part of Albert's office, startled her. She got up to investigate. The area which had been the kitchen was in fact still a separate room, although smaller, and gave onto the side door, which in this case, opened not onto a driveway, but the garage. The door was bolted.

Next to the door was the boiler for the central heating which Frankie immediately identified as the cause of the sudden noise. At that moment she looked behind her.

In her mother's house there had been a pantry under the stairs and here she saw that in this house it was now a closet. The door was easily opened. She looked at the floor. There was a keyhole. She bent down. Oh, if she had a key.

'Frankie?'

A voice came from behind.

She jumped up and turned around. Albert was standing behind her.

'I didn't hear you come in,' she said.

'I didn't know where you were. What are you doing?'

'What's under the floor?' she asked.

'There is a small cellar.'

'There isn't a cellar in my house.'

'I imagine there is, Frankie. The two houses are exactly the same.'

'No, they aren't. You have a garage. We haven't.'

'Yes,' replied Albert. 'Because, I added the garage on when I renovated the house. I had to get planning permission for it. It's not part of the original structure. But the cellar was there when I moved in. It was closed up, but the builders found it. I thought of having a wine cellar, but never got round to it.'

'Can we open it?'

Albert pushed a switch on the wall and a trap door opened in the floor. There was a bright, electric light and a steep staircase leading down.

'The builders installed all this. I never go down, it must be very dirty.'

The room was a cement floor with unadorned brick walls. Completely empty, no plumbing. Nothing like the basements in the houses in Iowa. It was bigger than she expected but still only about the size of her mother's kitchenette. There was a musty smell, mixed with damp.

'I never saw what use it might have,' said Albert. 'There is no natural light and it always seems a little damp.'

They went back upstairs into the living room. The television was still on. Frankie sat down and watched the news.

'You must have the same thing in your house,' said Albert.

'I'm sorry, what did you say?'

'You must have a cellar in your house,' repeated Albert.

'A cellar, why?'

'Like the one here,' he said.

'Like what?'

'Well if the houses are the same, you must have the same cellar as I have,' Albert insisted.

'Albert, what are you talking about?'

'The cellar.'

'What cellar?'

Albert looked at her and laughed.

'Never mind. I'll explain later. I have to get something. I'll be back in a moment.'

A few minutes later he came back with a small holdall.

'Shall we go next door? I've thought of something and I'd like to check it.'

They were standing in the kitchenette. Next to the side entrance there was a door which led to the pantry under the stairs. They opened the door.

'What are you looking for?' asked Frankie.

'I think there may be a cellar,' replied Albert.

'Why do you think that?'

'Because there's one in my house.'

'Really. I didn't know that.'

He bent down and moved his hands over the floor, which was made up of very short planks. One plank was loose and easily removed. He found a handle underneath and pulled it. A trapdoor sprang open. He took an electric torch out of his bag and shone it down revealing a metal ladder.

'Look Frankie. Your cellar. Let's go down and investigate. Wait a moment. I'll go down first.'

He crawled down the ladder.

'All right. Come down.'

It took her only a moment to descend the ladder. Albert was shining his torch around the little underground room. White kitchen tiles covered the walls. The floor was also tiled.

There was a light fixture on the ceiling and Albert found a switch next to the ladder. The room was suddenly bathed in soft white light.

'This is amazing,' said Frankie. 'I've lived in this house all my life. I've never seen this room before. But what is it for? There's no furniture here, no cupboards, nothing in here at all.'

'Maybe you've seen it and you don't remember.'

'You mean like the house near Fallowfield?'

'Or maybe your parents used it during the war as an air raid shelter. And haven't used it since.'

'I don't think so. Someone's been here since 1945. I'd say it was cleaned not long ago. Well whatever it is, I'd like to get out now. I'm beginning to feel claustrophobic.'

She quickly crept up the ladder. Albert close behind her. They closed the hatch, the larder door and went back to Albert's living room. The TV was still on. An old Esther William's movie.

'Oh,' cooed Frankie. 'I've always loved this movie. My mum took me to see it at the cinema when I was little. We always went to see Esther Williams. They were my mum's favourites. And this was filmed in Mexico.'

'And the cellar, Frankie? What have you thought about the cellar?'

'The cellar again? What cellar? Why do you keep going on about the cellar?'

Albert looked at the television.

'Oh is that Esther Williams? She usually swims, doesn't she? But she seems to be bullfighting. I've never seen any of these films. I remember going to see "Abbot and Costello Meet Frankenstein" with my mum and my auntie. They never show that on TV.'

They watched the film until the end.

## Chapter Fourteen

Tuesday morning Frankie went to get the post. A letter from her father's lawyer about papers she had to sign. Lots of late Christmas cards. One from her husband's parents. How they missed her and how welcome she would be if she came to Des Moines. She swallowed hard and opened the rest of the post.

Several cards from people she knew in America. And an Epiphany card from her former employer. They must have English Tea together this week. She was taking the liberty of calling Mr. Tucker to make the arrangements.

Then a note from Beryl. Could they have lunch on Tuesday? She was off work that day and if she could manage it give her a ring and they would see each other in the Village or go into town. Anywhere, but an American restaurant.

An hour later she was on the bus going into town.

She had phoned Beryl from the phone box near the bus stop and she would meet her later, but first there were one or two things she wanted to do.

Albert had not been at home, she imagined he was walking his dog. Somewhat relieved by that, she had popped a note through his letterbox letting him know she would be out for the better part of the day. She did not like giving explanations, but thought she owed it to him.

After making a withdrawal at the bank, she wandered into the large bookshop which she remembered was next door to the bank in the city centre. She spent some time browsing titles and found Albert's novels.

At first she could not believe it when she saw his name on the dust covers of the books. On the back of one of them there was a photo. He looked somewhat younger but she would have recognized him anywhere. She picked them up tenderly and placed them carefully on the cash desk. She asked the assistant to wrap them in brown paper and put them in a bag.

She then made her way to the little Italian restaurant where she had arranged to meet Beryl.

Her friend was already sitting at a table drinking what looked like a vermouth.

'I'm drinking Cinzano, but I've almost finished.'

Before Frankie could say anything she had called the waiter and ordered another for herself and one for her friend.

'Oh, Cinzano Bianco. I went to Rimini last September with a girl from the consulate and we drank Cinzano everywhere. Oh, what a beautiful drink.'

'Haven't seen you since New Year,' said Frankie. 'Did you get home all right? I phoned you the next day but your mum said you had a business meeting.'

'Well, yes.' Beryl laughed. 'A "my business" meeting. I had a date with an American guy I met at work. We went out for lunch. I told my mum I had to sign some papers and things. So I could leave the kids with her.'

'I thought you didn't like Americans.'

'No, I don't like America. If they want to take me out to posh restaurants in England, I like them fine. How's your French boyfriend?'

'He's not my boyfriend, I hardly know him.'

'Good. Because I thought I ought to tell you. He took you home and then dropped off that Spanish guy. But we got to my turn and first he wanted to come into the house with me and then, when I told him I lived with my mum, he wouldn't let me out of the car. If I were you, I'd stick with the boy next door.'

Beryl continued.

'What interested me was not his Gallic charm, but the book he was writing. He knew all about the aliens crashing their spaceship in Germany before the war. Apparently the Germans thought they could make a secret weapon out of things they found. And the Americans took it all back to the States in 1945.'

'I knew all that from my husband, but what I didn't know is that there were some Germans who escaped to South America and that they went through Spain and the other guy who was with him, the Spanish one, his family used to help them. And they brought these secret weapons with them. And left them in Spain for safe keeping. And this Spaniard's family still has them. But they need three discs. They know they are in England. That's really why he's here, in England. He has to get them back.'

'And they told you all that?' asked Frankie.

'No, they didn't. Bernard told me after his friend left. He'd been drinking, I think. Some people get very loose tongued. Raymond always did too. That's when he would tell me about what he knew. I told Bernard a lot of things anyway and that made him talk, I think. He thought he might get more out of me.'

'Did he tell you why they needed these discs?'

'No,' replied Beryl. 'I couldn't get any more out of him.'

'I want Chianti Rosso,' Beryl said to the waiter. 'A bottle?'

She looked at Frankie quizzically.

'Why not?' replied Frankie.


Beryl and Frankie left the restaurant.

'I can't spend too much time today as I have another business meeting after lunch,' quipped Beryl. 'I'll be in touch.'

As soon as they separated Frankie looked for a telephone and ordered a taxi home.


She went into her mother's lounge and sat down. Not only had she drunk before lunch, and had quite a lot of wine during lunch, but Beryl insisted on drinking grappa afterwards because Hemingway used to drink it in some book about Italy.

Although she was still feeling euphoric when she got into the taxi, she was now beginning to do, what she might have described, as feeling her age. She closed her eyes and fell asleep.

When she awoke, the room was dark and cold. She turned on the light, drew the curtains and went upstairs to freshen up. Since she had arrived, she had been sleeping in the back bedroom. But she had formed the habit of clothing herself and making up in front of the dressing table in another bedroom which faced the street.

Before turning on the light, she went to the bay widows to draw the curtains. She looked down at the street. Under a lamppost, across the road, on the corner of the street, she could make out the figure of a young man in a belted raincoat. He seemed to be staring at her house. She closed the curtains and turned on the light.

Frankie opened the door of her house and began to walk down the path to the front gate. She looked up the street. The man had not moved. She walked next door to Albert's house. The outside lights were on. She rang his doorbell. There was no answer. She rang again. No sounds from inside the house. No one had drawn the curtains. There were no lights inside.

Albert was not home.

She began to walk back along the garden path towards the gate. She looked up the street again. The man was gone. She walked out the gate and made her way to her own front gate.

She looked towards the end of the road. There, under another lamppost, was the man again. She opened the gate, walked quickly up the path and put her key in the lock. She turned it, went in, shut the door and bolted it behind her.

She could feel her heart beating inside her head. Panting, she could hardly breathe. How did the road where she lived, suddenly look so empty. She went into the lounge and sat down, exhausted.

She sat there, she could not say how long. She felt suspended between reality and fantasy. In her mind, she went over again all that had happened since her arrival. Des Moines seemed now so far away and yet this moment she was living was so surreal. Not for the first time, she wondered if she should call the police. To tell them what? That a man was standing under a lamppost down the street. But she knew he was watching her house.

Time passed but she felt rooted to her armchair.

And then she heard the heavy doorknocker. Once, twice, three times. She did not move.

Knock all you want, she thought. I am not moving.

'Frankie. Frankie. Are you there? It's me Albert. Where are you?'

She stood up and ran to the door, opened it.

'Oh, Albert, thank goodness.'

She burst into tears.

He closed the door behind him and put his arm around her.

'Whatever is the matter? What's happened?'

'Oh nothing,' she said. 'It's just I saw a man across the street looking at the house. And I went to your house looking for you and there was no one there and the road was empty and there he was down the street again, looking at me and I thought that that was him knocking on the door just now. I was all alone and I'm so tired of living between one mystery and another. I sometimes thought my life in Des Moines somewhat dull but this is too much for me.'

Albert went out into the road and rapidly returned.

'There's no one out there, Frankie.'

'Well, there was. Where were you?'

'Where was I?' he laughed. 'I was at my mother's. Where were you? I may ask now. I got a note that you would be out all day. But you didn't say where.'

'I went out for lunch with my friend Beryl. The girl Bernard finished up with, on New Year's Eve.'

'Oh yes. So he did finish up with her after all?'

'Well, really I don't know. But she began to tell him all she knew about the German secret weapon and the alien spaceship in Germany and he told her about the discs.'

'What did he tell her?'

'That these Spanish people, the ones that helped the Nazis after the war, they are the ones who want the discs. They must be the people who are paying Gallagher. He can't want the discs for himself. Whatever for? To do black magic? I don't think so. He's buying them for someone else. Maybe Salvador or his family.'

Albert sighed.

'So we're back to square one again. Just when we thought Bernard and that Salvador were taken care of. Why did Beryl tell you all this?'

'Why wouldn't she? She's been telling everybody else all about this business, her husband's involvement, her interviews with the FBI, ever since I first met her again a few weeks ago. We go out dancing and any lad who comes close to her is told the whole story. The whole city must be talking

155

about it, except no one listens to her, because it's all about aliens and crashed spaceships. Maybe that's why she tells me, because I take her seriously.'

Albert interrupted.

'Now I have news for you. Mrs. Petersen rang. Can we have tea with her? Tomorrow or the day after. Both of us. If you say tomorrow, I'll ring her now or better still I'll ring my agent's secretary and ask him to arrange it.'

'All right.' said Frankie. 'Tomorrow it is. Afternoon tea or high tea?'

'Oh, afternoon tea with scones.'

'Great,' she said. 'Do you think she has anything to do with all this?'

'I wouldn't be surprised in the least.'

## Chapter Fifteen

'Where is this place where we're going to have tea with my boss?'

It was Wednesday morning and the two friends were walking down the hill to the river. Marlen seemed very excited that the two were together.

She ran in front, then circled, ran around Frankie's legs, barked happily and then ran forwards and then backwards. There was a bitter wind that blew in one direction and then in another. A heavy smell of coal in the air. But the day was sunny and the vegetation, as always, a deep green.

'It's a place in town. I've never heard of it, but my agent's secretary has described it in glowing terms. We should dress up.'

'Oh,' replied Frankie. 'We'll dress up anyway if we're going downtown.'

'You're going downtown with Petula Clark?'

Albert laughed

'You see how American you've become,' he said. 'No one says downtown here.'

'Petula Clark does. You don't know how many times I think about that song when I go downtown. And it cheers me up too. There's even a part where she talks about nipping into a cinema. And I did that too. Then I met Auntie Flo afterwards.'

'That must have really cheered you up.'

'Well, yes it did,' she said. 'Not at first, but I realised it made me think I had people who cared about me.'

'I care about you Frankie. You know that.'

She threw her arms around Marlen who was nudging her legs again.

'Yes, I know and Marlen cares about me, don't you,' she shouted.

Marlen escaped her hug as quickly as she could.

There were some empty benches on the river bank.

'Would you like to sit down a moment?' asked Albert.

'I always enjoy the view here,' she replied.

She looked up at the other side of the river. There, at the entrance of the footbridge, was a man. Blond hair, a belted raincoat. He was watching them.

'Albert. The man from the other night is on the other side of the bridge. He's watching us. And I know who he is. He's Gallagher's Scottish employee. The one from Edinburgh.'

Albert did not look up at first. And when he did, he stifled a yawn and looked first in one direction and then in another. Then, without really looking in one direction, he said;

'Yes, I'd recognise him anywhere. And you say that's the one who was in our road, last night?'

'Oh, yes, I'm sure of it. And that's the coat he was wearing.'

'Let's casually cross the bridge. Start laughing a lot as we pass him.'

The three of them began crossing the bridge. Marlen as full of beans as before. Being with another person was almost like being on holiday for her.

As they got to the end of the bridge, Frankie began to laugh, perhaps almost hysterically, she thought.

They passed the young boy and suddenly Albert grabbed him.

'All right, pal. What do you want? Why are you following us? You'd better tell me or I'll cut your balls off.'

The dog began to bark loudly and growl. Two men nearby stopped to look at them. Another went up to the two and said:

'I say, this kind of thing.'

Albert snapped at him.

'You want some too, buster?'

The man backed off.

'Who sent you? Come on. Speak quickly!'

'It was the Spanish bloke. He was with Mr. Gallagher. He said to follow her everywhere.'

'You tell Gallagher that we only deal with the Spanish bloke. No more middlemen. Do you hear?'

'Aye.'

'And if I ever see you around here again. You're toast. Do you hear?'

'Aye'

'Tell me. What will happen if I see you around here?'

'I'm toast.'

'Good. Now buzz off.'

The lad moved off towards Fallowfield, as quickly as he could. The small group which had gathered moved away. They sat down on another bench and Marlen laid her head on Albert's leg.

'I can't take much more of this,' said Frankie.

'Sure you can. You and Petula Clark. Twin spirits. And this afternoon we're going for this Petersen woman.'


The tea rooms were situated in the centre of town, in what had been a Victorian Mill. They walked up the two steps to the entrance where they were asked their names and escorted to a table.

Although they were early, Mrs. Petersen was already seated and waiting for them.

She stood up when she saw them and greeted them warmly, hugging Frankie and shaking hands with Albert.

'Sit down, please. I'm so delighted you could come. Both of you. This is the third time I have been here now. I just love these English cream teas. I took the liberty of ordering before you came. Because the teas are delicious but the service is very English. Slow and meticulous. Real slow.'

The room was very small and it was already full of people.

Mrs. Petersen was right. Despite ordering early there was still a long wait.

The American woman spoke a great deal. She had been to Shakespeare's birthplace and chatted about the village, his cottage and whether or not he had been the author of his plays. Albert was able to offer opinions about all this. Frankie smiled occasionally but was unable or unwilling to participate very much.

After the tea and food had arrived Mrs. Petersen turned to Frankie and asked,

'You're very quiet today. That's not like you.'

'Frankie had a rather bad experience last night,' replied Albert. 'She was alone at home and she thought that there was a person following her and then standing in front of the house watching her. Luckily I came to visit and this person disappeared. But I think she is still upset.'

'I would have called the police immediately. And I keep several small hand guns near my bed.'

Frankie smiled.

'Well my parents never had a telephone and as I don't know yet what I'm going to do I haven't had one put in yet. It's quite expensive and there is a six month waiting list.'

'Oh, a little like the cream teas,' said Mrs. Petersen, smiling.

'Yes,' said Frankie, 'and in England people don't keep guns in their bedrooms, or anywhere else for that matter.'

'Well, I'm very sorry to hear about this. Would you like some more tea? Apparently, you pour the hot water in the pot and you get more tea out.'

She enjoyed playing with the tea service and dolloping out clotted cream.

For an American, thought Frankie, she was quite an expert. And she had been quite sympathetic about Frankie's bad experience and seemed not to have known anything about that or the incident with the Scottish boy that morning.

'Tell me Mr. Tucker. Are you working on a third book? Can I ask that?'

The American popped another scone onto her plate and began to nibble while she waited for Albert's answer.

'Most certainly. In fact, I am working on another book.'

'Another detective thriller? Can you tell us what it's about?'

'Well sometimes the plots change as it goes along. This one is about Nazis leaving Germany after the war. On their way to South America they are met in the Pyrenees by Spanish secret agents working for Franco. These take them to Madrid. There they leave secret weapons they have brought from Berlin. In return the Spanish government escorts them to Portugal where they get on ships bound for the Americas.'

'It sounds fascinating. I can't wait for it to come out.'

'Well it's going to take some time. I haven't got everything worked out yet. But I'll send you a signed copy.'

'That's very nice of you.'

Frankie looked at her former employer.

'Mrs. Petersen, how are you getting on at your hotel? Have you played lots of golf?'

'No, I didn't play golf more than one day. In fact I've changed hotels. I'm now in the Northern.'

'Oh,' said Frankie, 'that's very sudden.'

A cloud of unhappiness came over the older woman's face.

'I don't really know if I ought to tell you as this man Christopher is a friend of yours. But I didn't know him. Only, that he was an associate of my late husband, who as you know, was a financier in Des Moines. Well, he had many associates and friends abroad. But a few days ago, I found out a few things about this guy which I didn't like. So, I made an excuse about wanting to stay downtown for a few days before going to Edinburgh and booked out.'

'What did you find out, Mrs. Petersen?' asked Frankie.

'Well, he said you were a friend of his daughter, and you, Albert talked about business with him, but I think I better warn you. He's a crook. But a real crook. He was a bootlegger after the war and there were all kinds of other things. That's how he got the money for his hotel. And he's got little thugs working for him. I've seen them hanging around the hotel.'

Frankie took her hand.

'I am not a friend of his daughter's. I've never met his daughter. And Albert really has no business with him. We went to see him the other day, it's true. But we have nothing to do with him. And yes. We think he's a crook, too.'

'Oh, you've taken a weight off my mind, liebchen. I was so worried that you had got involved with such a shady guy. And I didn't know how I was going to tell you.'

The conversation moved on. Mrs. Petersen proved to be quite entertaining. She spent some time chatting about Iowa in the thirties and forties. Stories about well-known people she had known. For Frankie it brought back memories of the mornings she had spent with her when she was the American woman's personal assistant in Des Moines.

This was a woman who had known everybody and could arrange anything. And for the moment, it seemed Mrs. Petersen was not a crook and not in league with their enemies.

Sometime later when they were back in the car Albert asked Frankie;

'Were you surprised that she had left the hotel?'

'When she told me I was flabbergasted. I thought you were going to trap her with your comments about people following me or the Germans being helped by Spanish spies. But her reactions all seemed perfectly innocent. She didn't seem to know anything about all this. And then, when she told us that Gallagher was a crook.'

'That's how I felt. I thought she'd start spilling her clotted cream when I told her about the plot of my new book. But she just ate it all up.'

'Well you know she was very nice to me in Des Moines. Very generous. And when Chuck died, she was very good to me. And although I stopped working for her, she used to check up on me, make sure I was all right. Oh, it's just with all this; I've become so suspicious of everybody. And her sudden appearance and staying in that hotel.'

Albert parked in the car park of the Crown.

'Let's have a drink. I think we've earned it after all that tea.'

## Chapter Sixteen

It was just before lunchtime Friday morning when Frankie heard the heavy doorknocker. She was cleaning, something she had been putting off, mainly because she still felt as if she were interfering in someone else's house.

There was a grey haired man in uniform at the door, instantly recognizable as a GPO employee.

'Mrs. Frances Blakeley? I've come to install your telephone.'

'My telephone? I didn't order a phone.'

'Ordered and installation paid for. Normally there's a waiting list. But your company must have paid a supplement for immediate installation. Let's see.'

He put on his glasses, opened a ledger and read to her.

'Petersen and Bradbury, Des Moines. USA. That's your company, isn't it? Most American companies like to have their employees on the phone.'

'Yes,' she answered with a smile. 'That's my company, all right.'

'Now,' the man went on. 'In this country people usually put the phone in the hall. On a hall table, next to the door. But you Americans usually prefer them in the living room.'

'I'm not really American,' Frankie replied.

'Well, you could have fooled me. You certainly don't come from around here.'

'I'll have it in the lounge,' she replied.

Two hours later, Mrs. Petersen rang.

'I'm so relieved you have a telephone. Any more problems you call the police immediately. They've got a special number here. It's just 999. You dial that if you have any more schmucks standing in front of your house. I'm taking a night train to Scotland. Booked a sleeper. Say hi to Albert for me. I'll call you up when I get to my hotel.'

The first person she rang was Albert. He answered immediately.

'Hiya. When did you order a telephone?'

'Mrs. Petersen ordered it from her company. And she paid for it. First person to phone me. Just to let me know that the phone number for the English police is 999.'

'Don't they phone 999 in America?'

'No, it just depends on where you live. It's a different number everywhere.'

'Anyway, it was jolly good of her, wasn't it? It shows she does care about you.'

'Look,' Albert went on. 'You've caught me on the run. I'm taking my mum to Timperley. She's spending the weekend with a friend who lives there in one of those bungalows. Mum always takes Marlen with her. Makes her feel safer as the place is a bit out of the way. Anyway she's waiting for me. I was going to go for a hike by the river afterwards. Do you want to come?'

'I don't think I can, I'm cleaning the house Albert. It's been a month and I haven't done much at all up until now. I was in the middle of it when the telephone man came. I'll be at it all day.'

'All right. Hey, give me your number, I'll phone you later.'


Half an hour later dressed in a pair of corduroy trousers and a heavy sweater, Albert made his way down to the river.

Although it was January, the morning was warm. Very little wind, blue and intermittently sunny as the white clouds moved slowly across the sky.

Normally, when walking with his dog he would cross the footbridge and carry on walking to Fallowfield, but now being alone he decided on a longer route. He turned right and followed the path along the river bank.

Without thinking of anything in particular, he glanced at the flowing water, sparkling in the sunshine, the birds on the opposite bank and a small boat in the distance.

Suddenly something hit him hard on the back. He fell to the ground face down. He realised almost at once that someone had attacked him. He automatically moved his elbows backwards and pushed his attacker over. He stood up. There were two of them. Although vicious looking and moving fast, neither of them was very big. He made short shrift of the first one who ran away, and he pinned the other one down.

'Who are you? Who do you work for?' he asked.

The reply was a barrage of insults and expletives some of which he had not heard since he was in the army.

'London, aren't you? That's why you have that foul mouth on you.'

Unrelenting, he glanced round to see if he had an audience. There was nobody else around.

The man was wearing a sports jacket. He stuck his hand into the inside pocket and pulled out three passports. On the other side was a holster and an automatic.

'Quite the little secret agent, aren't we?'

He looked around again. They were quite alone. He left what he had found on the grass next to them. He grabbed hold of the man's arm and twisted it behind his back. He squealed with pain.

'If you want to see any of this stuff again, you tell me the name of your boss. I'll see he gets it.'

He twisted his arm a little more and looked at his victim.

Young guy, early twenties, fair hair, cut short, tanned skin as if he spent a lot of time in sunny places, thought Albert.

'Come on. What's his name?'

'Salvador Jimenez.'

The name came out as if he were speaking another language. No London accent here, thought Albert.

'And where do I find him?'

He gave him an address in town. A well-known luxury hotel not far from the tea rooms they had visited the day before.

'We were supposed to bring you to him anyway,' chirped his attacker. 'He wants to see you.'

Albert twisted his arm a little more.

'All right buzz off out of it. If I see you again, I'll break your arm for you.'

He let him go and the lad moved off, limping.

Albert picked up the gun first of all and hid it in his trouser pocket. He then looked at the passports. Spanish, British and French. Same photograph in each but different names. He put them in his back pocket and walked back to his house. There were people walking towards him, down the hill now, but no one seemed to have seen the attack or was interested in him.

Albert went home. Upstairs there were only two double bedrooms each one with a private bathroom. Although he slept in the back bedroom he went into the other one. The decorative wooden floors were covered with little rugs. Under one such rug he touched a small wooden plank. A mini trap door opened and he placed the automatic next to the one which he had confiscated from Salvador. He closed it. Replaced the rug. Found his car keys, went to his car and drove off.

He came back home two hours later. He sat down in his office and examined the material he had. The three passports he put to one side. Then he examined the copies he had obtained with photo stat machines. So as not to arouse suspicion he had gone to three different places. The copies he hid and the passports he wrapped in brown paper, making a package, which he tied with string.

He changed and put on a dark suit and tie. Combed his hair back using hair cream. He was now ready for his meeting with Salvador.

He left his car on the same side of the street as the hotel, some five yards away from the entrance.

Carrying the small package, he walked across the road and found a dark doorway leading to premises which had been closed long ago. It was just beginning to get dark.

He stood for a while, watching the entrance. And then turned right, walked some distance and crossed to the other side. Walking quickly, he entered the building.

'Good afternoon, sir. How can I help you?' The doorman smiled courteously, but firmly. No one entered the building without his consent.

'Oh. Good afternoon. I have a package here which I am to deliver to Salvador Jimenez.'

'Well leave it with me; I'll see he gets it.'

'No, I have to deliver it personally.'

'Could I have your name, sir?'

'Albert Tucker.'

'One moment.' The doorman spoke a moment on the phone.

'You may go up, sir. Do you know the suite number?'

'No, I'm afraid that's not possible. He'll have to come down. I'll wait outside. I can't leave my car as it's parked on a double yellow line.'

'I'll call him.'

Albert went outside walked down the street, crossed and returned to the dark doorway. And waited.

Some ten minutes later, three men came out of the building and moved in different directions. One to the left, another right and the last crossed the road coming close to where Albert was standing. He could not see Albert, who stayed back in the shadows. He stood in front of the doorway.

Suddenly Albert grabbed the man from behind and left him unconscious. He placed his hand under the lapel of his coat and, sure enough, found another gun in a holster. What a collection, thought Albert. He hid him in the doorway and moved back himself just in time. One of the other two men passed by whispering his friend's name. Albert hit him on the back of the neck with the gun and dragged him, too, into the recesses of the doorway.

Five minutes later the door of the building opened and another man ventured out. Black hair, slicked back. Overcoat hung over his shoulders as if it were a cape.

It was Salvador.

Albert turned left and walked a few yards down the street and crossed to where he had parked his car. He looked up the street. From where he was standing he could see Salvador standing in front of the steps of the entrance of the building and then, to his right, the third man further up the road.

Salvador did not see Albert as he was looking straight in front. But the other man saw Albert immediately and rapidly made his way towards both of them.

Albert jumped into the car, started the engine, and drove along the pavement towards Salvador, opened the passenger door, pointed a gun at him.

'Get in or you're a dead man,' he roared. Salvador did as he was told. Albert pulled off leaving the bodyguard with a long and wondering frown.

He stopped the car a moment and without letting go of his gun, frisked the Spaniard.

He was clean.

He drove on without speaking. He stopped in an empty car park behind a disused warehouse.

'Well,' said Albert. 'It seems we meet again.'

Salvador did not look at him, but made a kind of sneering noise.

'What a tangled web we weave when first we practise to deceive. Wouldn't you say that? You've been lying to us all the time haven't you?'

Salvador turned to him. His expression was fixed in a smug sneer.

'How much did Gallagher tell you he would give you for the discs?' he asked. 'All three of them? Twenty- five thousand? We'll give you more. That's all we want. The discs. Look, all you see here is me. You think that by beating me up you'll solve your problem. You Yankee types always think you can solve the mystery by slugging someone. But you can slug me but you can't slug a whole organisation, Mr. Tucker. So I would think very seriously about just accepting the money. Or you and that cheap broad of yours will be; how did you put it? Toast.'

Albert looked at him.

'What organisation are you talking about? Who do you work for?'

'That is none of your business, Mr. Tucker. But I warn you. You and that gormless girl are in serious danger unless you produce the discs.'

Albert hit him hard in the face, knocking him out.

He started the engine and drove north into a country lane. He pushed him out of the car and drove home. He still had the passports and two more guns. He had not got a great deal more information, but he certainly had defended a lady's name.

No one was calling Frances a cheap broad.


At four o'clock Frankie phoned Albert. No answer. About half past four she had finished cleaning and she rang again. Still no answer. She went upstairs and got ready to go out.

It was now after five and she made her way to his mother's house. She had never done this before; visit uninvited.

Auntie Flo was home alone, but, as it was almost teatime, expected Albert any moment. She led Frankie into the dining room and sat her at the table near the roaring, open fire.

The television was on. A programme with a studio full of cheering children and two comedians. Auntie Flo laid a place for her. And poured her a cup of tea.

'Our Albert's late,' quipped Auntie Flo. 'He usually calls if he's not going to come or if he's been held up. Vera went to Timperley for the weekend. To visit an old friend who lives in a bungalow, like my mother-in-law. She always takes Marlen does our Vera, when she goes there. The dog makes her feel that much safer.'

The children's shows finished and the news programmes began. Suddenly the phone rang. Auntie Flo went into the hall to answer it.

'Our Albert's going to be a little late, pet. He'll be here in about forty minutes. I'll make another pot of tea and we'll wait for him.'

'Where is he?'

'Don't know, he was in a phone box. I'll be back in a moment, love.'

It was seven o'clock and the doorbell rang. Auntie Flo stood up.

'Oh, this'll be him now.'

She left the room.

'We haven't touched anything, your Frankie's still here waiting for you.'

Albert came in. He was still wearing a long overcoat. He looked very tired, but smiled cheerfully, when he saw Frankie sitting at the table.

'I didn't know you were coming to tea. Sorry I took so long.'

'I was worried,' replied Frankie. 'I rang you on my new telephone. And you didn't answer. And so I came round, thinking you'd be here. And when you didn't come for your tea, I thought something had happened to you.'

He smiled broadly.

'Don't worry, but something did happen to me. Don't say anything. I'll tell you all about it later. Nothing to worry about.'

Auntie Flo came in with their tea. Fried fish fingers, peas and chips. She put some brown sauce on the table.

'I've made it all fresh. I'll make some more tea.'

After they finished tea they walked back to the pair of semi-detached houses where they lived.

Frankie looked at him and asked,

'Well, what happened to you? Are you going to tell me?'

'Come into my house Frankie and I'll make you a gin and tonic.'

They went into the living room. Frankie sat down on a bar stool whilst Albert looked for glasses.

As they sat at the bar sipping their drinks, Albert began telling her all that had happened that afternoon.

'I can't believe this,' said Frankie. 'And me cleaning all this time. Oh I've put you in terrible danger. You had a very nice life before you met me. Oh Albert, I'm so sorry.'

'Not at all. I had a very dull life. And I didn't know what my third novel was going to be about. I haven't had so much excitement since I was in the army.'

## Chapter Seventeen

Saturday morning Frankie went into the kitchenette to make her breakfast. She looked at the door of the pantry and decided to open it.

There on the floor, under a loose plank, just as Albert had described the night before, was the handle to the trap door leading to her cellar.

She climbed down the ladder, found the light switch and looked around the little room. Then she climbed out leaving the light on and the trap door open, made her breakfast and sat down in the lounge in front of the electric fire.

She concentrated on the cellar, determined to remember. She went upstairs, prepared and took a bath, got ready to go out. She went back to the kitchen, turned off the light and closed the trapdoor.

Satisfied that the cellar was now etched in her memory, she picked up the phone and rang Albert.

Although Bernard lived in another town and county, it was only a thirty minute drive to the address on the business card he had given Frankie.

Bernard lived in a ground floor flat in a leafy neighbourhood of modern looking maisonettes.

Albert pulled up on the opposite side of the road.

'Do you think he's at home?' asked Frankie. 'He may be working or simply have gone away for the weekend. I can't see his car.'

'Let's wait a little, see if there is any movement,' suggested Albert.

They sat for some minutes in the vehicle, when Frankie said;

'Look, the front door's opening.'

The door opened and a man, immediately recognizable as Bernard, emerged.

'Maybe he's going to his car. If so we'll follow him.'

Albert started the engine. Bernard sauntered down the road, paused in front of a little shop and went in. Albert turned off the engine. They waited and Bernard came out and began walking back home carrying a newspaper.

He went in and closed the door behind him.

Frankie got out of the car. She crossed the road, went up to the front door and rang the doorbell. Bernard opened the door.

'Hiya, just came round to see how you were getting on. Well, yes, I will have some tea.'

She walked into the house.

'Put the kettle on Bernard.'

She closed the door behind her. She immediately walked into a living room. To the left of the front door there was a large picture window giving onto the street. At the other end of the room was a door which opened on to a kitchen. Another door which was closed she imagined was to the bedroom.

There was a settee and two arm chairs, a coffee table and a television set. The newspaper he had just bought was open, and spread on the floor in front of one of the armchairs. No fireplace, but the flat was obviously centrally heated.

Bernard picked up the paper he had been reading, folded it and still without speaking carried it into the kitchen. No sooner had he disappeared, when the doorbell rang again. Frankie opened the door. Bernard came back out.

'Oh look. Albert's here too. So it's tea for three, Bernard.'

Bernard still did not speak but noises from the kitchen suggested he was indeed making tea. Some minutes later, he came out with a tray. He grinned at them.

'Oh haven't you sat down yet? Please, make yourselves comfortable.'

He placed the tray on the table. They all sat down. Albert and Frankie on the settee and Bernard in an armchair. Bernard began to pour the tea. When

179

he finished, he sat back in the chair and grinned at them. He seemed quite relaxed. He began speaking.

'I really didn't expect to see either of you again. I thought you had made it clear that we were both of us to stay out of your way. And yet here you are, with your tongues hanging out, asking for tea and biscuits. I may add that my biscuits are chocolate, not digestive.'

'Well,' said Albert. 'This time, we would like some truthful answers to our questions. Are you really writing a book about the German Secret Weapon, Bernard?'

'Yes, I am.'

'Is Salvador Jimenez collaborating with you on this project?'

'No, not really. I thought he was. He first came to see me some months ago. He said he had heard I was working on a book about the Haunebu disc and offered to work with me. I was a little suspicious because very often all people want to do is steal your ideas and get information out of you. But he brought that disc, the one you found in the wood. It looked like the disc in the photograph I had, but of course it wasn't authentic. It came from Spain. He had used it several times apparently.'

He paused to sip his tea and continued speaking.

'He once went to the old people's home where the old chap, who had lived next door to you, Frankie, was living. The poor old fellow was not very lucid, but when he showed him the disc, he kept on repeating that you Frankie knew where they were.'

'When you came to England,' Bernard continued, 'he wanted to show you the disc to see your reaction. However, although the old man knew what it was. You didn't. You had no idea.'

'But,' said Frankie. 'I knew where to find it, didn't I? How did I know?'

Bernard looked at her.

'Salvador said you had been hypnotized. By experts, in Sheffield. It's not the disc. It's the place. The house where you found the disc, the house in the wood near Fallowfield, it is circled on a map which I haven't got. Salvador had the map. But, obviously, the disc means nothing to you.'

'Bernard,' asked Albert. 'How does Salvador know all this? Where did he get the map?'

'That, I don't know.'

'And another question. Why was Salvador so willing to threaten us with a gun, to recuperate a metal disc which, you now tell me, is not authentic?'

'He told me it belonged to his family and was very valuable. And it is connected, I don't know how. I didn't know he was going to pull out a gun. We were not really friends. He had helped me with details about my book, that's all. Really all I wanted to do was finish it and have it published.'

He picked up his cup and drank the tea which remained.

'Things have become terribly complicated. I'm really sorry I ever met him. His family supports the dictatorship in Spain. My family was socialist and we always supported the Resistance. Really I have nothing in common with this bloke and his politics.'

The doorbell rang.

181

Bernard put his finger on his lips and gestured that they move into the kitchen. They followed him. He began whispering.

'Please, can you just go out the back door here? I don't want my visitor to know you are here.'

'Who is it?' asked Frankie. 'Salvador?'

'No,' answered Bernard, 'Beryl.'


Frankie looked at the cigarettes she had found in her handbag. Probably her last pack of American cigarettes. She took one out, lit it and offered the packet to Albert.

They were sharing a table with three strangers in the Crown. It was Sunday lunchtime and Frankie was on her second and last pint of bitter.

The girl sitting opposite at the table spoke to her.

'You're American, aren't you? I knew it as soon as I heard your accent. And you're smoking what my sister smokes. She lives in Florida. Where are you from?'

Frankie felt powerless when faced with this kind of question. In the end she just acquiesced.

'Des Moines, Iowa.'

'Oh where's that?'

'In the Midwest. Lots of cornfields.'

She braced herself for the inevitable questions.

'How long are you here for?'

'I don't know, maybe a few months. I'm not really American. I just lived there for three years.'

'Do you like it better there? I have a friend who works at the American Consulate. She used to live in Kentucky but didn't like it at all. That's why she divorced and moved back here.'

'Oh, I liked it quite a lot. I was quite happy there until my husband died.'

'Oh, how awful, I'm so sorry to hear that.'

'It's all right. It's been some time now.'

'This friend of mine is now going out with a French boy and seems really smitten.'

Albert looked at Frankie.

'Finish up; I have to get the cider.'

Frankie finished her ale, said goodbye to the girl and the two left the pub.

'Did you hear what she said?' asked Frankie. 'That was my friend Beryl she was talking about and Bernard.'

'How does she know her?'

'Beryl lives round here.'

Auntie Flo had made Sunday dinner. They drank cider and listened to the comedy hour on the BBC during lunch. Auntie Flo then turned on the television. There was always a war movie on Sunday afternoons. This one was about escaping from a German POW camp.

Auntie Flo and Albert seemed to love them but Frankie made her excuses and wandered off home.

It was already dark when she got to her front door. She put the key in the lock and suddenly someone called out her name from the side of the house. She jumped.

Her heart beating inside her head, she turned and looked around.

## Chapter Eighteen

'Oh, Beryl, what a fright you gave me.'

She looked at her. Beryl's abundant, flaming red hair had been replaced by a short curly blonde cut.

But it was her face; tears mixed with makeup that made her appear such a sorry sight.

'Whatever is the matter? Come in and tell me about it. I'll put the kettle on.'

Beryl sat down on the sofa. Frankie brought in the tray and poured tea for both of them.

'After the New Year do, I started going out with Bernard. He is ever so nice to me, Frankie, and I really like him. Anyway I went to see him yesterday at his house. We were just chatting, having a drink of something French he gave me, when someone began knocking on the door. He had a window next to the door and he looked through. He put his finger over his mouth to hush me, gave me my hat and coat and pushed me out the back where he had his car parked. We drove off as fast as we could. He took me home. Said a gang was after him and I wasn't to come back for a while and he would call in a few days. Anyway the next day I called him and no one answered. Then I called again and a man answered. He sounded American. I asked for Bernard. He said Bernard didn't live there any more. I went there this afternoon. It's true. He doesn't live there. There's been a fire. The house is all burnt out.'

'Burnt out?'

'Yeah, there'd been a fire. I think they burnt his lovely maisonette. And worst of all. Where is Bernard? What have they done to him?'

'Have you thought of going to the police?' asked Frankie.

'Bernard wouldn't hear of it when I said that yesterday. He's mixed up in something and said no police. He works for a newspaper, he might be thrown out of the country, lose his job. And at the consulate, I can't get mixed up with anything to do with police and foreign criminals. You know what the Yanks are like about those things.'

She began to sob.

'Oh, Frankie, if something's happened to him. Poor Bernard. Do you know anything about this?'

Frankie looked at Beryl.

'You've changed your hair.'

'Yes, I wanted something a little more with it. More fashionable.'

'What did Bernard tell you about all this?' asked Frankie.

'You remember Salvador, don't you? Didn't you dance with him on New Year's Eve? He told Bernard that he worked for a Spanish newspaper, but Bernard thinks that's just a front. Yes, he works for a newspaper but really he's here looking for something else. Small discs maybe about four or five inches in diameter each one and there are three of them. Salvador's family has a kind of machine. The three discs fit into three different slots. Like a vending machine. When they are inserted, the machine begins to work.'

'And what does it do?' asked Frankie.

'Well, that's it. Bernard says he doesn't know. But it came from Germany. But there's more. They need this large cartridge case. The machine only works if it's connected. And they've lost it. Someone's taken it.'

'Do they know who?'

'Bernard thinks he knows, but he wouldn't tell me. Said it was better that I didn't know.'

There was a knock at the door. A look of panic crossed Beryl's face.

'Don't answer it. Please don't open the door, Frankie.'

Frankie went to the door. It was Albert. She quickly apprised him of Beryl's visit and her fears for Bernard.

Albert came into the lounge and they were introduced. Beryl went over her story.

'Well, someone must know what happened to his house. Firemen, the police,' he said.

'Bernard wouldn't want me going to the police. And I don't want to get involved in anything.'

Frankie looked at her.

'How many people know about you and Bernard? Because the police might want to talk to you anyway. To find out about the fire.'

'Only you two, I didn't even tell my mum. Well, especially not my mum. Oh, my mum. Look, I'll go to the bathroom and freshen up; I'll have to be getting home. You're not on the phone, are you, Frankie? Oh, yes, you are. You've got it in the living room. Let me phone my mum, first.'

'Shall I drive you home?' asked Albert.

'No, I came over in the car. It's Bernard I'm worried about. But he did say he might not call for a few days.'

Beryl made a brief call home and then went up to the bathroom.

She came down, her face made up again, and left.

'Albert,' said Frankie, 'the girl in the pub knew Beryl and she knew about her French boyfriend. So I imagine she's told lots of people.'

'I don't think anything's happened to Bernard. But they certainly destroyed his house. But I don't know why. Maybe they were looking for something and it all got out of hand.'

188

'Well, we know something else now,' said Frankie, 'the discs are nothing like we thought. They're little. And that means they could be anywhere. If I am the key to the whole operation they could be in the house. And that disc we found that belonged to Bernard and Salvador. Could that be the empty cartridge that they need? Do you still have it in the garden shed?'

'Yes, it's locked up there. But the truth is, I haven't looked at it since the day Bernard and Salvador came. So much has been happening, I've hardly even thought about it.'

'Well it's dark now,' said Frankie. 'We'll check on it tomorrow.'

'No, I'll check on it now. I have lights in the garden.'

There were lights in the garden but he still needed a torch to open the shed. He turned the key in the lock and opened the door. He shone the torch down at where he had left the disc.

Before they entered the garden they both knew what they were going to find and so it was no surprise to them that the shed was empty.

'It was a silly place to leave it,' said Albert. 'Especially as Bernard saw us in the garden. I wonder who took it. Bernard or Salvador.'

Something on the grass next to the shed drew Frankie's attention. She bent down and picked up a crumpled cigarette pack.

'And if it were neither of the two? But someone who smokes Woodbines? That would explain why Bernard didn't have the disc. And why Salvador and his merry men, not believing him, were searching his maisonette.'

'And how did Bessel know where it was?' asked Albert.

'He might have been watching us. Hidden behind a tree or something the day we were opening it. We weren't being very careful. This is really our fault.'

'My fault,' insisted Albert.

'Oh, Albert, you have been so good to me.'

She threw her arms around him and hugged him tightly.

Albert looked down at her. Her sweet little face looked up at him. He looked into her beautiful blue eyes. He bent down and kissed her. She threw her arms around his neck and responded with unexpected passion. He kissed her again. And again, holding her tightly.

'Let's go into the house,' he whispered. 'I'll turn out the garden lights.'

They went into the house and turned out the lights.

## Chapter Nineteen

The ringing of the telephone woke her up. She ran down the stairs to the living room and answered breathlessly.

It was Mrs. Petersen. She had called her the night before but no one answered. She just loved Edinburgh. She was in a hotel opposite the castle. She had even tried haggis which she thought tasted like something Jewish her mother used to give her.

Someone had tried to convince her to drink some Scotch whisky but she stayed with ginger ale.

She had met two other American women travelling together on the train coming up and they had arranged to have lunch together in a place near the castle. She discreetly enquired if Frankie had had any more problems with what she called 'Peeping Toms'.

She sent regards to Mr. Tucker.

It was still very early in the morning. Frankie wondered if Albert was awake yet. She felt as if her life were full of contradictions.

She was in love with Albert, but still remembered Chuck. The events of the previous night came flooding back to her although really they had never left her.

She had wanted to wake up in her own house, but nevertheless she realised how very lonely she had been and how she never wanted to feel like that again.

She wanted to see Albert, love him, talk to him and, at the same time, she wanted to stay at home and not see anybody. She had woken up with such strength, and now, she weakly began to cry.

She went upstairs, ran a bath, bathed and went into the front bedroom to the dressing table. As she looked out the window she saw a man across the street looking at the house.

It was Bernard.


Albert woke up early and wandered down to his office. Here, there was a long table which served as a desk. A pile of blank sheets of paper he kept to one side of his automatic typewriter, and to the other an office tray for typed manuscripts. Next to it, another tray for discarded pages.

He sat down at the table, slipped in a sheet of paper and began to type.

The story took form, as he placed his detective in a small, grubby office full of cigarette smoke. The door opened and the woman, for whom he had always been waiting, wandered into his life.

The telephone started ringing behind him. At first, he thought of ignoring it, but then realised it might be Frankie. Maybe to tell him it was all a mistake and she never wanted to see him again. No, surely not. All the same, he picked up the phone with trepidation.

'Albert, pet,' Auntie Flo sounded worried. 'Didn't want to wake you love, but your mum's called. We've been on the phone all night. She's sure there's a fellow following her about. Every time she goes out with the dog, she sees the same man. She didn't want to say anything to her friend but she wants to come home. She's told her friend I've had one of my turns and she has to go back. Can you go and pick her up, love?'

Albert promised to go over as soon as he could. He set the phone down and sat looking at what he had written when the phone rang again. He answered this time with annoyance, sensing that his inspiration had disappeared.

'Albert?'

It was Frankie. His voice softened.

'Oh, sorry, I thought it was Auntie Flo. I was writing and she phoned me with some ridiculous story of mum being followed. I have to go and pick her up from Timperley. Do you want to come with me? We could stop for breakfast somewhere on the way over.'

'Yes,' she answered, 'that would be nice. But Albert. I was standing in my front bedroom and I saw Bernard standing across the street looking at our houses.'

'Well, at least he's not dead. What do you think he wants? Can you see him now? Look out your front window.'

'Yes. He's across the road. But he's just standing there. What does he want?'

'Hold on. I'll go and ask him. I'll call you back, all right?'

He went upstairs, washed quickly and put on his brown corduroy trousers and fisherman's sweater. A few minutes later he was out the front door and had crossed the road to where Bernard was standing.

'Good morning, Bernard. Would you like to come in? We'll have a little chat. I know Beryl is very worried about you.'

Bernard shrugged his shoulders in the way many Frenchman do when lost for words and followed him into the house. Albert showed Bernard into the living room.

He went into the office, telephoned Frankie very briefly as he did not want to leave the man alone.

Bernard was seated on the settee. His usual cheerful expression had disappeared and he looked decidedly glum.

'Would you like a cup of tea?' Albert enquired.

'You wouldn't have anything a little stronger? I need more than that.'

'What would you like? Whisky? I have a bottle of French red wine that's open. Would you like some?'

'Yes, a glass of red wine, please.'

Albert gave him a glass of wine. The sound of the doorbell startled Bernard and he looked round in alarm.

'That'll be Frankie.'

Albert opened the door to her and she came into the house.

'Hello, Bernard,' she said.

He stood up and kissed her on both cheeks. He then sat down or more precisely seemed to collapse on the settee.

He began speaking.

'After you left my flat, Beryl came to visit me. We were chatting and drinking something when I heard noises on the doorstep. I couldn't see but I thought it might be Salvador and his men. Beryl and I went out the back way and we drove to Beryl's house.'

'Yes, Beryl told us all this,' said Frankie. 'But why are you so afraid of Salvador?'

'He thought I had the disc. The empty one that you have.'

'And don't you have it? Didn't you take it out of Albert's shed? It's not there now. And if you haven't got it, who has? Because someone's taken it.'

Bernard looked at her.

'I thought you had it. Salvador thinks I have it though.'

'Why does he think that?' asked Frankie.

'Because he thinks I took it from you.'

'Why?' asked Albert.

'Because he asked me if I knew where it was. I said I might know but then he told me to steal it. I ignored him, of course. I wasn't going to do anything like that. I'm just writing a book, I'm not a criminal.'

'So someone else took it,' said Frankie.

'Yes, but not Salvador, apparently,' Albert said ruefully. 'It really was all my fault.'

'No, it wasn't,' Frankie took hold of his arm and squeezed it.

She looked at Bernard.

'And that's why they burnt your house down?'

Bernard shrugged his shoulders.

'It's not my house, I rent it. I know it's insured. I had only been there for a few days. There was a problem with damp in the cellar and there was a paraffin heater there to dry it. I imagine they had a mishap when they were searching down below. Better the house than me. And I've hidden my car. I came here on the bus.'

Albert looked at his watch.

'We have to go and pick up my mother and bring her home. Where do you want us to leave you Bernard?'

He gave them the address of a small hotel. The three of them got into the car. And dropped Bernard there.

There was a small coffee shop just outside Timperley. Albert parked in a car park not far away. They sat down at a table, near a window, from which on the other side of the main road, a large park and some playing fields could be seen.

Albert sat with his back to the window but Frankie could see two different groups of people watching and playing football.

A waitress brought them some coffee and rolls. They felt they had much to talk about, not least the morning's events, but neither said very much.

'You know, I woke up inspired and immediately began writing my novel,' said Albert. 'I was really getting into my stride when the phone rang.'

'Oh, I'm sorry. I interrupted you.'

'No, not at all. It was Auntie Flo to tell me to pick up my mum. I thought it was you. That's why I answered.'

'Oh, Mrs. Petersen called me this morning from Edinburgh. She ate haggis yesterday and thinks it's Jewish.'

'I've never eaten haggis. In fact I don't really know what it is.'

'It's typical of Scotland. A sheep's heart wrapped in sheep's tripe cooked with oats. It tastes much better than it sounds. And Mrs. Petersen liked it. She sent you her regards. You made quite a hit with her.'

Albert looked up.

'There's a phone near the cash desk. I'll pay and tell my mum we won't be long.'

He was a long time. Frankie gazed out the window, watching the boys playing football. It was a cold, grey day and the spectators moved about a lot, maybe, she thought, to keep warm.

Albert came back. He sat down at the table.

'Well, that's a turn up for the books. My mum got fed up waiting for me and took a taxi home.'

'Oh, no. Is it so late?'

'No not really. But she's home now anyway.'

'First I phoned to see if I had any messages. The secretary said my mum had called twice. So I phoned her. First the friend in Timperley who said she'd left and then our house. Auntie Flo answered the phone and said she could see she was getting out of the taxi.'

Frankie looked a little worried,

'Do you think she's upset?'

'I don't know. Who cares? Now that we're here I think we could go for a drive. I know some pretty villages near here. Let's go.'

He took her hand. They left the coffee shop and walked to the car.

## Chapter Twenty

Bernard woke up shivering. The hotel room was cold and there was only one blanket on the bed. He looked at his watch sitting on a side table. It was three a.m.

He could not take in that the house he had been living in had been destroyed. Luckily, he thought, it had been a short term, temporary arrangement and all his notes and writings, of which there were a great deal, were either in France or in his flat in London. Clearly, the men who had searched the maisonette did not realise this.

He got out of bed, put on his slippers and dressing gown and went to the wardrobe. He pulled out his case. Inside was a bottle of Johnny Walker. He opened it and looked for a glass. Not finding one, he took a swig. And then another. He replaced the cap and put the bottle back.

As he was placing the bag back in the wardrobe he heard a noise on the other side of the door. Some muffled voices. The key moved in the lock and the door opened.

Two men entered quickly. One grabbed him from behind and the other pushed some kind of cloth into his mouth. Then something was pushed over his nose. He lost consciousness.

When he woke up it was morning. Light was streaming in through a window which seemed to be located near the ceiling of the room. He was lying in a bed. He sat up in the bed and then sat with his legs hanging over the side. Rather like a hospital bed, he thought. Very high up.

He managed to slide down and began to walk around and examine the room. It seemed to be some kind of basement which would explain the high windows. The walls were simply bricks and mortar, no plaster. The door at the far end of the room was dark and metallic looking. Next to the door were some boxes that might contain or had contained bottles of beer and other alcoholic drinks. Maybe he was in the basement of a pub, a restaurant or a hotel.

He tried the door and as he expected it was locked.

Obviously he had been kidnapped but by whom and why? And what were their plans?

The door opened and two men came in. Both of them looked young. One slim with short blonde hair and the other, also with fair hair, but a much darker complexion than the other. They grinned at him but there was nothing friendly in their expressions.

The first one looked at him. Bernard recognised him. Not long ago he had offered him money for the discs. And now he was here threatening him.

'Have you slept well? Comfortable bed? Och, you struggled hard enough last night.'

Bernard could tell he was Scottish. The other one began laughing and speaking with a London accent.

'Who do you work for? What do you want from me?' asked Bernard.

'Who do you work for?' he asked Bernard. 'Oh, yes, you work for Salvador Jimenez, don't you? Well, not any more. Salvador died last night. Of heart failure. Poor Spanish laddie. Must have had a weak heart. And when his three friends disappeared and never came back. Too much grief for a Spanish heart.'

The Scot assumed an expression of sorrow.

'What happened to his men?' asked Bernard.

'Están con los peces, Bernard,' said the other boy, suddenly speaking Spanish.

Bernard looked at him.

'You mean you drowned them. All three of them?'

'First we got rid of the three bodyguards. No one will ever miss them. Or look for them at the bottom of the Mersey.'

He lit a cigarette and gave one to his companion.

'Then,' added the Scottish boy, 'We had Salvador all to ourselves. And he told us everything. And then we gave him a cocktail. But he couldn't take it. Heart failure.'

201

'Solo nos quedas tu, macho,' quipped the other. He blew out cigarette smoke as he spoke, trying to look sinister, Bernard thought.

'Why do you speak to me in Spanish?' asked Bernard. 'I'm French but I do speak English.'

'Salvador said he always spoke to you in Spanish.'

'Look, I don't know what you want. I want to go home.'

The Scot laughed.

'You haven't got much of a home left, have you? Chuan here knocked over a paraffin heater when we were searching your cellar. Almost didn't get out. Why did you have a heater full of paraffin in your cellar?'

'The owner was trying to dry it out. Get rid of the damp. What did you say his name was? Sounds Chinese.'

'It means John. In the language of my village. In the Pyrenees. It was my father's name too,' Chuan replied peevishly.

'Fascinating,' replied Bernard. 'Now can I go home?'

He looked at the two young men. The Scot was quite tall, slim almost lanky. Chuan, much shorter, broader but neither looked like formidable opponents. Together he had no possibility against them. But all things being equal, he was in with a chance against either of them. Although of a slight build he kept himself fit and these two probably smoked too much. What would keep them going was their cold blooded viciousness.

He looked again at the boxes of bottles by the door. One box was open. He moved slightly closer to where the two men were standing.

'Look, I don't know what you want from me. Just let me go home.'

Chuan gave a nasty laugh.

'I'll ask the boss what we are to do with you.'

He left the room.

Bernard stood looking at the Scot.

'Where are we? In a pub basement?'

'Why do you say that?' asked the other.

'More than anything because of that small door up there in the corner.'

The Scot turned around and looked up.

'I don't see anything.'

In a split second, Bernard grabbed an empty bottle and hit the Scot hard on the back of the neck, breaking the bottle in two. The Scot staggered, but remained on his feet. He turned around.

Bernard remembered his father's words when recounting his experiences fighting in the Resistance, when you're fighting for your life, you don't take half measures.

He pushed the jagged edges into the Scot's stomach and twisted the bottle. There was a look of surprise on the man's face and he fell to the ground.

Without stopping he picked up another bottle and opened the door.

He was in a long, dark corridor, illuminated by the occasional bare light bulb. The windows in the room where he had been imprisoned were on the right. So he turned in that direction, walking slowly, listening all the time.

He came to a wooden staircase which he climbed.

The door at the top of the stairs refused to budge when pushed. He was seized with panic. So near, yet so far, he thought. He calmed himself down, he was not dead yet. He examined the door. It was bolted from the inside.

In a moment the door was open and the cold air blew into his face.

He crept out of the building into the sunlight. He was in a car park. Empty of course, as the pub, if that was what it was, had not yet opened.

A gate to his left was open and led to a main thoroughfare. Next to the gate was a bus stop and as luck would have it, a bus, which was just moving off.

He ran, grabbed hold of the vertical bar and pulled himself up onto the platform. He went inside and sat on one of the long seats in the entrance.

The relief Bernard felt was enormous but short lived. He looked down and realised that he was still dressed in his pyjamas, dressing gown and slippers.

And his dressing gown was stained with something which he realised was blood.

There was only one other passenger downstairs. Seated behind the driver, he had not even noticed the Frenchman in his pyjamas. Bernard moved from where he was and sat in another more discreet place next to a window.

A few moments later the conductor had come downstairs.

'Fare, please.'

Bernard reached into his dressing gown pocket and found half a crown and a number of thrupenny bits. The evening before, which now seemed so long ago, he had left change there in case he had to pay or leave a tip for the room service in his hotel.

Luckily, the money was still there.

He named the street where his hotel was located and paid the sixpenny fare.

The conductor did not appear to notice his attire. So far so good.

The bus began to fill and by the time he left, people had already begun to stare and certainly the sight of a man getting off the bus dressed in pyjamas, dressing gown and slippers was bound to raise more than a few eyebrows.

He scurried to his hotel, entered the foyer, asked for his key at reception.

He approached and entered the hotel room with great caution. As far as he could see nothing had been disturbed. He quickly washed, got dressed, packed his things, checked out and nipped into a passing taxi, which took him to the station.

Here he bought a ticket to Euston station.

Before he got on the train he bought a newspaper and made some phone calls.

He then found his carriage, sat down. Five minutes later, with a lurch, the train began to move. He opened his paper and sat looking at the headlines for some time, not reading any article at all.

He was still not sure what his next move should be. He had had a very narrow escape and could not guarantee that he was now out of danger. He realised he may have been followed.

There was even the question of what had happened to the Scot. Had he killed him? Would he be wanted for murder? Who were his kidnappers working for? Certainly not Salvador. He had bought the newspaper to see if there was any news about Salvador's death. Of course, there was nothing at all.

He suddenly felt rather hungry. It was now midday and he had eaten no breakfast. He left the compartment where until now, he had been entirely alone and made his way to the restaurant car, sat at a table and ordered some lunch.

The waiter placed a plate of onion soup in front of him. Onion soup always lifted his spirits. After the main course, he decided not to bother with dessert but to finish with a cup of coffee.

Another diner sat down opposite him. He looked up from his coffee. It was Chuan.

He did not speak, but continued drinking his coffee.

The waiter placed the bill on the table. Without looking up, Bernard looked at the bill and placed some money next to it.

The waiter came by, picked up the money.

'I'll get your change, sir.'

'No, that won't be necessary,' replied Bernard. 'I wonder if you could direct me to the bar? It's still open, isn't it?'

'Thank you very much, sir. The bar is this way. If you would like to follow me.'

Without looking at his table companion Bernard followed the waiter to the next carriage. There were a number of drinkers although the wagon was far from full. Bernard ordered a Bacardi and Coke. As he spoke he glanced behind him. Chuan was standing near the door watching him.

Bernard wondered if someone had come with him. His first impression was that Chuan was alone. His partner hopefully was dead or at least so wounded that he had to stay at home. Very possibly, this was a job Chuan would prefer to manage by himself.

Bernard paid for his drink poured the Coke into the glass, left it on the bar and walked to the WC at the end of the carriage.

Once the door was closed he took the empty Coke bottle out of his pocket, smashed off the end and put it back into his jacket pocket. He opened the door of the WC. Another passenger was waiting to enter and Chuan was right behind him.

Without establishing visual contact Bernard continued walking. To his left were more compartments. At the end of the carriage there was a space between this one and the door of the next carriage. Bernard waited where he thought he was out of sight. He stood with his back to the next carriage so as to be facing the passengers coming from the bar.

He heard footsteps and loud voices. Two men passed. He heard the footsteps of another person, a cough. And then saw him pass into the next carriage. It was not Chuan.

The next person was.

He appeared suddenly and startled Bernard who had momentarily been lulled into a false feeling of security. He turned and glared at the Frenchman. Grabbed his left arm and twisted it behind his back.

Bernard's eyes filled with tears of agony, but he remained silent. With his free arm he took the bottle and rammed it into Chuan's stomach twisting it just as he had done in the morning, now so long ago.

Chuan immediately released his grip and fell banging his head against the door of the carriage. Bernard seized his opportunity, opened the door and somehow pushed the body out of the moving train

No half measures, he thought. He closed the door again. He looked around, now terrified that someone had seen him. But he was quite alone.

He still had the bloody Coke bottle in his hand. He opened the window and threw it out. He closed the window.

'Are you all right, sir? Do you need help?'

He turned around. A grey haired guard was looking at him.

'You're covered in blood, sir. Have you had an accident?'

Bernard looked down. His right jacket sleeve and the cuff of his white shirt and his right hand were blood stained.

'I had a nose bleed. Terrible nuisance but something I'm prone to, I'm afraid. But I'm perfectly all right. If you excuse me, I'll go and wash.'

He opened the door of his compartment. It was still empty. He opened his case and took out a clean shirt and sports jacket. He changed his clothes.

He emptied the pockets of the stained jacket and pushed both the jacket and the shirt out the train window. No point in carrying evidence with him. He calculated he was half an hour from London. He closed his suitcase, sat down and thought about his next move.

Of one thing he was certain. He did not know if the Scot was dead or simply wounded. Chuan was certainly dead. And he had killed him. For the moment, he imagined, there were no witnesses. Nor had the body been found.

But this was all a matter of time. Without doubt his best option was to leave the country.

From Euston station, he made his way to Victoria station by underground. Then he went to the ticket office.

Next train to Paris was at ten o'clock, arriving about eight thirty in the morning. Luckily he had withdrawn a considerable sum before booking into the hotel and had sufficient funds to last him until his arrival in France.

He looked at his watch. It was now after six and the best thing would be to have a light supper.

There was a pub nearby in Victoria Street where he knew they served suppers. The Albert. He ordered some food and a beer and sat at a table facing the door.

People wandered in and out, mainly London office workers coming for a drink at the end of a work day, before commuting back to their homes in the outskirts of the city.

The toilet was situated at the back of the pub in a basement. He went down and immediately when faced with a couple of narrow, empty corridors, realised this had been a mistake. He entered, washed, dried his hands and face and turned to leave.

At that moment another man opened the door. Bernard moved back, alarmed. The man smiled and that was enough. Bernard hit him hard in the stomach several times. The man fell and began to vomit.

'Mate, what's wrong with you? Oh fucking hell, you're a fucking lunatic.'

Bernard turned and rushed up the stairs and out of the pub. He did not go directly to the station but took several side streets. He stopped at a newsagent's and bought an evening newspaper. He then arrived at the station, took his case out of the left luggage office and went to his train. Half past nine. He sat down in a compartment and began to read the paper.

By the time the train began its journey to the coast the compartment was half full. Two French couples who seemed to be friends and an elderly English vicar.

A train guard came in and looked at their tickets. The French people spoke French with everyone but Bernard preferred to continue speaking in English. He wanted to be as inconspicuous as possible. Especially after making the clumsy mistake of attacking an innocent man in a London pub.

He stood in a line at passport control waiting to board the ferry. The queue moved slowly. He wondered if they were looking for someone. Maybe for him.

Two uniformed policemen stood watching the travellers. He gave his passport to the official. The man looked at him, unsmiling. He looked at the photograph in his passport and looked at him again. He handed the passport back to him. Not even a stamp.

Bernard moved on down a ramp and onto the ferry, leaving his luggage in the hold and climbed up into the passenger section.

It was now quite late, and he sat down and tried to close his eyes. Five minutes later he was awake again as he watched the people move about him. Maybe he should not try to sleep at all. Perhaps he was being followed.

He looked up. A strange fellow was looking at him. Large head, bald, middle aged. Dressed in a jacket, shirt and tie. Obviously north European. Maybe German or Scandinavian.

Bernard looked in another direction but then, like a magnet, the man caught Bernard's gaze. The man stood up and began walking. Bernard looked in a different direction. He looked up.

The man was there, next to him.

'Excuse me, sir. May I ask you if you are Dutch, from Amsterdam?'

'No, I'm not. From London,' answered Bernard.

'Oh, I'm so sorry. You see my wife,' he pointed to a middle aged, brown haired woman Bernard had not even noticed; 'she thought she knew you. Obviously our mistake. So sorry to trouble you, sir.'

Bernard stood up and began to walk. He climbed some stairs and found he was in a bar. Being in international waters it was open all night and duty free prices applied. But Bernard did not want to drink anything; he had to keep his wits about him.

He asked for a cup of tea and sat at a table. His hands were shaking a little. When he finished his tea he followed the arrows to French passport control located near the hold. Here they looked at his passport and gave him a disembarking card. He must be safe now.

In very little time the ferry docked, he picked up his suitcase and, on the other side of the customs shed, found the train to Paris. It was now about three thirty in the morning. He closed his eyes, and someone touched his shoulder,

'Monsieur, nous somme deja arrives a Paris.'

He opened his eyes. The train had stopped and the passengers were all leaving.

He grabbed his suitcase, walked towards the exit and into the centre of Paris. He felt safe now. Chuan was dead. The Scot even if not dead was in no position to harm him. No one had followed him.

Even if the police found the dead body they probably would not connect it with him. And even if they did, he was in France.

And he was no longer a Frenchman in London but now a Frenchman in France.

Like a needle in a haystack.

## Chapter Twenty-One

It was Saturday lunchtime when Albert and Frankie pulled up outside the pair of semi detached houses, where they lived. The first time, thought Frankie, that she had ever taken an impromptu holiday.

More than that, without any luggage at all. They had had to buy new clothes, suitcases, toiletries.

And they did not talk about their mystery at all, although Albert mentioned a book he had read once about a married couple who were detectives. It was called Partners in Crime.

During one of their many romantic dinners he had proposed that is how they should describe themselves.

Frankie opened the door. A lot of post on the hall table. She carried her things into the dining room, left them on the table and then made her way into the kitchenette to put the kettle on.

Once she was comfortable, in front of the little electric fire in the lounge, she went through the post.

Two postcards from Mrs. Petersen who had enjoyed her time in Scotland and had decided to move on to Paris in the company of a new friend, one of the two women she had met on the train to Edinburgh.

There were some other letters. She looked at them curiously for a moment when the telephone rang.

It was Albert.

'We seem to be back in business as partners in crime, I have quite a lot to tell you. Would you like to come over for a coffee?'

'I was going to have a cup of tea. But I also have some letters to open.'

'Well let's have coffee together. Bring them over and we'll examine all the evidence together.'

A few minutes later she was sitting at the bar in Albert's living room.

Albert was preparing coffee.

'First thing I did was call my agent's secretary. He had a message from Bernard. He called on Tuesday. It was a little confused but he was no longer in his hotel. He had been kidnapped during the night, had escaped and was now on his way to London.'

'And today is Saturday. Who kidnapped him and where is he now?'

'I don't know. Perhaps we should start opening the post. Look this one is addressed to me. It's posted in France. Looks like Paris. Wednesday.'

He opened it.

'It's from Bernard.'


"Dear Frankie and Albert,

Just a note to let you know I am well. After my experience on Monday I have decided to leave England for a time. Perhaps you might explain things to Beryl.

Yours etc. Bernard."


'Not very explicative, is it?'

'No,' replied Albert. 'He doesn't know who might read it.

He set the letter alight and placed it in a large ashtray.'

'Why did you do that?'

Albert smiled grimly.

'There is no evidence that we know where he may be. Another letter. Oh this one is addressed to you Frankie.'

He opened it.

'Oh it's a newspaper cutting. From a Spanish newspaper. Salvador Jimenez correspondent for this newspaper bla bla bla, son of bla bla bla has been found dead in bla bla bla in the north of England bla bla bla from a heart attack. Remains to be brought back to Madrid. Burial on Wednesday next.'

'I didn't know you spoke Spanish.'

'Enough to manage a newspaper article. I've learnt the basics of several languages. I told you my life was very dull until I met you. Now I'm a partner in crime. Before I used to walk Marlen and do language courses. More importantly, who sent this to you? And what happened to Salvador?'

He looked at the envelope again. There was nothing else. He looked at the postmark. It was difficult to make out, but the letter had a British stamp on it.

'Oh, Frankie this one's for me. It's from a residential home.'

He began reading.

'The old boy who used to live here. He'd like to see us. Or rather the letter is addressed to me but because he doesn't know you are here. He is too ill to write himself, but someone in the home has written for him.'

He showed her the letter.

He looked through the other letters. Bills and circulars most of them. And then there was one left. Addressed to Frankie.

He opened it. Two typewritten sheets of paper.

'You should read it first, Frankie. It may have nothing to do with the matter in hand. And I don't want to interfere in your personal affairs. I was getting a little carried away, I think.'

Frankie took the letter and began to read it.

'I don't know if I understand this.'

She gave it to Albert.

'Have a look at it. Tell me what you think.'

Albert spent some time reading.

'I think you should go. I'll go with you if you like.'

'No, I wouldn't go alone Albert. Do you know Sheffield?'

'I've been there but I don't think I've been to the University Officers Training Corps headquarters. Did they say exactly what you were invited to?'

'It simply says that my father and mother were always invited to this commemoration ceremony. As they are now deceased they would like to invite me and a guest if I so desire to come in their place. My father used to spend a lot of time in Sheffield.'

'When is the ceremony?'

'At three o'clock, Thursday 28th January. But there's a lunch at one o'clock. In the barracks.'

'All right. Let's see what happens. Now I think I should make an appointment to see the old boy who used to live here. And then perhaps we should contact Beryl. She'll be worried about Bernard.'

'Better still I'll ring her and see if she wants to go out for a drink this evening. I don't think I want to discuss this on the phone.'

'You think someone might be listening to our calls?'

'I don't know,' replied Frankie. 'But let's not risk it. I'll go home and phone Beryl.'

'Auntie Flo's invited us to lunch. I think she wants company and she has been keeping an eye on our houses all week. My mum's taken the dog to Timperley again for the weekend.'

'I thought she was worried someone was following her over there.

'Well apparently not. Let's go to the Crown, have a pint or two and then have lunch at my house. It's bound to be a roast if she's invited both of us.'

217

Frankie opened her front door, went into the lounge, sat down and dialed Beryl's number.

Beryl answered the phone. Unusually, Beryl was not very talkative. The voices of the children could be heard in the background. Beryl left the phone a moment to close a door. When she came back it was all much quieter.

Without going into too much detail, Frankie said she had been away for the past few days and wondered if Beryl was free to go out for a drink that evening.

This chirped her up a little. And they agreed to meet about seven in the Royal Oak, a smart pub in the centre of the Village.

'I wonder why Mrs. Petersen suddenly decided to go to Paris.'

Frankie and Albert were sitting alone at a table in the Crown, drinking bitter from pint jugs. Frankie opened a packet of Rothmans that she had bought at the bar.

Her last pack of American cigarettes was empty and perhaps now no one would think she was American.

'Well, she's a wealthy American on holiday in Europe. Paris is the next step after London.'

'Yes, I know,' said Frankie. 'But she never mentioned she was going to Paris. And suddenly we get a letter from Bernard in Paris and then Mrs. Peterson's going there too.'

'Does she know Bernard?'

'Well, she knew Gallagher,' said Frankie.

'Did he know Bernard?'

'I don't know. Neither he nor Salvador seemed to know Bessel. But someone offered Salvador money for his disc. And that might have been one of Gallagher's agents.'

'Anyway,' said Albert. 'Tomorrow morning we'll go to see old Uncle Willy.'

'What time?'

'Nine o'clock.'

'That's very early, isn't it? That's a time for a job interview or an exam.'

'The lady I spoke to said it's better to visit him early on. As the day wears on, he tends to fall asleep. Uncle Willy is more on the ball in the morning.'

'How old is he?'

'Just turned eighty, but he's been quite ill these last few years.'

A group of four sat down at the same table. Albert got up and bought two more pints.

Frankie lit another cigarette.

'You're Frankie Cooper aren't you? Don't you remember me? My name's Betty, Betty Condren. Well, now it's Betty Froebel. I'm just visiting my mum for a few days. I live in Germany with my husband. Didn't you go to America?'

'Yes,' replied Frankie. 'I married an American, but he died some time ago and I've come back to England for a while.'

'Oh, how awful. I am sorry to hear that. What, you're visiting your mum and dad?'

'They died very recently, in a car crash.'

'Oh, Frankie. I'm so sorry. I really seem to be putting my foot in it, don't I? I was so glad to see you. Have you decided to stay here, then?'

'For the moment, yes.'

Albert came back with two more pints.

'Oh, Albert. This is an old school friend, Betty, I'm sorry what did you say your married name was?'

'Froebel. My husband is German, from Karlsruhe. I work there as a teacher, I teach British military children on the base there.'

'Oh, how interesting. This is Albert Tucker,' Frankie hesitated for only a moment, 'my boyfriend. We've been going out together for some time.'

'Oh, how do you do?'

She introduced the man sitting next to her, a serious looking man, with short brown hair and a forehead set in a wrinkled frown, as her brother.

'What do you do, Mr. Tucker?'

'I'm a writer.'

'Really. I knew I had heard that name before. You didn't write, "Life Makes You Weep", by any chance?'

'Yes, that's me. I confess.'

'There was another one, too? I can't remember. Something like "Jack and Jill went up the Hill"?'

' "Four and Twenty Blackbirds".'

'Oh, yes. I loved that one. I wanted my husband to read it but he can't speak English well enough. Has it been translated?'

'Into three languages. French, German and Dutch. But they're working on more.'

Albert had now finished his pint and was eager to leave. He never enjoyed talking about his books. He told Frankie that it was getting late and Frankie explained that they had a luncheon date. Betty insisted on writing down Frankie's phone number.

'It's so difficult to stay in touch with old friends,' she said, 'We seem to pass like ships in the night. And Mr. Tucker it has been an honour to meet you.'

Frankie braced herself for the reply.

'The honour is all mine.'

They left the pub and hurried to the off-licence.


At seven o'clock sharp Frankie was sitting alone at a table in the Royal Oak. Although it was still early the lounge bar was filling up. Frankie was sipping her tomato juice and Worcestershire sauce when two young men sat opposite her at the same table each one holding a jug of black stout.

Both of them were in their mid-twenties, very blonde hair, short, back and sides, dressed in dark modern suits.

This was obviously the beginning of a Saturday night pub crawl that would finish late, maybe two o'clock in the morning, in some club.

Beryl walked in and saw Frankie almost immediately. She walked over to the table and sat down. She glanced at the two men.

'How are you Beryl? Would you like a drink?'

'Frankie, could we go somewhere else? I want to chat. Do you mind? Maybe even a coffee? We could have a drink later.'

Frankie finished her juice and the two of them left the pub.

'Sorry Frankie, but I knew those two at the table and I didn't want to talk with them there. There's a little coffee bar around the corner in London Lane. We'll get a table there.'

'Frankie,' she went on. 'I can't begin to tell you how distraught I am about Bernard. He's just disappeared. I'm sure something's happened to him.'

Beryl took a sip of her coffee. Frankie touched her arm.

'That's why I wanted to see you. We got a letter from him. He's in France. But we think he's all right. I didn't want to tell you on the phone.'

'Why ever not?'

'Well, we've been away all week but on Tuesday he called Albert's answering service and left a message. Monday night he was kidnapped from his hotel.'

Beryl stifled a scream.

'He escaped and caught a train to London,' said Frankie. 'The next thing we knew was a very short letter stating he was in France for a time and to let you know he was all right.'

'He told you to contact me? Have you got the letter?'

'We burnt it.'

'Why did you do that?

'Look Beryl. You really mustn't tell anyone about this. I'm going to be quite clear. If you tell another person that Bernard is in France he may be killed and you will be responsible.'

'Why does anyone want to kill him?'

'We don't know. But someone tried to kidnap him. He's escaped from the country. You have to wait until he contacts you.'

Beryl looked at her friend.

'What are you mixed up in? You and Albert and Bernard? Is it about these discs? Was it Salvador who kidnapped Bernard?'

'Salvador is dead.' answered Frankie. 'He died of a heart attack, last week. Someone sent me a cutting all about it from a Spanish newspaper.'

'Well,' said Beryl, 'it's such a relief that you have news of Bernard. Thank you so much for telling me Frankie. You can't imagine how I felt when I saw what they had done to the little house he had. Anyway, we'll wait and see if he gets into contact. I think I could manage a drink now. But not the Royal Oak. Let's go to the Daylight, lots of youngsters. They have a jukebox and play Beatles and Rolling Stones.'

'Fine,' said Frankie, 'but seriously, Beryl, not a word to anyone about Bernard. His life may depend on it.'

Beryl nodded, but said nothing.

'Let's go,' said Frankie.

## Chapter Twenty-Two

The care home where Uncle Willy lived was an Edwardian house set in extensive grounds. Green lawns, gardens full of ferns, bushes and evergreens. Lots of trees.

Frankie imagined it would be cool and leafy in the summer.

They parked behind the house and then walked round to the front door. They were greeted by a plump, businesslike woman, fiftyish, smartly dressed in a dark skirt with matching jacket. She seemed to be waiting for them and led them into a large sitting room.

Uncle Willy was in a wheel chair on the left hand side of the fireplace listening to a tall, old fashioned radio.

Frankie went up to him.

'Uncle Willy, do you remember me, Frankie Cooper, your next door neighbour.'

The old man looked at her and smiled.

'Yes, of course I remember you Frankie. I was so sorry to hear about your parents. I didn't know you were in England. They said you had got married and gone to America.'

'Yes, but my husband died, so I've come back.'

'Well, I'm sorry to hear that Frankie. Lots of sad things happen over the years. You know my niece died too. That's why I had to come and live here. What with my leg and all my problems I couldn't manage on my own.'

He looked at Albert.

'And this is the fellow I sold my house to. Someone told me that you've changed it quite a bit. Gutted it, they said.'

'Frankie,' said Uncle Willy. 'Did they write to you from Sheffield? About the ceremonies?'

'Yes. I got a letter this week.'

'Good,' the old man began to pant a little, 'Frankie, you must go. And you must speak to Captain Mark Ryder. You say you've spoken to me. He'll tell you about the discs. And where they are. We had a code. You tell him I told you these two words. Neptune. Broomstick. Can you remember that?'

'Yes. Neptune. Broomstick.'

'Good,' he began to breathe more heavily again. 'Look, I'm going to have to take my medicine again. And then I'm done for. I'll have to sleep. Getting old isn't fun, Frankie. I'm so glad you could come. Sorry about all the people you lost, but remember it isn't worth moping about them. Put it all behind you. Remember. Neptune, Broomstick.'

He breathed in deeply.

A young woman came into the room pushing a medical trolley.

Frankie and Albert left the old man.

They got into the car and Frankie burst into tears.

'I'm so sorry,' she said. 'I wasn't crying for him. He was an old guy who lived next door and I hardly knew him. It was Mrs. Davis who was so kind to me when I was small. It's just that I suddenly remembered all these people who have died. And this mystery I can't escape from, and I don't even understand why I'm so mixed up in it. Last night, I spoke to Beryl as if I were some character from an American gangster movie.'

'Anyway,' said Albert. 'Another mystery solved. Uncle Willy really was her uncle.'

'Yes, I suppose so,' smiled Frankie. 'Today's Sunday. It was roast lamb yesterday. Is it going to be roast beef today? Or aren't I invited?'

'At some point we may have to pick Auntie Flo's brains, said Albert. 'Find out what she knows. Today at lunch, as my mum's in Timperley, we could try pumping her for information. But first, let's go to the Crown.'


Auntie Flo opened the door.

'Oh, I'm so pleased you're here, Albert and you've brought your Frankie, too. Hello pet, you're always very welcome here. My goodness me, how lovely you look. Oh, and you've brought cider, too. Look, I'm glad you're both here because I've invited a friend for dinner. He's never been here before and I wanted you to meet him, Albert. And you too, Frankie, love.'

They walked into the dining room.

There was a man sitting next to the roaring fire. He stood up when they came in and walked towards them smiling.

'My name's Jack Smith. How do you do?'

He was not very tall, although somewhat taller than Auntie Flo. His hair was completely white and his large glasses fit neatly on his nose, giving him the appearance of a country vicar, thought Frankie. His smile was very friendly although it was obvious that he was somewhat nervous.

'How do you do,' replied Albert, shaking hands.

'And this is Albert's Frankie,' gushed Auntie Flo. 'Isn't she a lovely lass, Jack?'

'She's a cracker, all right. Flo does nothing but talk about you, love.'

'Jack and I have been seeing each other for some time,' explained Auntie Flo. 'And I thought it might be a good idea if you got to know him. So I invited him to Sunday dinner. Another day he can come and meet Vera. That way it won't be so many people at the same time. Jack likes Ken Dodd, too, so we can turn the wireless on and listen to the comedies while I get the dinner on the table.'

Auntie Flo switched on the radio, which had the advantage that no one was obliged to talk. Albert poured four glasses of cider. Auntie Flo wandered to and fro with dishes of food.

The four of them laughed through the two radio programmes. By the time they were finishing their lunch they had become firm friends. Auntie Flo then turned on the television and they watched an old comedy with Gregory Peck about a million pound bank note.

Frankie realised that this was not going to be the day that they were going to pump Auntie Flo for any information.

Well, she thought, there would be other days.

228

After the film, the two of them left the house and walked back home.

'Gosh, Albert, it's like she knew, isn't it? You couldn't make it up, could you? The day we decide to put her under the third degree she introduces us to her beau. How long do you think this has been going on, by the way?'

'Oh, I don't know. She's always been very independent, in spite of living with her sister. My mum's very independent too, you know. But I don't think she wants to introduce him to my mum. I don't know why. My mum's two years younger but I think she looks up to her.'

'Albert, I just saw a light turn off in the front bedroom of my house. I've got a burglar.'

'Are you sure?'

'Yes,' she replied. 'As we were coming I noticed that a light was on and was wondering if I'd left it on. And then suddenly it went off. There's someone in the house.'

'Give me your key, Frankie. I'm going into the house. I'll give you mine and you stay at my house till I get back.'

'No way,' said Frankie. 'I'm going in with you. I don't see why you should have all the fun.'

At the front of the house there was a gate which opened onto a path which led to the front door. Further along there was an opening in the wall, not closed by a gate, which was the driveway which led to the side of the house, the kitchen side entrance and then the garden.

Albert and Frankie stealthily entered the front garden through the driveway, crossed the little front lawn and crept up the double step to the front door. Albert slipped the key in the lock and noiselessly turned the key.

The door creaked when they opened it. A shadow leapt off the staircase and pushed Albert who fell to the ground with a thud. The intruder pushed Frankie aside, ran out the door and down the street.

Frankie frantically looked for the light switch. The room flooded with light and Albert who had hit his head on the hall table was sitting up and rubbing it tenderly.

'I'm afraid he got away.'

Frankie closed the door.

'Go and sit down in the lounge. I'll put the fire on and make you a cup of tea.'

Albert sat down, still a little dazed. Frankie went into the kitchenette.

'Albert. Look,' Frankie shouted from the kitchen. 'Come and look!'

Albert rushed to the kitchen. The pantry was open and the trap door leading to the cellar had been raised.

'I'm going upstairs first to have a look around,' said Albert.

'Well, everything looks tidy, at least,' he said when he came down.

He went into the dining room.

'And they didn't come in through any of the windows, downstairs. The back door is bolted. I'm going into the cellar. Have you got an electric torch?'

Frankie found one in the cupboard next to the pantry. He took it and went down the stairs. Frankie followed him.

'I remember there was a light switch down here.'

He found the switch and the little room filled with light. Nothing had changed except for an open door on the wall aligned with the back of the house.

'There is a tunnel under the garden. Did you know that?' asked Albert.

'No,' replied Frankie 'It might lead to an old air raid shelter. I don't really remember the bombings. My parents told me that they had stopped by the time I was four. I only remember one and we all hid under the dining room table. There hadn't been time to get to the shelter.'

She stopped and thought a moment.

'But I think the shelter was clearly in the garden,' she said. 'We didn't go through the cellar. And I do remember when they got rid of it. That's when they landscaped the garden with all the ponds and those silly gnomes.'

Albert inspected the tunnel entrance. The four walls of the cellar were covered in white tiles and the secret door appeared to form part of the wall, but now opened into the tunnel. There were two hinges only visible from inside the tunnel and the door handle itself was only accessible from outside the room.

How did one open the door from inside the cellar, thought Albert. This was not immediately evident.

'Well our intruder could have got in this way or he was looking for something down here. Or both. Let's explore the tunnel. Wait down here a moment.'

He climbed up the ladder and quickly came back with a dining room chair. This he placed across the doorway in such a way that the door would not suddenly close.

Albert shone the torch through the open door and they cautiously stepped into the tunnel.

The floor was made of concrete. The tunnel was a semi-circle of white corrugated iron, high enough for two or three men to walk upright without difficulty.

After a short distance the entrance to another passage appeared on the left hand side.

'I was expecting that,' said Albert. 'I bet that one leads to my cellar. Shall we have a look?'

The passage led to a parallel tunnel.

'There are two tunnels,' said Albert. 'One from my cellar and the other from yours. They are connected but separate passageways. That means there may be two separate entrances to our houses. Let's go back to your house Frankie. We can find out where these tunnels lead in the morning when there's light.'

'Albert, we've got to find a way of securing the entrances. Otherwise these people can come and go as they please.'

232

Once back inside Frankie's cellar they found no visible locks on the door. When closed, the door merged with the wall and seemed impossible to open from the inside.

'It's completely invisible,' said Frankie. 'I know there's a door there because I've seen it.'

She began to push the tiles on the wall with the palm of her hand. One actually moved as if on a spring. And the door opened.

'Well at least we can now open it from the inside,' she said. 'But there still seems no way of locking it.'

They climbed up into the kitchenette. Frankie found a heavy trunk in the cupboard under the stairs and Albert placed it over the trap door.

'I think Albert that we should go over and look at your cellar now.'

'Yes, I was thinking the same thing.'

They went into the small room at the back of Albert's house and opened the flap in the floor. Albert turned on the light and they both climbed down the stairs. Frankie went to the wall which gave onto the back of the house and began to push the bricks as she had done the tiles. First one, then another, the door opened.

They closed the door, climbed out of the cellar and secured the trap door as they had the other.

Frankie sat at the bar in the sitting room whilst Albert made some coffee.

'I wonder how many times there have been people in our houses without us knowing. They've been able to wander in out as they pleased. And when we were sleeping. Oh, Albert this doesn't seem to have any end to it. And why are there tunnels under our houses? And where do they go?'

'Well,' said Albert. 'We'll explore them in the morning. But I imagine they were built by the Ministry of Defence, during the war. They built lots of tunnels. But mainly in forests and woodland. In the early forties they thought there might be a successful invasion. They built tunnels and secret underground fortresses so that a possible British resistance might be able to sabotage enemy installations. But why they built these tunnels, I don't know.'

He put a cup of coffee in front of her and she began to sip it.

'Albert, she said, 'would you mind awfully if I stayed here tonight? I really am scared of sleeping in my house.'

He smiled and took her in his arms.

'I was going to suggest the very same thing. You'll be much safer here. And we'll begin exploring the tunnels tomorrow.'

234

## Chapter Twenty-Three

'Pardon, Monsieur, vous êtes de Paris?'

Bernard was standing in the sunshine outside the Gare d'Austerlitz. A blonde woman, early twenties, slightly tanned in spite of it being January, heavily made up, well dressed, what the French called 'chic', was speaking to him.

'I'm sorry?' he said in his best English.

The girl immediately dismissed him almost as if he had never existed. Maybe she had wanted to interview him for a newspaper. But she wanted a Frenchman, not a tourist.

It was his third day in Paris. He was feeling more confident. Nobody seemed to be looking for him.

He went into the enormous station and retrieved his suitcase from the left luggage office. His train to Lyon departed from platform five in twenty minutes.

He bought two newspapers, one French, one English, found his train and sat down in the reserved seat. He unfolded the newspaper and began to read.

As far as he knew he had killed two men. He expected to find some information in at least one newspaper. But no one seemed to care. No one was looking for him.

This, he realised, should make him happy. Yet at the same time it filled him with worry. At least, if he had information he would know what to do.

It was about four o'clock in the afternoon when the train pulled into the station in Lyon. He picked up his suitcase, the same one he had brought from the north of England and made his way to the exit.

He got into a taxi outside the station and gave the driver an address. Half an hour later the taxi pulled up outside a house on the outskirts of the city.

The light red brick house was surrounded by a high wall of the same colour. Once the taxi had gone Bernard went to the gate in the wall and pushed the doorbell. He waited a moment and then pushed again.

Almost immediately a small, wiry, middle aged woman with short, brown hair came to the gate, looked at him and without a word opened it. She gestured that he should enter. Bernard went in and she closed the gate behind him. He followed her to the front door of the house. He entered first and then she followed.

There was a large entrance hall and three dark, wooden, bare armchairs next to the door. She pointed to the chairs.

'Sit down and wait.'

She left him and climbed an enormous central staircase leading to the next floor. He watched as she strode determinedly up the stairs. She was wearing a white blouse and a long brown skirt which fit very tightly around her narrow waist.

Bernard waited. Some ten, fifteen minutes passed when a door opposite the chair where he was sitting opened and a man of about the same age as Bernard came out. He extended his hand and shook Bernard's effusively.

'Welcome to France, welcome to Lyon, Bernard. So nice to see you again. Come, we'll speak in my office.'

The two of them went in and his companion closed the door behind them.

They sat in a small room on either side of a wooden desk, cluttered with papers and files and a wide, overflowing ashtray.

The other man pulled out a packet of Gaulloise, lit a cigarette, and offered another to Bernard, who refused it.

'Oh, yes, our cigarettes are now too strong for you Englishmen.'

'Neither strong nor weak, Jean-Paul,' replied Bernard. 'I don't smoke too much. I play tennis and it's bad for my game.'

'So what happened to our friend Salvador Jimenez? Did you get the information we required?'

'Salvador is dead,' replied Bernard.

'You killed him?'

'No, of course I didn't kill him.'

Bernard rapidly recounted the events leading to the burning of his house, his kidnapping, his escape and the death of his captors.

Jean-Paul leaned back in his chair and blew smoke out of his mouth very slowly.

'Well, my friend. You are very lucky to be here. You met some very dangerous people and you dealt with them, I must say, most courageously. Are you sure you haven't been followed? How did you come here? By taxi?'

Bernard nodded.

'That may have been a mistake. But no matter. We are quite protected here. But my question is, for whom were these two men working. Evidently they were not working for Salvador. The English girl, did she give you any information?'

'The Scotsman, two weeks before he kidnapped me, offered me money for the disc. When I told the English girl about this, she mentioned a name. Daniel Bessel.'

'Bessel? Daniel Bessel? I can't say it sounds familiar. And no other names were mentioned?'

'No.'

'Well, as we don't know if the house is being watched, we'll take you out to a car waiting outside a restaurant in a street some distance from here. Margaux will go with you.'

He touched a button on his untidy desk and the door opened almost immediately. A young blonde woman walked in. She returned Bernard's friendly grin with a serious expression almost a scowl, her mouth set in a small pout.

'Margaux, this is Bernard. He's just come from England. Please take him to the car waiting in the Equilibres Café.'

Without further ado Bernard left with the young woman. She led him out of the office to some steps, leading to a basement floor.

Down a long corridor with doors to different rooms and then a series of descending stairs to a very large number of what seemed to be ancient tunnels.

Bernard had little time to observe his surroundings as it was dark, the only light being provided by the torch held by his silent companion.

She walked briskly and Bernard had difficulty keeping up.

Some forty minutes later, the two arrived at a door. The woman produced a key, opened the door and led him up some steps. Suddenly they were in the middle of a bustling café. They sat down at a table. A waiter appeared and the woman spoke for the first time.

'Two draught beers please.'

She looked at Bernard.

'When the beer comes you will drink a little and then go out. A yellow Renault will be waiting. You get into it. The driver's name is Francois. He will take you to your hotel. You go in, ask for the key to room 316. You can go out for dinner if you want, but you must take breakfast at the hotel. Someone will come for you at nine o'clock, tomorrow morning.'

Bernard did as he was told. He took a few swigs of beer, got up, walked out of the café into the waiting car. They drove off.


'Have you been to Lyon before?'

Francois was a thin man of about thirty. A gaunt, swarthy complexion. He was sitting behind a steering wheel, but Bernard could still see that he was quite tall.

'No, I can't say I have. I'm from Amiens. I've been living in England for some time. In fact, although I was born in Amiens, I lived in England until I was seven years old.'

'So your English must be very good.'

'Well,' said Bernard. 'I speak English almost without an accent. Most people don't realise I'm foreign. What surprised me was the trip to the café. Through a tunnel.'

'Oh, Lyon is riddled with tunnels. They were first built in the Middle Ages but the Résistance used them a lot during the war. Most people know little about them. If you were followed to the house, they will spend a long time waiting for you to come out.'

He pulled up.

'Here is your hotel. I'll come for you tomorrow at 9:00. Wait for me here.'

Bernard collected the key at the desk and went to his hotel room. He undressed, washed at the basin in the corner of his room and then lay down on the bed.

He looked at his watch. Half an hour had passed. He must have fallen asleep. It was now after six. He got dressed and went down into the street.

He spotted an Italian restaurant at the end of the road. He went in, sat at a table and ordered some food. He got up and walked towards the toilets at the back of the restaurant.

Here he found a pay phone. He was completely alone. He picked up the receiver, made a call and then returned to his table. A few minutes later the food arrived.

After dinner he ordered coffee and an Italian brandy. He sipped the brandy and reflected on his situation. Here in Lyon, for the moment, he was safe. Unlikely that anyone from England even knew where he was.

Except perhaps Albert, Frankie and Beryl. And, whomever Beryl may have told. Well, that was a risk he had wanted to take.

And no one knew that he was here in Lyon.

'Bonsoir, monsieur.'

Bernard looked up. Long, straight, black hair hanging across her shoulders, a small mouth formed into a little smile. Dark, penetrating eyes. Dressed in French clothes but unmistakably Italian.

He stood up and kissed her on each cheek.

'Hello Adriana. Please sit down.'

The waiter suddenly appeared.

'Grappa, please.'

Adriana beamed at the waiter who stood almost mesmerized for a few moments.

'Yes, of course.'

'I came as soon as you telephoned,' she said. 'Why are you in Lyon?'

'Some men came to my house to search it and accidentally burnt it down. Then I was kidnapped from the hotel I had gone to. I managed to kill one of my captors and took a train to London. I was followed by the other kidnapper and killed him, too. So, when I arrived in London, I decided to take the next train to Paris. No one seemed to be following me, so when I deemed it safe, I came to Lyon to get new orders.'

'Well you have been busy. You've turned into another James Bond. Your mission was to collect information, not to kill everyone.'

'I didn't kill everyone, only two very bad men. My father always said that when you are fighting for your life you don't take half measures.'

'But you killed Salvador Jimenez, too, didn't you? Or doesn't he count? He was the man you were supposed to investigate. Find out what he was doing in England.'

'He died of natural causes.'

'That wasn't my information. Someone went to the hotel building where he was living with his three bodyguards. The bodyguards have disappeared. No one knows where they are. For the British they are Spanish and must have left the country. Salvador suddenly had a heart attack. The British will be convinced, but we know better, don't we Bernard? And I heard this was your doing.'

'Who told you that? Look, I was kidnapped by two guys, a Scotsman and a Spanish guy called Chuan who told me that the three body guards, how did he put it? "Están con los peces.'"

'In Italian we say they sleep with the fishes.'

'And he said they had given Salvador a cocktail which provoked a heart seizure.'

'They told you that before you killed them?'

'Don't be cute, Adriana,' Bernard said. 'I had never killed anyone in my life and I never want to do it again. I still don't think about it. I always console myself with, it was them or me.'

Adriana laughed.

'Oh you always were very sentimental Bernard. It always starts with little things. One or two and then you can't stop. There will be more. Many more. And you'll even start to like it. If you don't already.'

She looked at the waiter.

'Two more grappas, please.'

Adriana beamed at him again. Bernard felt warmed by her presence, by the intensity of her eyes and her small lips.

'Bernard you must go back to London and stay there for a while. You are not a police suspect. These men you killed. They have just disappeared. They are common criminals and no one will be looking for them. But, they worked for someone and you must find out who. Don't go up north yet. We'll tell you when you should go north. Jean-Paul wants you to go back to the little flat you have in London. They'll tell you about it tomorrow at

243

breakfast. Give your English girlfriend a ring. What's her name? Sheila? She'll keep you informed, won't she?'

'Her name is Beryl. You think it's a good idea to call her?'

'Oh, yes. She's a friend of the English girl, isn't she? You are too useful in England. Anyway, thanks for the brandy. I have another appointment.'

They both stood up. He kissed her again on both cheeks and she left.

He sat down again and finished his brandy. He paid his bill and walked out into the street. Too early to go back to his hotel and now more confident after his interview with Adriana, he wandered into a side street and entered another café. He sat at a table and ordered a glass of red wine.

There were newspapers near the table where he was sitting and he took one. Twenty minutes later he had finished his drink and asked for his bill.

As he looked up he saw that someone who had been sitting at the bar and evidently looking at him, suddenly got up and left the premises.

Blonde and chic, he recognised the woman who had spoken to him outside the station in Paris.

Three hours later Bernard was sitting on the train to Paris. He had never returned to the hotel. Francois drove him to the station, accompanied him to the left luggage office, where his suitcase had been left for him, and then went with him to his train.

Francois was convinced they had not been followed. Bernard, of course, had his doubts and was prepared for anything.

# Chapter Twenty-Four

Frankie was in the back bedroom of Albert's house looking through the window. The river was hidden behind grey fog. A sad, cold day. She went downstairs.

Albert was sitting in his office. He had two or three books open in front of him and was taking notes.

'What are you doing?'

'Oh, I was just looking for information about tunnels. It's much as I said before. The Ministry of Defence built them mainly in wooded areas and near strategic installations so that, in case of invasion, resistance fighters would be able to strike the enemy without being detected.'

'You think they built the ones here?' she asked.

'Oh, I'm sure of that. They probably got the idea from the French Resistance. They also had tunnels, but built in the Middle Ages. They used them to attack the Germans, too.'

'So these tunnels in England were never used?'

'Thankfully, no. But they can still be found all over the place.'

'I'm a little worried about exploring these tunnels together. Last night both of us went in. I think we should go in separately and one of us should wait by the door. Make sure it stays open.'

'You think going in together was a bit reckless, do you?' asked Albert. 'I was thinking the same thing. You stay by the door and I'll go in alone. At least the first time.'

An hour later found Albert creeping through the tunnel under his house. Shining his torch from one side to the other, he was not sure what he should find.

According to the information he had researched, some of the tunnels might lead to secret military bunkers. Others were simple escape routes.

This one seemed to lead to an opening behind a bush. The wind in his face and the light at the end of the tunnel confirmed this.

It was a short walk back to where Frankie was waiting.

'No, problem, here,' he said. 'This leads to a hole behind some bushes. It's all quite safe. Do you want to have a look?'

Once in the open air, they stood in front of the bushes which covered the large aperture. It was quite hidden from view.

'There must be another entrance to the tunnel to the other house,' said Frankie. 'Let's see if we can find it.'

Frankie walked in a straight line from the bushes in front of Albert's house, to where she imagined she would find the entrance to the tunnel which led to her house.

She found nothing. No openings nor bushes. In a straight line, leading down from her kitchen, on the side of the hill, was the stump of what had been an enormous oak tree, maybe six feet in diameter.

She began touching the stump, moving her hand around the sides, feeling for invisible levers. As she moved her fingers down she found a hole on the right hand side. She felt for and found, what seemed to be a handle which she pulled. The top of the trunk swung aside.

'Albert,' she said, 'come over here. I've found it.'

They stood looking at the large entrance that had been hidden by the almost vertical tree stump.

'I'm going in,' said Albert. 'Why don't you wait here and make sure the door here stays open.'

Almost immediately he emerged once again.

'This leads to a bunker. Take the torch and go in. I'll wait for you here.'

She walked into the tunnel. Cement floor. The tunnel itself was just like the other one. Constructed of white, corrugated iron.

Fairly quickly she came to a wall with a door. She opened it. Just as Albert had said, there was an underground room, with furniture, a table, chairs. She shone her torch around.

At the far end of the bunker was another door. She walked towards it and turned the handle. It was locked. She inspected the four walls again hoping to find, perhaps, another exit.

She shone the torch on the table and chairs. The table was empty. She sat on one of the chairs and looked at the rest of the furniture. There was something oddly familiar about the table. She felt underneath and instinctively her hands found a drawer. She pulled it and it opened under the table. She put her hands inside, fearing she might find something disagreeable.

She touched something metallic, small, circular. Three objects, very similar. She pulled them out and placed them on the table.

She spent some minutes inspecting the discs.

They were each some three inches in diameter. Covered in or made of silver metallic material. A different symbol differentiated one from another. The symbols themselves meant nothing to her. They were not numbers nor letters from any language or culture that she could recognise.

She sat studying them. Touching them. Were these discs the key to everything?

'Frankie,' Albert called out to her. 'Are you all right? You were taking so long that I thought I'd better look for you.'

'Oh, I'm glad you've come Albert. Look I think I've found them. They were in a drawer in this table. Albert, these are the discs.'

She showed them to him.

'Each one has a different symbol on it. What could they mean?' she asked.

'They aren't symbols I've ever seen before. Frankie, what are we going to do with them? We can't leave them in the house. And we can't leave them here. I have an idea.'

He put the three discs into his jacket pocket and the two of them returned to the entrance of the tunnel. Luckily, there was no one about. They pushed the tree trunk back into its place, and walked back to the house.

# Chapter Twenty-Five

The next few days were uneventful. Two postcards from Mrs. Petersen in Paris. A letter from her mother in law in Des Moines.

The weather was quite warm during the day and Frankie spent some time in her garden. Sweeping the paths, cleaning the gnomes and sitting on the bench at the bottom of the garden, lost in thought, as she gazed at the river and the people moving up and down the hill and over the bridge. She would not go back into the house until it was almost dark.

It was already Thursday. She opened the side door to the kitchenette. The phone was ringing.

'Hello.'

'Oh, hi, liebchen. It's me, Ruth Petersen. How are you?'

'Oh, hi. I'm fine thanks. How's Paris?'

'Well, it has its good points and bad points. Any more Peeping Toms?'

'Oh, no, I've had no more problems.'

'And how's Mr. Tucker? Is he busy writing his novel? I can't wait to read it.'

'Actually he has been very busy these last few days. Last night we went out to a pub for a few hours but he's been spending most of the day writing.'

'So, you're at loose ends, perhaps? Good, that's what I wanted to talk to you about.'


Frankie was sitting in the lounge bar of the Old Cock in Fallowfield. It was here, she thought, that she had seen Albert Bessel for the first time. She remembered how she had fooled him into thinking she had left the pub.

That was how her adventure, if it was really an adventure, had begun.

She lit a cigarette and looked around the pub. Outside a plaque placed its origins in the sixteenth century. The ceiling, supported by dark, wooden beams, was certainly very low. There was also an eerie sensation of being surrounded by spirits. But, perhaps, that was only in her imagination.

Still, she would not like to spend the night alone in such a place.

Albert came to the table with a pint of beer in each hand. He placed one in front of her. They were sitting at a large table, but for the moment they had it to themselves.

'I didn't tell you, Mrs. Petersen phoned me from Paris.'

'That must've set her back a bit. First she pays for your phone to be installed and then she makes overseas phone calls. Money is no object if she wants to talk to you.'

'She wants me to go to Paris. Stay with her for a while. Act as her personal assistant for a few days.'

'Did she say why?'

'Not really. I was thinking about that afterwards. I never really did very much when I worked for her in Iowa. And I couldn't really get her to explain what she wanted me to do in Paris. Just that she had a series of business meetings and she needed someone she could trust.'

'Can we trust her? That's the question. We've also got this business in Sheffield next week.'

'I told her that I had an important meeting next week. She only wants me for the weekend, she said. I'll be back on Monday night. She's already bought my tickets. I pick them up tomorrow night when I go the airport.'

She looked at Albert and said, almost apologetically;

'Look, if I can, I have to be nice to her. She's always been very good to me and I want to stay in her good books. Also, I've never been to Paris before. Personally, I think she just wants company.'

'Don't tell her anything. About the discs, or Gallagher, or Bernard, the meeting in Sheffield. Nothing. I don't know if you should go. Maybe I should go with you. In case you need help.'

'I think I can manage a weekend in Paris.'

A group of five, three men with an older couple who might have been their parents, sat at the table.

One of them asked Frankie if she knew anything about the history of the pub. Frankie knew what she had read on the plaque outside and Albert a little more.

One of the three men began chatting about local history, on which he seemed quite an expert.

It was not until they were in the car driving home that Albert broached going to Paris once again.

'I think what I can do is to take a different flight and stay in another hotel. If you need me, you call me. Otherwise no one's the wiser. I'll fly out tomorrow morning.'

Frankie protested, in vain, she thought. Secretly she felt rather relieved. Having Albert on hand would make all the difference if things became difficult.

The next day, just as it was beginning to get dark, Frankie got into a taxi to the airport.

Despite a thirty minute delay she arrived in Paris before nine o'clock. Mrs. Petersen was not there to meet her but she had sent a driver who stood with a sign advertising her name to the world. Next to him stood Albert who, without showing any sign of recognition, watched her emerge into the entrance hall. He followed the two, first on foot to the waiting car, and then by taxi to Mrs. Petersen's hotel.

The driver parked in front of an expensive hotel in the centre of Paris. A uniformed doorman opened the car door, took her suitcase and led her into the foyer. She was then taken to the lift. Mrs. Petersen had a suite on the fifth floor.

She was shown into a large, ostentatiously decorated living room. A young woman who had been sitting at an ornate desk, next to the door, stood up when she came in.

'Good evening, Mrs. Blakeley. My name is Brigitte Dupont. I'm Mrs. Petersen's personal assistant.'

'Oh, how do you do?'

'Mrs. Petersen is at a business meeting this evening and may not be back until late. Let me show you to your room.'

Frankie's bedroom was large, elaborately decorated with a private bathroom. A quick glance around the room confirmed there was a telephone and a television.

Frankie looked at her watch. Half past eleven. Of course, it was later than she had thought. There was an hour's difference between England and France. The telephone rang.

She picked it up expecting to speak to Mrs. Petersen. It was Albert.

A short call just to give her his hotel and number. She hung up. Half an hour later she was asleep.

She was roused by the ringing of the telephone.

'Hello.'

'Morning call, it's seven o'clock.'

Half an hour later, she entered the lounge where Mrs. Petersen was sitting eating breakfast. On seeing Frankie she stood up and greeted her effusively.

'So sorry I wasn't here last night. But it couldn't be avoided. Sit down and have some breakfast. The food here is so much better than in England. But then the French are famous for their cooking.'

Frankie had not had anything since lunch the day before and ate a hearty breakfast.

Mrs. Petersen chatted happily about her travels. She had just come back from a fashion show in Florence which was why she was not in the hotel the night before.

The telephone rang. Mrs. Petersen answered it. She spoke rapidly in French and then put the receiver down.

Frankie looked at her.

'I didn't know you spoke French, Mrs. Petersen.'

'And German, of course. And Yiddish. But now, I almost always speak English, liebchen. There is someone who wants to see you. Which is why I asked you to come.'

There was a knock on the door.

'Oh, here he is now,' said Mrs. Petersen. 'Come in.'

The door opened. And a man walked into the room. He grinned when he saw Frankie sitting at the table.

'Hiya Frankie. I bet you didn't expect this surprise.'

'No, Bernard,' she said. 'I didn't.'

## Chapter Twenty-Six

Frankie looked from Bernard to Mrs. Petersen and back again.

'Well now we've all met perhaps you two can let me know what's going on. I don't believe Bernard that this is just about your book. And Mrs. Petersen, you brought me here under false pretences.'

'No, I didn't my dear. I want you to act as my personal assistant for a few days. I've given Brigitte a short vacation. Now that Bernard is here you are the only person I know I can depend on.'

'How do you want to begin?' said Frankie. 'Since probably the day I arrived in England, about six weeks ago, I have been lied to, by just about everybody. And now this. What are you planning to tell me now? Bernard has changed his story so many times.'

'Frankie, none of us has been totally honest, have we? Not even you.'

Frankie looked at Mrs. Petersen.

'That is unfair. I have been harassed and assaulted and have kept any information I may have acquired to myself sharing it only with my boyfriend for my own protection. I have no interest in your affairs except as they affect my safety and that of people I care about.'

Frankie looked at Bernard and then the American woman. A feeling of impotent rage overcame her. She wanted to throw a tantrum on the floor to scream and kick her legs like a baby.

And yet she remained composed. She stood up, went to her bedroom. When she came out she was wearing her coat.

'I'm going out for a walk. This is all too much for me and I need to clear my head.'

She went to the door. Opened it. And turned around.

'One more thing. If I find that I am being followed, I will throw myself into the arms of the first policeman I see.'

Bernard and Mrs. Petersen did not say a word. She closed the door behind her.

Albert's hotel was a short taxi ride from the centre of Paris. The entire hotel was located on the second floor of an old fashioned apartment building. There was no lift and Frankie walked up two wide staircases to the reception area.

Albert was not there, but he was expected back shortly. Frankie sat on a long, narrow settee in the entrance and waited.

Half an hour passed. The reception area was a hub of activity but Albert did not appear. The young boy in reception assured her that he would not take long.

Frankie had seen a café in the street below and after leaving her name, told him she was going to have a coffee and come back in fifteen minutes.

She turned and began walking down the staircase which led to the first floor landing. Albert was walking up. He smiled when he saw her and Frankie threw her arms around him.

'I have to pay in advance in reception. Otherwise they want to keep my passport and I'm not wandering the streets of Paris without it. It took me ages to change money. How is Mrs. Petersen?'

'I have news. But pay your bill first. Then we'll go and have a coffee and I'll tell you all about it.'

Albert insisted that he knew a better café than the one Frankie had seen near his hotel. It was in the next street. They walked in, sat at a table.

A waitress came, took an order for coffee.

'Mrs. Petersen has given her regular personal assistant, who I think is French, time off these next few days. She wants me to substitute her as I am the only person she can trust.'

'All right. What's she got planned?'

'Someone called while we were having breakfast and she told him to come up. You'll never guess who came in.'

'Gallagher?'

'No, Bernard.'

259

'Bernard?' said Albert. 'What has he got to do with Mrs. Petersen? What did you say?'

'Oh, I ranted a little and then got my coat on and said I needed some air. They didn't say anything. Of course, I wanted to see you and plan our next move. I've been thinking about it. I think you should come back with me.'

'Yes, so do I. Two heads are always better than one. Otherwise they'll have the advantage over you. But how does Bernard know your boss?'

'Well, perhaps they'll tell us.'

'More lies?' Albert laughed. 'This Bernard is a slippery customer. And your Petersen woman another one.'

They got out of a taxi in front of the elegant hotel where Frankie was staying. The doorman took them to reception where a uniformed employee telephoned Mrs. Petersen. They were then taken to her suite.

Bernard and the American woman had not changed position. The breakfast trolley had been cleared away. Mrs. Petersen stood up smiling when she saw them come in.

'Oh, Mr. Tucker, this is a pleasure. I didn't know you were in Paris, too.'

'There seems to be a lot we didn't know about,' replied Albert. 'Mrs. Petersen, you haven't been honest with us, have you?'

'Well,' she laughed. 'We have none of us been very honest, have we, Mr. Tucker? Not since your fortuitous encounter with us in that American restaurant. I realised that wasn't a coincidence. And I didn't believe the synopsis of your book, either. But we all have another thing in common, I believe. We are the good guys.'

'We are the good guys?' asked Albert. 'And who are the bad guys?'

Mrs. Petersen laughed loudly.

'Oh, Mr. Tucker. You know who the bad guys are. Christopher Gallagher is a bad guy. And Bernard tells me you had Salvador Jimenez sized up as soon as you saw him.'

'And we included Bernard and you in the group,' Albert replied. 'And personally I don't see why we should change our minds, do we Frankie?'

Frankie nodded. She sat down in a chair which she found next to her.

'I am now convinced,' said Frankie, 'that all this began long before I left Des Moines. This job you offered me as personal assistant was simply a pretext.'

'Surely you are not going to be so ungrateful. Frankie, I couldn't have loved you more if you had been my own daughter. Of course, I wanted to look after you. And I had promised your father.'

'My father? Oh, is there some point where you can begin the story? And finally tell us what is going on. I am so fed up with these mysteries and not knowing who I can trust. What did my father have to do with you?'

Mrs. Petersen picked up the phone.

'I'm going to order some coffee. We should all relax a little.'

She spoke into the receiver in French. Put the phone down.

'Tell me Frankie. Do you know anything about Alderney?'

'I've never heard of it.'

'It's one of the Channel Islands. Invaded by the Germans in 1942. They brought in workers, voluntary workers they called them. There was of course nothing voluntary about them.'

'Jews?' asked Frankie.

'Oh, yes, some were of course Jews and what they called Mischling. People who had Jewish ancestors and didn't even know it. Like Bernard here and his family. But there were lots of other prisoners here. Spanish republicans who had escaped to France from the Spanish war. Russian and other prisoners from the east. But, yes, many Jews, some of my family died there and some of Bernard's folks too. Worked to death and then the bodies flung into the sea. No one knows how many died there.'

For a moment she stopped. Frankie thought the American woman was going to cry. But her expression only became unusually serious.

'But, more importantly, no perhaps that is the wrong word here; these people were very important, but more pertinent to our conversation.'

She stopped again; there was a knock on the door.

Bernard went to the door and opened it. He was pushed back into the room and onto the floor. Three men entered. Bernard got up slowly and was pushed again towards where the others were sitting. The men moved round the room and stood in a semi-circle surrounding the group. Dressed in dark suits. Dark hair, expressionless.

'Are these your bodyguards?' asked Frankie.

'I know nothing about this', replied Mrs. Petersen. She addressed the intruders. 'Who are you? What do you want?'

One of them, the tallest and the only one sporting a small beard spoke.

'Oh, but you know what we want.'

Frankie identified his accent as Spanish.

The man continued speaking.

'The three discs, the girl has brought them with her, hasn't she?'

One of the men grabbed Frankie from behind and flourished a knife under her throat. Frankie felt the blade stroke the lower part of her neck. She wanted to struggle but found herself paralysed with terror. This is the end she thought. They are going to kill us all.

Suddenly the man released his grip. Frankie turned around in shock. He was lying on the floor behind her with a hole in the centre of his forehead.

Mrs. Petersen was sitting in her chair with a revolver in her hand. Her expression was even more serious than before.

'Now the two of you move into that corner over there. And get on your knees.'

Her accent had suddenly become much less American and more German. Frankie was not sure if it was because she was nervous or because she wanted to add dramatic effect.

She gestured with her pistol. She fired again; another noiseless shot brought the man with a beard to the ground. Frankie saw a gun fall from his hand. The other man moved into the corner, his hands above his head.

He kneeled.

There was a knock on the door.

'Who is it?' cooed Mrs. Petersen.

'Room service, madame.'

'One moment.'

Mrs. Petersen moved towards the corner where the surviving intruder was kneeling. She suddenly hit him hard on the back of the neck with her pistol.

He slumped to the floor.

The American then opened the door to a young, uniformed, French maid. Mrs. Petersen took charge of the coffee service and closed the door behind her.

'Well,' she said, 'let's drink our coffee in the other room before it goes cold. I also asked for a plate of cakes and another one of these delicious cookies. It would be a shame to waste it all because of a little unpleasantness.'

Bernard wheeled the coffee trolley into the adjacent room. Frankie and Albert followed him. Another elegant, but smaller, living room. Frankie and Albert sat down on a small sofa. Bernard continued standing.

Mrs. Petersen began to pour coffee and hand around biscuits and cakes. Frankie felt as if she were in a state of shock. Even Albert had been stunned into silence. As always in moments of crisis, Frankie began to feel suddenly quite hungry. She took the plate and dutifully nibbled a biscuit.

Mrs. Petersen went back into the other room and made a call, speaking rapidly in French.

She returned and sat down. Bernard still standing, walked across the room, looked out the window and sipped his coffee. He avoided looking at Albert and Frankie.

The American woman, although relaxed, still wore an unusually serious expression.

The telephone rang and she left the room to answer it.

'Oh, yes, show them up,' they heard her say.

'Mrs. Petersen,' asked Frankie, 'what are we going to do about these dead bodies and the man you slugged? Are you going to call the police?'

'No, liebchen. Some of our people will take care of them.'

There was a knock on the door.

'Oh, here they are now.'

She left the room closing the door behind her.

'Well, Bernard,' Albert spoke for the first time, 'you and Mrs. Petersen certainly seem to be experts at this. You're all members of a spy ring then, are you?'

'Not really spies. I belong to a group of people based in Lyon. Our parents and relatives were in the French Résistance. Or they were victims of the Nazis. My family were in the Résistance, then captured taken as forced labour to Alderney. Most of them perished there but my father managed to escape and survive the war. He died only a few years ago.'

Mrs. Petersen came back into the room leaving the door open behind her.

'I was saying to Bernard that you two seem quite expert at this business. I had no idea we were getting involved with spies.'

'Not exactly spies, Mr. Tucker. We are the children, of the victims. My father died in Alderney. My mother died before she arrived. Bernard's father

265

escaped from Alderney towards the end of the war. But the rest of his family was not so lucky, if that is the word.'

'What's so important about this island?' asked Albert. 'I've never heard of it.'

'They expelled its very small native population,' replied the American. 'And then used the island to research experimental, secret weapons. One of these was this machine, in which everyone suddenly seems so interested.'

'What does it do?' asked Frankie.

Bernard, who had been staring out the window, turned and replied.

'It looks like the disc you found in the house near Fallowfield. In fact that disc was a replica. It was hollow and no more than a kind of model.'

'Why did Salvador bring it from Spain?' Frankie asked, 'and why was it so important for him to get it back, if it was only a model?'

'And who took it out my shed?' asked Albert.

Bernard frowned and continued speaking.

'As far as I know, two copies were made. The first copy was the one you had in your shed. It was crude and really not an authentic replica. At the end of the war it was taken to Spain by one of the Germans who Salvador's family helped. What you called the Ratline, that day we were all together in Frankie's living room. I have no reason to doubt the story Salvador told us.'

'Well, if it was so crude why did he want it back so badly?' asked Frankie.

'Because Salvador was told to get it back. He received orders from some organisation in Madrid. They must have wanted it for something. It was after all the only replica.'

Albert laughed humourlessly.

'Oh, so he was only obeying orders?'

'If you like,' said Bernard.

'You said there were two replicas,' said Frankie. 'What happened to the other one?'

Mrs. Petersen looked at her.

'Your father, Frankie. He took the machine back to England. To Sheffield. He found it in the castle which Himmler had restored for his own use in the thirties. He had been using it in his peculiar black magic ceremonies. It was covered in symbols.'

'What did the symbols mean?' asked Frankie.

The American sighed.

'We don't really know. According to your father the German soldiers in the castle thought that the machine had come from an alien spaceship which had crashed in Freiburg in the thirties. The Nazis were full of bull and liked to manipulate their people.'

'Anyway,' said Bernard, 'your father came to think that he made a mistake and the machine he took back to Sheffield was a copy.'

'And what happened to the real one?' asked Frankie.

'That's the mystery. We don't know,' Bernard replied. 'But the people who have the machine, the real one, are interested in you Frankie because they think you are the key.'

'Why?' cried Frankie.

'The machine has a slot, much like the one for coins in a vending machine,' said Bernard. 'Well, really there are three and they are rather bigger. Three small discs have to be inserted. To turn the machine on. No one knows where the small discs are.'

'And why would I know?'

'When your father took the machine,' replied Bernard, 'he also took the discs. The machine, the replica, that is, was in Sheffield for some years but eventually was taken to Virginia. But the small discs disappeared.'

Mrs. Petersen looked at Frankie.

'You remember when your parents came to Des Moines, don't you? They spent time in Virginia first. The American government had been in possession of the replica for a long time. They had been told it was a worthless model but they insisted it had come from an alien spaceship.'

'Why did they think that?' asked Frankie.

'Well in Germany there was an American military base where they investigated these things.'

'In Karlsruhe?' asked Frankie. 'Were they investigating there?'

'Yes, exactly,' replied the American. 'It was there. There had been so many rumours of flying saucers. Even a black sun, an alternative source of endless energy. Rendered even less believable because it was all mixed up with notions of black magic.'

Bernard interrupted.

'There were flying saucers of a type, but they were German weapons. They looked like larger versions of the disc your father took. But really they had nothing to do with outer space.'

'But,' said Frankie, 'you still haven't explained what this machine is for. Why do people want it? And which people are these?'

'That's what we are investigating, my dear,' replied Mrs. Petersen. 'I went to England to see that crook Gallagher. Bernard was investigating the Spanish journalist. But he was working for different people.'

'And Mrs. Petersen,' asked Albert. 'Why are you doing this? Why aren't you just enjoying your life in Des Moines?'

'For two reasons Mr. Tucker. In May, we celebrate the twentieth anniversary of Victory in Europe. Many say, "oh, it's been twenty years now, let it go," but we cannot let it go. It hasn't finished. Look at this guy Jimenez, from Spain, still working for the Nazis under a Spanish dictatorship put in power by them. And the other reason. All the war criminals who escaped from Germany. Helped across the Pyrenees and into Portugal and then South America. Argentina was really popular. First the criminals arrived, established themselves and then they brought their families.'

Bernard interrupted.

'The point is. They're still at it. Salvador was getting his instructions from someone in Argentina.'

'All right, said Albert. 'but Frankie's parents have gone. It has nothing to do with her. Why are you involving her?'

'Because Frankie knows where the three discs are,' replied Mrs. Petersen.

'No, I don't,' replied Frankie.

## Chapter Twenty-Seven

For a while no one said anything. Bernard walked once again to the window and Mrs. Petersen lit a cigarette. The silence was broken by a knock on the door. Mrs. Petersen left the room, closing the door behind her.

Frankie looked at Albert.

'What do we do now?' she asked. 'I don't know what to make of any of this.'

Bernard answered her.

'You were hypnotized, Frankie. I don't know when, maybe when you were a little girl. Your father told you where the discs were and it's buried deep inside you. There are key places which activate your memory. They were all marked on a map. That's why you found the house near Fallowfield.'

'Are the discs there?'

'They might have been. Or these places form part of a sequence. You go from one to another until you find the discs.'

'And what happens if we find them? What then? We haven't got the machine. They are better hidden.'

'Maybe so, but until we have the discs you will be in danger.'

Frankie looked at him.

'Why? Are you or your friends going to kill me?'

'No,' said Bernard. 'But the people who have the machine, the bad guys, as Mrs. Petersen says, will do anything to get them.'

'We should go to the police,' said Frankie. 'That's what I wanted to do from the very beginning. And now with those dead men in the other room.'

'Oh, don't worry. They're all gone now.'

'That's for sure,' Albert said and added bitterly, 'I don't know how we got involved in murder.'

'Not murder. Self defence,' replied Bernard. 'And as for the police, forget it. They won't believe any of this, unless they've been paid off. And then you really will be in trouble Frankie.'

'I meant the British police,' she retorted. 'I know about continental policemen.'

Bernard shrugged his shoulders and began to laugh.

The door opened and the American came into the room.

'I can't keep you here all day, liebchen. I promised that you would see Paris. But after that nasty incident this morning I've decided to send someone with you. For your protection. Come, both of you.'

All three of them wandered into the other room. A man wearing a hat and belted raincoat seemed to be waiting for them.

'This is Sebastian who will show you round Paris. And take you to lunch. There is a car waiting below.'

The American woman ushered Frankie and Albert out of the suite before they could protest.

'This wasn't exactly how I had imagined our weekend in Paris,' said Frankie.

They were sitting in an upmarket restaurant. The waiters in attendance had poured wine and served the first courses, which seemed to have been chosen before they arrived.

'We've already seen all the landmarks one is supposed to see in Paris. Now we're going to eat an expensive French lunch. And two murders and some guy trying to cut my throat. And it's only one thirty. And Albert, I'm the one who dragged you into all this.'

'Oh, don't worry about that. I told you you've changed my life. I'm not going to tell you any more because someone may be listening to our conversation.'

Frankie looked at him, but could interpret nothing from his expression. However she said no more. They ate in silence.

When the second course arrived, a waiter opened another bottle of wine and poured two glasses.

'Oh they're pairing the wine with the course,' said Frankie. 'Chuck and I used to go to a French restaurant in Des Moines where they used to do that.'

'You had French restaurants in Iowa? I thought you said you could never go out.'

'I meant the bars were tacky and they had no pubs. But there were some nice restaurants. And Americans always love anything French, of course. This wine is a little strong, isn't it?'

'Frankie,' said Albert. 'Where has Sebastian gone? Can you see him?'

'He was behind you near the door. But he seems to have disappeared.'

Albert stood up and looked around the dining room. Most of the tables were empty, although there were two or three couples seated at tables some distance away.

'Frankie,' he said. 'We have to go. Something's wrong.'

'Do you need anything, monsieur?'

A waiter spoke to Albert.

'We're leaving. Bring our coats.'

'Certainly, monsieur. Un moment, s'il vous plait.'

The waiter moved off towards a door which Albert thought led to the kitchen. He looked at Frankie. She was still seated on her chair but slumped over the table. He looked down at his feet, suddenly so far away.

Time passed.


Albert realised when he opened his eyes that a very long period of time had gone by. A noise which he perceived to be some kind of boat on the river. River? He was still in Paris.

He was sitting on a bench on a path overlooking a river. The river Seine of course, he could see Notre Dame through the mist in the distance. And Frankie? What had happened to Frankie?

He looked at his watch. It was just before eight o'clock. Sunday morning? How long had he been asleep? Since two o'clock the day before. The wine. They had drugged the wine and kidnapped Frankie.

What had happened to their body guards? Was this the work of Bernard and the American woman? It seemed unlikely.

He stood up and looked around. Although he was very thirsty, he felt remarkably clear headed. The effects of the drug must have worn off completely.

He could now see sleeping forms on the other benches along the path. He shivered. At least these other people were covered in blankets. Even wearing his overcoat he was cold.

Church bells began to ring. He looked in one direction and then the other. The path along the river was quite empty. Above, on the embankment he could hear the sound of traffic. He was alone in Paris.

Frankie had been abducted. Perhaps his only allies were Bernard and the American woman.

Near the bench where he had awoken he saw a staircase which led to the street above. This he climbed.

He was now in a street with traffic. Cars, taxis passed. He took a taxi to his hotel.

He walked into the building. The hotel was on the second floor at the end of two very wide staircases. As he climbed the stairs his spirits began to sink. Frankie had disappeared. He had failed to protect her and had allowed himself to be gulled by such untrustworthy people as Bernard and Mrs. Petersen.

He had no notion of what his next move should be. How does one begin looking for a missing girlfriend in Paris? Go to the police? Hire a private detective? What would you do in one of your novels, Frankie would have asked him.

He walked into the reception of his hotel. Next to the door was a long narrow settee. In one of his novels, she would have been sitting there waiting for him. Except this was real and she was really there.

'Frankie,' he said, 'how long have you been here?'

He sat down next to her, put his arms around her. She looked up at him and he covered her face with kisses. He hugged her in disbelief, and kissed her again.

'Are you all right?' he asked, 'how did you get here? What happened to you?'

She hung on to him, but did not say a word. He kissed her again, holding her tightly against him. He realised she was whimpering.

'I don't remember anything, Albert,' she sobbed. 'One moment we were in a restaurant and the next I was sitting on a bench in a park. I didn't know what to do so I came to your hotel. But I've only been here a short time.'

'Well if it's any consolation I don't remember anything either,' replied Albert. 'They drugged us. And we've been out for a long time. How do you feel?'

'I'm very wide awake, but very thirsty. Let's go to the café we went to yesterday and drink something, have some breakfast. Oh, Albert, thank goodness I found you. I thought something had happened to you.'

## Chapter Twenty-Eight

'What I don't understand,' said Bernard 'is why you invited Frankie to Paris. She doesn't know where the discs are.'

He looked at Mrs. Petersen. So typical of his idea of an American business woman. Stout, pushed into tight clothing, hardness in her face which, in spite of her sugary speech, revealed her true character.

This woman, once he had received his final orders from Francois, was his contact in Paris.

'Oh, I'm sure she does. She's found them and now she's hidden them. And that boyfriend of hers has helped her. They're not in either of the houses. We've searched them from top to bottom. It was a mistake to steal the replica from the shed. That made them feel vulnerable. If they've found the discs, and I'm sure they have, they're well hidden in some other place. We've got to get it out of her.'

'Will your men be able to do that?'

'Oh, possibly.' Mrs. Petersen replied. 'They've managed this kind of thing before.'

Bernard thought back to his first years working in the local newspaper in Amiens, living with his father and stepmother. Both of them had been full of stories about the war, the Résistance, the work camps.

But, he wrote articles about weddings, village festivals in a local paper.

Then he met Adriana, an Italian. She had come looking for him because he spoke English and they wanted someone to work for them in London. He was easily seduced, first by the sensual Italian woman and then the offer to work in Paris.

Two years in Paris and then London. No real mission at first. He was, what they called a sleeper, waiting for orders.

And then they sent him north to befriend Salvador. Find Frankie and find the discs.

Now Salvador was dead. The discs were nowhere to be found.

And Frankie was in the hands of this strange American woman whom he had orders to obey.

'Anyway,' Mrs. Petersen continued, 'we have little left to do here and our cover, as they say, has been blown. Pack your bags, you are going to London. Your plane leaves this afternoon. I shall go back to Edinburgh with Mrs. Potts this evening.'

'Who is Mrs. Potts?' asked Bernard.

'One of the women I met in Scotland. We came to Paris together and it seems she is returning now and I thought I might go with her.'

'Oh,' replied Bernard, 'and what about the English girl?'

'Oh, she won't remember anything about her interrogation. And when she comes to, she may very well come back here. Brigitte will see to her needs. But I do believe that Paris is no longer safe for either of us.'

'Is it safe for Frankie and Albert?' asked Bernard, 'are we just leaving them to their fate? They really are friends of mine.'

'I love Frankie as if she were my own daughter,' cooed Mrs. Petersen, Bernard thought dishonestly. 'But there are more important things at stake. Believe me she's well looked after with Albert Tucker. Now get packing, monsieur, or you'll miss your flight.'


Bernard sat on a train as it pulled out of Charing Cross station. Although his newspaper's offices were just off Fleet Street in central London, his flat was situated in a village in Kent, a fifty minute train journey from Canterbury, where he had spent his early childhood.

This allowed him to commute to town as often as deemed necessary and, at the same time, leave him close to familiar surroundings.

Another advantage now, was that very few people knew where he lived and this made surprise visits from old enemies unlikely.

His flat was only a fifteen minute walk from the station. As he wandered home he remembered, not for the first time, his car. Maybe his first move should be to travel up north and get it out of the car park where he had left it.

And see Beryl. If she still wanted to see him. His orders were to stay in London, but he could manage to go and come back in a day.

He climbed the stairs to the apartment which was on the first floor of a modern two storey building. He put the key into the lock, opened the door and turned on the light. He breathed a sigh of relief. Nothing had been disturbed. It was just as he had left it. So, no one knew where he lived.

A small living room, a kitchen and two bedrooms one of which served as an office. He went into the kitchen found some ice and a glass and returned to the living room.

He opened his bag and took out the bottle of whisky he had bought at the airport. There was a large portable radio on a table next to the settee. He turned it on and listened to the French news.

One advantage of living in the south was the easy reception of French radio.

The next day was Sunday, he thought. He could easily get an early train. Perhaps he could have lunch with Beryl. A late Sunday lunch. He stood up, put his coat on and walked down to the street. There was a phone box on the corner of the road where he lived.


Bernard felt very confident when he alighted from his train on Sunday. No one had followed him to the station, he had travelled on the tube, caught the train from Euston station. No attempts on his life. And perhaps now, he could collect his car and drive back to London.

He joined a queue at a bus stop near the station. Buses tended to be more infrequent on Sundays and the line was rather long. The man behind him in the queue was reading a newspaper and the headlines caught his eye.

Winston Churchill had died early that morning. Well, that was a great spirit gone, he thought. He continued reading the article and the owner of the newspaper glanced up and their eyes met. The man started and looked back at his paper.

Bernard turned around. The bus came and he began walking.

'Room for one more inside, pal,' said the conductor.

'Sorry,' he said to the man behind in a flat cap carrying his newspaper. 'There's another one coming right now.'

Bernard got on the bus and it moved off. The conductor was right. There was another bus immediately behind them.

He got off the bus in the Village close to where Beryl lived. He had arranged to meet her in a coffee shop nearby. It was still early so he began walking to the car park where he had left his car.

Sunday morning and the normally busy, shopping street was very quiet. Bernard felt relaxed, almost happy, he thought. No people about, no traffic. The world seemed to belong to him. The noise of an ambulance made him turn around.

He saw the headline from someone's newspaper again, announcing Churchill's death. A man was leaning against a tree reading the paper.

Flat cap, belted raincoat. The same man. Bernard was now alert.

He turned the corner at the end of the road. There was a small railway station used by local commuters to other large cities during the week. Now it was almost empty, but Bernard remembered that it had two entrances. He walked in very quickly and left through the rear exit.

He found himself in a back street. He wandered back into the main road and stayed hidden whilst he watched the station entrance.

The man emerged looking somewhat dismayed. Obviously he had not found what he was looking for. He made his way across the street. Bernard followed him at a distance. The man turned the corner into the next road.

The Railway Inn was near the corner and seemed to be open. The man walked in. Bernard stood across the street watching.

A small group of people coming from the opposite direction entered the pub. Five minutes later a few more. Bernard crossed the road and sauntered in.

The lounge bar was divided between two rooms each on either side of the bar. Bernard located the man immediately, sitting next to an old fashioned fireplace. He did not see Bernard as he was engaged in conversation with an older man at his table.

Bernard looked at his companion. Early sixties, he thought, greying black, wavy hair, with a very prominent, hooked nose. The man was smoking a cigarette held in white, bony fingers.

He kept out of sight in the adjacent room. He bought a drink and then sat down at a table, which allowed him to watch the door, whilst at the same time avoid being seen.

As he sipped his beer, he pondered over the identity of his pursuer. Only Beryl had known he was coming. And this man was waiting for him at the station in town.

At the far end of the room, he could see the entrance to the toilets and a pay phone next to it. He stood up, put his hand in his pocket and pulled out some change.

Beryl answered almost immediately.

'Oh, mon cherie. I knew it was you.'

She sounded somewhat breathless as if she had been running.

'Oh, I just called to say I was going to be a little late. Maybe half an hour. Don't leave home until I call you.'

'That's OK. I'm still not ready. Is everything all right, Bernard?'

'Beryl, did you tell anyone I was coming?'

'Oh, I know you told me not to. But I had to tell my mum.'

'Anyone else?'

'No, of course not. Bernard is everything all right?'

'Don't worry. I'll see you later.'

Bernard hung up and walked back towards the bar. The pub was quite full now. He looked over to where the two men had been sitting. The table was empty. He walked back to the telephone and opened the door to the toilets.

At the end of a short corridor, there was an exit into an empty back street of small, terraced houses.

Certain now that he was not being followed, Bernard continued on his way to the car park where he had left his car.

## Chapter Twenty-Nine

Albert and Frankie were sitting at a table eating croissants and drinking hot coffee.

'What do you think we ought to do now, Albert? Go back to Mrs. Petersen's hotel? Confront her and Bernard? Do you think they are responsible for this?'

Albert shook his head.

'There are several possibilities. The first and most obvious is that Mrs. Petersen arranged your kidnapping to find out where the discs are.'

'But,' protested Frankie, 'I told her I didn't know where they were.'

'She may think you're lying.'

'Well, I'm not. I don't know. You've never told me where you put them, so I can't tell anybody, can I?'

'That's true,' replied Albert. 'But perhaps I told somebody. I don't know what they did to us. Did they inject us with some kind of truth serum? Or did they just interrogate you? I really don't remember anything, try as I may. It's all completely black. Frankie, did you leave your passport at the hotel or have you got it with you?'

Frankie opened her handbag.

'Everything's here. My passport, my money. They didn't take anything from me.'

'I don't think we should go back to your Mrs. Petersen. We should go home.'

He looked at his watch.

'Look, it's half past nine. There's a train leaving Gare du Nord at half past ten. That'll get us into Victoria Station, London at half past eight. We'll be a lot safer there.'

'OK. Do you want to go back to your hotel to get your stuff?'

'My shaving stuff and a pair of trousers and a small case? No. I've got everything I need with me. Something tells me we should get out and quick.'

They stood up and walked to the cash desk and paid. They went into the street and hailed a passing taxi. Twenty minutes later, they were walking into the station.


The train to Calais pulled out of the Paris station on time.

They were sitting in an empty compartment. Albert lit a cigarette and offered one to Frankie. She refused it and snuggled down on his shoulder and fell asleep. Albert continued smoking and watched the corridor.

Occasional passengers wandered back and forth, but no one entered their compartment.

An hour passed, Frankie continued to sleep when a rail employee abruptly opened the door and demanded to see their tickets. He left, the train pulled up at a station and Frankie woke up.

She opened her eyes, looked at him and smiled.

'Oh, I'm sorry; I couldn't keep my eyes open. Is everything all right?'

'We've stopped at a station. The ticket inspector came in to look at our tickets. Nothing else. It seems very quiet, but that may be because it's Sunday.'

Frankie smiled at him again. The train lurched into motion. Frankie looked out the window. Farmhouses, fields and trees moved past almost hypnotically. She felt herself being lulled back to sleep.

Her reverie was abruptly interrupted as the door opened noisily and two passengers, a man and a woman in their fifties, Frankie thought, burst into the compartment, carrying two suitcases.

'You're English, aren't you?' said the man. 'I can always tell. It's something in the face. Where are you from? We're from Bolton, Lancashire.'

'And if I had said, no, we are Dutch?' replied Albert, good-naturedly.

'Wouldn't've believed you. You don't look Dutch. And from your accent I'd say you were from Lancashire too, or Cheshire. Posh part.'

'And where would you say I was from?' asked Frankie.

'Oh, you're American, aren't you? Well, I made a mistake there. But I was really looking at your husband when I said you were both English. On holiday, are you? Visiting from America?'

Here we go again, thought Frankie. Thirty seconds in the compartment and he wants to know all your business.

'Yes,' she said. 'We've spent Christmas with the family. Went to Paris for the weekend and we're going back to New York, the day after tomorrow.'

'New York. That's a big city.'

'Yes,' continued Frankie, 'but it's not the city. We live in a town upstate. Are you on vacation here in France?'

The woman sat down opposite Frankie and continued.

'Oh, we've been visiting English friends here. Well, he's English. Michèle's French. We've been friendly with them for years in Bolton. Then Brian retired, and they went to France. They bought a big, old house in the country. They keep chickens. We had fresh eggs for breakfast every morning.'

'You must find America very different to England,' said the man looking at Albert. 'What do you do there?'

'We work in a bank', replied Frankie, before Albert could open his mouth. 'Wells Fargo. You must have heard of it.'

288

'Can't say I have,' replied the man, 'though the name seems to ring a bell. But I never associated it with a bank.'

He stood up and unbuttoned his overcoat, folding it neatly on the seat next to him. He lifted the suitcases easily onto the rack above their heads.

He looked at them.

'You travel lightly, don't you? A weekend in Paris and no luggage.'

Frankie laughed.

'It was a little more than a weekend and we sent our stuff off in advance. We had rather a lot.'

'Going to pick it up when you get to London, are you?' asked the woman.

The woman had already taken off her coat, but had not removed her hat. Frankie could see she had greying dark brown hair. A small jolly face and a slim build.

Her husband was somewhat more corpulent, white hair and jagged features.

'No, we sent it off to New York.'

'Oh, I don't think we've introduced ourselves,' said the woman. 'My name's Susan. And my husband's Stan.'

'Oh, pleased to meet you', replied Frankie. 'Bernice and Homer.'

Albert exploded in a fit of coughing.

'I'm afraid my husband's not very well. I'm going to take him to the buffet and see if I can get him something. So nice to meet you.'

The two of them got up, picked up their coats and ambled out of the compartment.

The buffet car was nearly empty. There were a couple of bar stools free. They sat down and asked for sandwiches and bottles of beer.

Albert began laughing. Frankie did not share his amusement.

'I don't know if they are spying on us or not but I most certainly was not going to tell my life story to Ma and Pa Kettle just to be polite. Pair of nosy Parkers.'

'No, you're probably right,' said Albert. 'But somehow we'll have to keep out of their way until London.'

'Do you think someone has sent them?' asked Frankie.

'It's possible. If we've been followed. Even though we haven't been followed they may imagine we are on a train leaving Paris on our way to London and so have sent someone, on the off chance we were on the train. I couldn't say. So many things have happened since this all began.'

'Albert, why don't we get off the train at the next stop and catch the next one. I have enough money with me to buy new tickets. Maybe they'll change the ones we have. I'm not going to risk it with those two. There may be more of them on the train. Oh, for goodness sake, behind you, they're coming in now. Both of them. I knew this wouldn't last long. Well, that decides it. Next stop we get off.'

Stan and Susan waved and smiled as they entered the buffet car. Albert and Frankie stood up.

'Feeling better now?' Susan asked.

She twisted her face into an expression of compassion.

'He's still feeling sick,' said Frankie. 'I'm going to take him for a little walk. See you later.'

Before the others could answer they left the wagon.

Almost immediately the train came to a stop.

'Let's get off right now,' said Frankie.

She opened the door and jumped off. Albert followed.

'We'll nip into that bar and hide until the train's gone,' said Albert. 'Let's make sure they don't get off too. They may do if they see us.'

They stood watching. A few people got on the train. No one alighted. The whistle blew and the train began to move.

'Well, that settles that,' said Albert. 'They probably were from Bolton, after all. They'll wonder what happened to us. Now what do we do?'

Frankie was looking at a sign through a window which gave onto the inside of the station.

'Look,' she said. 'Car rentals. We'll hire a car and drive to Calais. Take the ferry and then get another one on the other side of the Channel to drive north. No more danger of spies on the train or who we might meet in London.'

Two hours later, they arrived at the port in Calais, found the rental office and left the car.

Although it was cold, the day was sunny and it looked like they would have a good crossing.

The ferry was on the point of departure and they were the last to board. They stood on the deck and Frankie watched as the boat moved away from the French coast. The wind blew through her hair and she began to feel cold.

She hugged Albert who put his arm around her and held her tightly. Was this ever going to end? And yet, Albert was right. She had felt more alive this last month and a half than she had felt in some time.

'I'm going to tell you something that may upset you,' whispered Albert. 'Don't look round and don't say anything. But that couple are on the boat. I don't know if they've seen us. But I have just seen them.'

'I don't believe it. How did they manage that? They are following us. They must have been waiting for us in the port.'

'Not necessarily,' replied Albert. 'They may not even be interested in us.'

'Albert,' she said. 'Everybody is interested in us and we have to be suspicious of anyone who speaks to us or seems to be following us. They could be working for Bernard's lot, Salvador's lot or for our Mr. Gallagher. Or some other group that we know nothing about. I've been kicked round so much in the last month that I don't regard anything as a coincidence now. What's the betting that in five minutes we've got them next to us asking questions again? Like, where's your luggage? Or how long have you been married?'

'You've told me yourself that northerners are very inquisitive,' said Albert. 'They might be quite innocent. Why did you tell them my name is Homer? If they come back I'll have to live with that name. Wherever did you get it?'

'They were the names of my neighbours when we first went to Des Moines. On one side Homer and on the other Bernice. Americans have funny names. Bernice's husband was called Gob. Would you have preferred that?'

'I'm supposed to be English, anyway. You're the American. You could've called me Bill.'

'They know who we are. And they want something. Just what their intentions are, I don't know. But not good. I'd like to just push them overboard.'

Frankie was getting visibly upset. Her eyes welled with tears. Albert put his arm round her.

'To the left of us there's a door which leads down to a kind of buffet. Without turning around let's move towards it.'

They nudged themselves to the door and walked down the stairs to the lower deck.

'Either they haven't seen us or they've got another plan,' said Albert.

'Or we are completely wrong and they are just a boring, middle aged couple on holiday, trying to make friends,' chirped Frankie. 'Look the rest room is over there. I'm going to freshen up a moment. I'll be back in a few minutes.'

She walked into the toilets. She went to a wash basin and began washing her hands and face. As she dried her face with paper towels she looked at herself in the mirror. How wrinkled and tired her face seemed. Were those bags appearing under her eyes? She appeared to have aged twenty years since the day she had left for Paris. Well she, decided, a little make up will do the trick. She opened her handbag.

The door opened behind her.

'I know Frankie, you look old,' Susan's face was behind her in the mirror. 'But now look again. You're young. What good, clear skin you have, the bags you thought you saw under your eyes, they've disappeared, haven't they?'

Frankie looked at herself. Yes, she was looking younger. Much younger.

'You see, how I give you good advice. Look how lovely you are. Now you haven't seen me have you? It was just an impression, wasn't it? I'm not really here.'

She came closer to Frankie whispered in her ear and walked out.

Frankie looked at herself in the mirror and deciding she did not need any make up, closed her handbag and left.

Albert was leaning against a pillar waiting for her.

'Everything all right? You suddenly look radiant. What happened to you in there?'

Frankie smiled.

'I don't know. I suddenly felt as if an enormous weight had been lifted from my shoulder. I feel much younger. I think that's it. Any sign of the old couple?'

'No, I'm beginning to wonder if I really saw them or if it was just my imagination.'

'Yes,' she said. 'I've been thinking the same thing. I'm sure we've attached too much importance to this. They weren't anybody.'

She moved closer to him, put her arms around his neck and kissed him. How safe she felt with him.

Albert took her hand and they walked back onto the deck. It was getting dark but they could still make out the white cliffs, Dover castle and the seaside town in front of them.

'This is the first time I've been here,' said Frankie. 'I went to France once with the school, but we came back through Dieppe and the ferry took hours to cross.'

'Yes, it must have been the route to Newhaven,' replied Albert. 'This is the shortest crossing. Look we're almost there.'

Travelling without luggage made disembarking much easier. They headed for the car rental office on the other side of the customs shed where a green Vauxhall Victor was waiting for them.

Frankie looked at it, nostalgically.

'My car in Des Moines was green. I was thinking that I should buy a new car if I'm going to stay in England. But not with gearshifts. It would have to be automatic. I never learned to manage a shift.'

They got in; Albert started the engine and pulled off. Some ninety minutes later they were driving past Buckingham Palace and looking for the route north.

'Albert,' said Frankie suddenly. 'Did you know Winston Churchill's died? This morning. I've just seen it at a newspaper stand.'

'Well, we were all expecting it. He was very ill. Well, that's an era gone. How old was he? Ninety, I think. Let's stop and have something to eat. There seems to be a place on the left up there and it's open.'

He pulled into a nearly empty car park which belonged to a large, well lit restaurant. Rectangular, windowed premises, housed in a low, modern building.

They sat down at a table near the cash desk, as far from the windows as possible. Although there were almost no customers, they waited some time before an employee appeared with a menu.

Albert spotted a pay phone near the cash desk.

'Frankie, I'm going to call and see if I have any messages. I'll be back in a sec.'

As Frankie perused the menu, she glanced up at Albert chatting on the phone. He was writing something down and looking at her all the time.

Their eyes met and he smiled at her.

'Were you watching me?' asked Frankie, when he came back.

'Yes, I don't really want to let you out of my sight, Frankie. Nothing is going to happen, I'm sure, but I worry all the time.'

'What were you writing down?'

The waiter arrived to take their order.

'You didn't answer my question,' she said, when the waiter had gone.

'Let's eat first,' answered Albert. 'I'll tell you later.'

'No, tell me now,' she insisted.

'Well, I've arranged an appointment this evening with a hypnotist. She lives nearby and has agreed to see us.'

Frankie did not say anything. The food arrived and they began to eat, not speaking at all.

The plates had been cleared away, and the bill paid when she finally spoke again.

'What time is the appointment?'

'We'll go now. She's expecting us. I said we had to eat first and then would drive over.'

'OK. Well let's go.'

Albert stopped the car in front of semi-detached house, just off the main road.

'Well, here it is. 33 Burford Lane.'

They both got out of the car and walked to the front door.

Albert rang the bell.

They heard noises from inside the house. A light went on and the door opened. A middle aged woman with long, straight, blonde hair stood in the doorway.

'Good evening,' she smiled. 'My name is Emilia Winters. But I was told to expect only one person.'

'Good evening. Albert Tucker. How do you do?'

'I was told you would come on your own. Please come in, both of you.'

She turned to Frankie.

'What is your name, dear?'

Frankie had hardly spoken a word since she left the restaurant and was still tempted to maintain a sullen silence. She was not sure if she liked this woman.

'Frances,' she said. 'Frances Blakeley.'

The woman showed them into the front lounge. The room was warmed by a gas fire in the hearth. A three-piece suite around the fireplace and an upright piano against the opposite wall. Two or three paintings hung from the picture rails.

Vaguely religious themes, thought Frankie.

'Please, sit down,' said the woman. 'Now I understand, you have had a rather unpleasant experience. Was that just you, Albert or both of you?'

'Both of us,' replied Albert. 'We were drugged, abducted and there are some eighteen hours we can't account for.'

'Also,' he went on. 'We were accosted by two people connected with our abductors who tried to use some kind of hypnosis on us. I realised they had tried to hypnotise me but I fear they tried the same with Frankie.'

Frankie looked at him, a little bewildered, but said nothing.

'Where were you drugged?' asked Emilia.

'In a restaurant in Paris, on Saturday,' replied Albert.

'Albert, I'd like to speak to Frankie alone. Could you sit in the hall until I call you?'

Albert smiled encouragingly at Frankie and left the room.

The woman turned to Frankie.

'What may I call you, dear? Frances or Frankie?'

'Frankie.'

'And you call me Emilia, dear. Frankie I want you to listen to me. Why don't we go back to the restaurant in Paris? Did you fall asleep? At the table?'

'Yes,' Frankie replied. 'I couldn't keep my eyes open. I fell asleep.'

'Yes, I know, now this is very simple, Frankie. You are going into a light trance and you must only listen to me. Do you understand? You won't hear any other voices. Even if Albert speaks, you won't hear him. Or anyone else, just me.'

Frankie did not move or say anything, but stared at the woman.

'You fell asleep in the restaurant, but later they woke you up, didn't they?'

'Yes.'

'Now you are there now. Describe the room. What can you see?'

'A small room. Curtains. A light on the ceiling.'

'Are you alone?'

'No,' said Frankie. 'There is a woman.'

'Do you know her?'

'Yes, it's the woman on the train, Susan.'

'And what does she want?'

'She wants to know about the discs. She's asking about the discs.'

'What do you tell her?'

'I don't know where they are,' laughed Frankie, 'because I don't.'

'Why are you laughing?'

'Because I gave them to Albert. I had them and I gave them to Albert. So I don't know where they are. Albert has them.'

'Did you tell her that?'

'No, she never asked. She told me she would visit me in England and we would look there. She told me I was getting old and had to find them. Otherwise I would die soon.'

'Did you get old?'

'Yes, on the boat. In the restroom. I saw my face. In the mirror. Then Susan came and told me I was young again. Then she whispered to me. I had to give her the discs or I would become very old. Then she left.'

'Well, Frankie, listen to me. Susan was wrong. You are not old. You are very young. Susan was wrong about all of it. Do you understand?'

'Yes,' replied Frankie.

'Susan has no power over you. If you see her again, you will not listen to her. Do you understand?'

'Yes,' replied Frankie.

'Now. When I say the word Timatic you will fall into a deep trance until I wake you. Do you understand?'

'Yes,' Frankie replied.

'Good would you like some tea, dear?'

'Yes, please,' replied Frankie.

'Oh, Frankie, what time is it?'

'Half past nine,' she replied.

'Oh, that's a lovely watch, isn't it?' said Emilia, looking at Frankie's wrist. 'Is it a Timatic?'

Emilia smiled at Frankie.

'What time did you say it was, dear?'

Frankie looked at her watch. A quarter to ten.

'Fifteen minutes, dear. I'll get the tea.'

Albert came into the room.

'How are you?'

'Albert, I remembered all of it. And that couple on the train. We were right about them. And Susan tried to hypnotise me. That's why I've been so depressed. She made me think she could make me old. What an old witch! Did you know all the time?'

'It all came back to me on the drive to London. That bloke, Stan, began whispering to me when you were in the bathroom on the boat. He told me you looked really radiant and I had to tell you that. But when he spoke to me, I wasn't able to move. Then he left and you came out.'

'But later,' Albert continued, 'I remembered that he'd questioned me in Paris. Tried to find out where you had hidden the discs. I told him you didn't have them. But he never asked me if I had them. So I didn't tell him.'

'Why didn't you tell me this when you remembered?'

'I didn't know what effect it might have. Then I remembered this lady and called the agency to see if we could arrange a meeting. I think I did the right thing. How do you feel now?'

'As if I had been cured of a serious illness,' smiled Frankie. 'What would I do without you?'

The door opened and Emilia entered followed by a young girl carrying a tray. The girl placed the tray on the low table in front of the fireplace and left.

When they finished their tea, Emilia looked at Albert and said;

'Albert, it might be a good idea if you and I had a little chat too. I'd like to make sure these people haven't left any surprises.'

Frankie left the room and found the bathroom. She stood looking at herself in the mirror. How was it possible that she had seen such terrible wrinkles in her face? She spent some time freshening up, then went downstairs and waited in the hall, until Albert and Emilia had finished their session.

It was quite late when they left Emilia's house. Frankie suggested spending the night in a hotel, but Albert wanted to get back that night, even if it meant arriving in the early hours of the morning.

## Chapter Thirty

Bernard looked at the sign at the side of the road. London a hundred and eighty miles. He continued driving. Another sign advertised a restaurant and petrol station. He slowed down and parked opposite some lorries, outside a sleazy looking café.

He got out of his car and looked at it. The roof of his convertible was still in place and he had not even thought about retracting it. He walked to the back and opened the boot. There were several pots of fresh honey which he and Beryl had bought during an excursion into the country.

So much had changed since that day, he hardly felt the same person, he had been so full of joie de vivre, so carefree.

And now he felt a deep gloom come over him.

There was a telephone box outside the café. He went in, closed the door behind him and dialed.

'Hello,' Beryl answered immediately, as if she had been sitting by the phone.

'Beryl, it's Bernard. Look, I can't come today, I'm being followed. It's too risky.'

'Are you in danger? Don't worry. Don't come if it's dangerous. Where are you?'

'Look, I'm all right but I really can't talk. I've got to go. I'll ring you later.'

He put down the phone and walked out of the phone box. It was beginning to rain. He walked back to the car, got in and drove off.

The rain continued and a light fog was beginning to settle over the road in front of him. He began to drive more slowly. A sign to his left advertised fish and chips, tea, coffee.

He slowed down and drove into the car park at the side of the road.

The fog was getting thicker. An estate car pulled in behind him and parked a few yards away. Without leaving his car, Bernard watched as two men got out. The driver of the estate was wearing a flat cap and belted raincoat. The other, early sixties, dark, greying hair and a hooked nose.

They slammed the car shut and walked over to the café.

Bernard sat behind the steering wheel, planning his next move.

The fog began to settle in thick clumps around the parked cars. Bernard got out of his car, opened the boot and took out a pot of honey. He walked over to the estate car, opened the petrol tank and emptied the contents of the pot into it.

He then got back into his car and drove off.

Ten miles later he once again left the main road and parked. The fog was getting worse and he could barely see more than a few feet in front of him. But more than that he wanted time to think.

His action of sabotaging the car was, he realised, perhaps a little foolish, although it did fill him with a deep satisfaction. Well, he admitted to himself, childish as well. Indeed the more he thought about it, the more he giggled. Well, maybe he was recuperating his joie de vivre. At least he had not killed them. Not yet, anyway. He giggled again.

And he realised that now he had neutralised these two, he was going to turn around and drive back. But he was not going to phone Beryl. He had to find another way to get in contact. Obviously someone had bugged her phone.

Anyway he had time.

## Chapter Thirty-One

Albert drove slowly through the thick fog and carefully pulled up near the pair of semi-detached houses where they lived. He looked at his watch.

Nearly five o'clock in the morning. Frankie was in the back seat, curled up, fast asleep.

He sat in the car. He had parked on the opposite side of the road and he strained to catch a glimpse of their houses, so hidden by the thick walls of dirty fog.

All he could see was the pale yellow glow of the two street lights outside their houses. How long had they been away? he thought. Two days. But yet.

He got out of the car and locked the doors. He opened the boot of the rented car, a small light turned on and he was able to find the lever for the car jack. He searched in vain for an electric torch.

Armed with the metal bar he made his way towards the entrance to Frankie's driveway, which he remembered had no gate. He wanted to avoid creaking metal, announcing his presence to anybody who might be there.

The two gardens were separated by a low wall. Albert moved rapidly towards the front door of his house, put the key in the lock and noiselessly opened it.

He stood in the open doorway, for a moment, and listened carefully. He stayed for some time, and then he heard it.

At first, he thought he was listening to the sound of his own breathing and then he realised it was someone else. Sleeping. Not snoring, but clearly the sound was of slumbering and it was coming from the settee.

His first thought was that it might be his mother or his aunt. But neither would have come without the dog.

He listened again. It was only one person. Were there others in the bedrooms? Should he go upstairs? Too risky. Stairs were always noisy. He moved towards the light switch and flicked it.

The sleeping man stretched on the settee, stirred and he looked up at Albert.

'Hello,' said Bernard. 'Isn't Frankie with you?'

He looked at Albert, quizzically, but there was an unfamiliar gravity in his expression.

'I thought you were in Paris,' replied Albert.

'Well, I thought you were there too. But, here we are. All together again. Unless Frankie is still in Paris?'

'Is there anybody upstairs?' asked Albert. 'How did you get in?'

'As far as I know I'm completely alone. I was followed this morning but I managed to shake them off. So I came here to see my friends.'

'Your friends? Why do you say that? I have to go out to the car. To get Frankie. I want you to come with me.'

'Why?'

'Because,' said Albert, 'I don't trust you and I'm not going to leave you alone in the house.'

Albert left the lights on but closed the door behind him. They walked to the car and woke Frankie. Bernard greeted her, but the unusually serious expression still had not left his face.

'What are you doing here?' she asked. Her tone was decidedly unfriendly. Bernard attempted a smile.

The three of them crossed the road and walked back into the house. Bernard and Frankie made themselves comfortable in the lounge and Albert went to turn on the heating. He came back and prepared coffee.

'Where is Mrs. Petersen?' asked Frankie. 'Did she come with you?'

'No,' replied Bernard, 'she's gone back to Scotland with Mrs. Potts.'

'Who the heck is Mrs. Potts?'

'She met her in Edinburgh and the two travelled to Paris together.'

'Bernard, what do you know about Susan and Stan?'

Bernard stared at her with incomprehension in his face.

'Nothing at all. Who are they?'

'They kidnapped Albert and me. In Paris. While we were having lunch in a restaurant.'

'Oh,' said Bernard. 'Yes, that was Mrs. Petersen's doing. She wanted to know where you had the discs. She explained that just before she sent me back to London. She told me she loved you like a daughter but that she had to get the discs.'

'Why aren't you in London now?' asked Frankie, coldly.

'I came up north to get my car. And to see Beryl.'

'Have you seen Beryl?'

'No.'

Albert put three cups of coffee on the bar.

'Why not?' he asked. Bernard went on to explain how he had been followed, and had come to the conclusion that someone was listening to Beryl's telephone conversations.

'And now,' asked Albert, 'why have you come here? As if we were all friends?'

Bernard tried to look hurt.

'I thought we were friends. I didn't know Mrs. Petersen was going to have you kidnapped. I had nothing to do with that. I have nowhere else to go. Beryl may be in danger. I have to contact her and I can't go to her house or telephone her. You are my only friends here. And I don't want to have anything more to do with that American woman. Or really anybody else connected with this affair. I don't care about the discs anymore. Or the remnants of the French Résistance. I want a quiet life.'

'Tell me about the men who followed you,' said Frankie. 'Can you describe them?'

'The man in the town centre was fairly ordinary looking. He wore one of those flat caps old men wear, although he wasn't that old. The other one I remember was much older. Black hair going white, a hooked nose and when he smoked these horrible long, white fingers, holding his cigarettes.'

Bernard looked as if he were going to be sick. Frankie started laughing.

'Yes, he's pretty horrible. That's Daniel Bessel.'

'How did you shake them off?' asked Albert.

'Oh, I lost them in the Village. Then I went to get my car. But on my way to London, I stopped to have something to eat. It was very foggy and they suddenly appeared in the same car park. I never went into the café. Once they had left the car, I poured honey into their petrol tank.'

'Honey,' exclaimed Frankie. 'Why? Where did you get honey?'

'The last time Beryl and I went out we drove past a farm where they sold it. Beryl wanted to buy some for her mother. But then she left it in the car. I wanted to slow them down. The honey would wreck the motor. My father always said not to take half measures, when fighting for your life.'

'Then I moved off as fast as I could,' Bernard continued. 'But it was then that I decided not to go back to London, but come north again and forget my missions. I'm not cut out to be a spy.'

'You're doing quite well,' remarked Albert. 'Do you know what happened to them? Did they carry on to London or do you think they turned back too?'

'No idea', replied Bernard. 'But I would imagine they continued on their way to London if they managed to repair the car or get another one. But I don't think they know where I live. Nobody does. And I'm sure because my flat in London was just as I left it.'

'I was thinking, Frankie. Tomorrow or really today now is Monday. Could you go to see Beryl, at work? No phone calls. They may be listening.'

Frankie looked at Bernard.

'All right. Tomorrow I'll go and see her.'

## Chapter Thirty-Two

Beryl worked in a large building in Market Street. Frankie got off the bus on the other side of the street, crossed at the traffic lights and walked up the imposing steps, past an American soldier and into a foyer.

Under an enormous American flag, there was a painting of George Washington and under both of these, standing at a counter, was a middle aged, balding American.

'Good morning ma'am. How can I help you?'

'Oh, good morning, this is the American Consulate, isn't it?'

'No, ma'am, it is not. There is no consulate in this city. This is the United States Commercial Office.'

'Oh, I wanted to see Mrs. Beryl Greylish.'

'Is Mrs. Greylish expecting you? Have you an appointment?'

'No.'

An expression of distaste made his lip curl slightly. He said nothing, but picked up a telephone.

'Could you give me your name, please?'

'Mrs. Frances Blakeley'

'Perhaps you could take a seat,' he said, making gestures towards some wooden benches, some distance away.

Frankie sat down and waited. A door opened and Beryl came out. She quickly walked over to Frankie, who stood up.

'Come into my office, Frankie. I was going to phone you but I didn't know you already knew. How did you find out so quickly?'

Frankie followed her friend down a corridor past several doors, some open, some closed, until they came to small office full of filing cabinets, where it seemed Beryl spent her working day.

Beryl sat down behind a wooden desk and Frankie sat on the other side.

'Everybody's in an uproar here with what's happened,' said Beryl. 'Luckily they haven't asked me about it. But I know they're going to keep it out of the papers. How did you find out?'

'I'm a little confused,' said Frankie. 'First of all I thought you worked in the consulate. The man at the desk said there wasn't a consulate in the city.'

'Oh, we call it that but it's really a commercial office and other things. But I can't talk about the other things. If I told anyone, I would lose my job. Not even my mum knows that.'

'I came with a message from Bernard. I don't know anything else.'

'Oh,' said Beryl, 'I see. Tell me. What's happened to Bernard?'

'He's being followed and thinks people might be following you too. And he thinks your phone's bugged. So he daren't phone you. He wants to see you.'

'Oh, I want to see him too. Where is he?'

'He's at Albert's.'

'I'll go over after work then. See him then. I'll call my mum; tell her I'll be late.'

'But don't mention Bernard, Beryl. They may be listening.'

'Don't worry Frankie. I know that.'

'Beryl, what is it that you thought I already knew, but I don't?'

'Look,' she said. 'I started talking and now realise I shouldn't have said anything. But you have a right to know. It's that woman you worked for in Des Moines. The one who went to Scotland.'

'Mrs. Petersen?'

'Yes, Ruth Petersen. She was being investigated by an FBI agent here, a woman, Doris Potts. They were both murdered yesterday in a hotel. In Edinburgh.'

Frankie almost stopped breathing.

'How awful. Oh goodness, how awful. Oh, I can't believe it. How were they murdered?'

Beryl shrugged.

'I'm not sure. They were together in the hotel room and someone shot them. There was another FBI agent in the hotel in another room. But I don't know any more.'

'Why were they investigating Mrs. Petersen?' asked Frankie.

Beryl went very quiet and looked at Frankie.

'Well, everyone said that it was about taxes. But now that this has happened. Maybe it was more than that. I can't tell you anything else. Poor Doris worked here. She was from Scarborough but she married a GI after the war and went to the States.'

'Was she working undercover?' asked Frankie.

Beryl looked down at the desk and then looked up again.

'Frankie, I'll go to Albert's tonight, to see Bernard and we'll talk then. Look, I really am not supposed to say anything about this. I'll see you to the door.'

Frankie walked down the steps of the building. She saw Albert standing on the other side of the street. She went to the traffic lights on the corner and crossed over.

They walked together without speaking. A casual observer might not even have realised that they were acquainted. At the end of the road there was a coffee shop.

Albert broke the silence.

'Bernard's waiting here,' he said.

They walked into a modern, L shaped café. The walls were covered with menus which boasted morning coffees, lunches and afternoon teas.

Bernard was sitting on a long bench at a table near a window, drinking coffee. Albert and Frankie sat down together opposite him, on another bench.

'Well,' he asked. 'How's Beryl?'

'Oh,' said Frankie. 'She's great. Some things I've just discovered. After weeks of telling me she works in the US Consulate I find out there is no consulate in the city. Of course there isn't. I remember now, I had to go to Liverpool to go to the consulate when I got my visa for America.'

'Well,' asked Bernard. 'If it's not the consulate, what is it?'

'Ahh,' said Frankie. 'There's the rub. They call it the United States Commercial Office. I think it's an undercover office of the FBI.'

'Get away,' said Albert, 'and they've got a loud mouth, like her, working there.'

Frankie snorted.

'Well, they told her not to say anything, if she valued her job and up until now she hasn't told anyone, not even her boyfriend, or has she?' she added, looking at Bernard.

'Not a word,' replied Bernard. 'I always believed she worked in the consulate.'

'Anyway, something she has told me,' Frankie went on. 'Mrs. Petersen has been murdered. In a hotel in Edinburgh.'

Albert and Bernard looked at her. For what seemed a very long time, no one said anything.

'What happened?' Albert asked at last.

'She was in a hotel with this mysterious Mrs. Potts who it turns out is some kind of undercover agent for the FBI, investigating Mrs. Petersen for tax fraud, but now Beryl thinks there was more to it. Someone popped both of them off.'

Bernard looked tearful and, when he spoke, seemed visibly affected.

'She told me Mrs. Potts was English. Mrs. Petersen, I mean. She told me she was an English woman she met in Scotland and had come to Paris with her.'

'They're all English women but married to Americans,' said Frankie. 'There are thousands of English women in America. Young GIs came here during the war and afterwards and married all the English girls.'

'They used to say overpaid, oversexed and over here,' added Albert.

'Your husband was in the military, too?' asked Bernard.

'No', replied Frankie. 'We met at university. Completely different. It had all finished by then. I'm a different generation.'

'I'm sorry about Ruth Petersen,' said Bernard. 'We had a long conversation about the war and our families. We were getting on very well. But at the same time this whole situation was becoming too much for me, and, with her gone, it's another little problem that has disappeared.'

'I think we all feel like that,' said Frankie.

'Does Beryl have a lunch break?' asked Albert.

'Yes, she always comes out at twelve. Returns at one fifteen,' replied Bernard, 'and finishes at four.'

318

'Well, its half past eleven now,' said Albert. 'Let's wait for her here. Would she come out the main door or are there special exits for functionaries?'

'I've always met her on the steps outside,' replied Bernard.

'Well, we can see the steps from here. Let's have another coffee and wait until she comes out. She might have something else to tell us.'

'Why don't we wait until she comes round tonight?' asked Frankie.

'I've got a hunch that we should keep an eye on Beryl,' said Albert. 'And I think I'm right. Look over there. Near the traffic lights, Frankie. Do you recognise anyone?'

Frankie looked across the street. Standing alone next to the traffic light was a short, thickset man in his fifties. Bald on top but with abundant red hair.

Some weeks had passed but she had no difficulty in recognising Christopher Gallagher.

'I would hazard a guess and say Mr. Gallagher is waiting for Beryl. Does he know her, Bernard?'

'I don't know,' replied Bernard. 'I've never seen this man in my life. Who is he?'

'Didn't Mrs. Petersen tell you about him?' asked Frankie. 'His name is Christopher Gallagher. He sent that strange man you saw, Albert Bessel, to offer me money for the discs.'

'Why would he want to see Beryl?' asked Bernard. 'She knows nothing about the discs.'

'Another question is why he would come personally. He usually sends someone,' said Albert.

Frankie watched as he strode across the street. Two men were coming out of the building. One of them, a young man, walked briskly towards Gallagher. The other, much taller and wearing a hat, moved in a different direction, but stopped at the bottom of the steps, sat on a low wall and lit a cigarette.

Gallagher and the young man shook hands, and began to walk together down the street in the direction of the coffee shop. Just outside the coffee shop, they stopped and stood several minutes engrossed in conversation. Gallagher suddenly laughed, shook the man's hand and walked off. The young man turned and ambled into the coffee shop.

There was a table free near the entrance and the man sat down. A waitress appeared and he placed his order.

He lit a cigarette.

'Twelve o'clock,' said Albert looking at his watch.

The three of them looked up at the entrance of the US Commercial Office. Almost immediately, the doors opened and several men and women, maybe as many as ten or eleven, emerged and made their way down the steps almost all of them coming towards the coffee shop. Some of them together and a few on their own.

Beryl was alone.

'She's coming towards the coffee shop,' said Albert. He stood up and looked around the restaurant. There were three empty tables on the far side, in an alcove, which would be hidden from anybody coming in through the main entrance.

'We'll go and sit over there,' he said, 'Until she's settled in.'

Bernard and Frankie moved to another table. Albert followed, but more slowly, and stood for a moment in the alcove, behind a wall, where he could watch the door without being seen.

The door opened and half a dozen people, including Beryl, walked into the café. They quickly dispersed and sat at different tables. Beryl was left by herself, but she looked up, smiled and waved at the young man, who had clearly been waiting for her.

He stood up, Beryl went towards him, smiling and the two embraced and kissed. They separated, Beryl smiled again and the two sat down. They began speaking, their heads together, hands touching, the intimacy of lovers, Albert thought.

He moved back towards the table where the others were sitting.

'Well?' asked Bernard. 'Did she come in?'

Albert touched his arm and gently moved him towards his surveillance point.

Bernard watched for some minutes and walked back towards the table and sat down opposite Frankie.

'Well,' said Bernard. 'Quite frankly. I may as well take my car and go home. I've been here in the north now for two days, being followed, risking my neck just to talk to Beryl.'

'What's going on?' asked Frankie.

'Oh, Beryl is carrying on with some bloke. The one, who was talking to your gangster. But I tell you, really romantic. Not just having lunch together.'

'OK,' said Frankie, 'Let's go and talk to them. Find out what's going on. You and me, Bernard. Albert you go and stand by the door. So her boyfriend can't just stand up and leave.'

She stood up and walked determinedly towards Beryl's table with Bernard in tow. Albert discreetly made his way to the entrance.

'Hi Beryl.'

Frankie smiled and waved at her friend as she approached the table. A grimace of surprised horror quickly twisted into a smile on her friend's face.

'Oh, hello Frankie,' she cooed. 'I didn't see you here.'

Bernard sat down on the bench, to the right of the young man.

'Hiya Beryl.'

'Oh and Bernard, too. What are you doing here? We're just going to have lunch. They do a lovely toad in the hole here, you know, Frankie.'

She looked at her table companion.

'Bernard's French so he wouldn't like traditional English fare. Coq au vin is more in his line.'

'Aren't you going to introduce us to your friend, Beryl?' asked Frankie.

'Oh, yes. This is Frankie Blakeley, an old school friend and this is Bernard, another friend.'

'And who are you, sir?' asked Bernard, turning to the young man next to him.

'Oh,' said Beryl. 'His name is John Pailthorpe. He works in my office.'

The man offered Bernard his hand. Bernard ignored it.

'Well it was nice meeting you, but I have to be getting back to the office.'

The young man, from his accent obviously American, made to get up and move towards the door. It was then that he found Albert sitting on the same bench to his left.

'My name's Albert,' he smiled. 'And we have a few questions, if you don't mind.'

'Oh, Albert,' Beryl beamed at him. 'You've startled John. Sitting down like that suddenly.'

She looked at John and continued speaking.

'Albert's a writer and he's Frankie's boyfriend. Lives next door to her. Always looking after her, he is. He looks ferocious, but he's as gentle as a lamb.'

'Well, I can get pretty ferocious too, buster.' The American turned to Albert. 'And I am not a lamb. What kind of questions do you want to ask me?'

Albert stared at him for a moment. Black hair, dark eyes, he was wearing a business suit. As Albert was sitting right next to him he noticed a bulge under the lapel of his jacket. A shoulder holster.

'I wanted,' said Frankie suddenly, 'to ask you, why you were talking to Christopher Gallagher just now.'

The man looked at her blankly.

'Who's that?' he asked.

'The man who you were chatting with in the doorway, before you came in,' Frankie said.

'I don't know his last name. His first name's Joe and we chat sometimes in the pub I go to, across the street. Don't know anything about him.'

'You shook hands with him,' Frankie said.

'Oh, yeah? So what? Americans shake hands with everyone. Not like you guys. It's no big deal.'

'And snogging with Beryl? Something else you Americans do with everybody? No big deal?' gushed Bernard.

'Oh, Bernard. Mon cheri.'

Beryl started speaking in French to Bernard who was getting visibly irate. Frankie and Pailthorpe looked at them and did not see Albert move quickly towards the American and pull the revolver out of his jacket and place it on the table in front of them.

'And this? Something else you Americans just do. No big deal? Have you got a licence to carry a gun in England?'

Albert spoke softly, but slowly.

Beryl staged a horrified gasp. Frankie giggled. Bernard said something in French.

The American grabbed the pistol and put it back in its place.

'OK, buster, that's enough.'

There was a hum of background noise that seemed to get louder. People were looking at them.

Albert once again spoke softly and slowly.

'No problem here, we'll just call a policeman if you like and you can explain why you are carrying a revolver in a public restaurant in England.'

The American went very quiet.

'OK. Let's all just relax. Just what do you guys want?'

'Well,' said Frankie. 'We've just seen you chatting and shaking hands with a man we know is a gangster. Then you are carrying on with Beryl who we thought was Bernard's girlfriend.'

The door of the restaurant opened. Albert looked up. A tall man wearing a hat came in, glanced at Pailthorpe and walked over to an empty table opposite them and sat down.

Albert recognized him as the man who had left the US commercial office at the same time as Pailthorpe.

Beryl moved to her left slipped off the bench and stood up.

'I'm sorry but toad in the hole or not, I'm not feeling hungry. John come with me. Albert please let him leave.'

Albert moved off the bench stood up and Pailthorpe slipped out and walked towards Beryl.

The tall man in the hat also stood up and walked behind Beryl and Pailthorpe. They stood for a moment looking at Albert, still on his feet and Bernard and Frankie sitting at the table. Then without another word, they left.

'Toad in the hole?' said the waitress.

## Chapter Thirty-Three

'I'm beginning to feel like I have no friends left,' said Frankie.

It was Wednesday morning and she was sitting at the bar in Albert's lounge, drinking coffee.

'Why?' asked Albert. He, too, was sitting on a stool reading the morning paper. 'You and Bernard seemed the best of friends yesterday when he left for London. I thought you seemed quite tearful.'

'Because, I don't think he's ever coming back and we'll probably never see him again. He'd only returned because he thought there was something going on for him with Beryl. Now he wants to be well shot of everything.'

She took a sip of her coffee and looked at Albert.

'But I was thinking about Beryl. I thought she was my friend and it turns out she's been using me all along. Just as she was using Bernard. Playing a double game. No wonder he had people waiting for him when he got off the train. And she was always pretending to be so gormless.'

She drank some more coffee and continued.

'Then there is Mrs. Petersen. You have no idea the mornings I spent with her drinking coffee and chatting about her life before the war. I always thought of her as such a sweet, generous old thing.'

Albert spluttered over the coffee he was sipping.

'Sweet? I can think of quite a few people who wouldn't consider her sweet.'

'She saved my life, Albert. And she paid for my telephone. Anyway she's gone now. Albert, who do you think killed her?'

'It may not have had anything to do with us or the discs or anything. Your Mrs. Petersen had her thumbs in a lot of pies. Look, she was being investigated by the FBI.'

There was a knock at the door.

Albert opened the door. A middle aged man in a raincoat, balding, about five foot six inches tall, he thought. Holding up his credentials in his hand he introduced himself as Detective Constable Good, CID.

'You are Albert Tucker, is that correct sir?'

'Yes, that's right.'

'May I come in a moment?'

'Yes, certainly.'

The detective walked into the living room and sat down in an armchair.

'This is my girlfriend Mrs. Frances Blakeley.'

'How do you do?'

'Would you like a cup of coffee?' asked Albert.

He was, as always, perfectly calm, speaking slowly and softly.

'No, thank you, sir. I was wondering if you could tell me about Daniel Bessel. Do you know him?'

'Bessel?' Albert paused in thought. 'There was a family of Bessels in Timperley that my family was friendly with. I don't remember any first names. One of them was a doctor.'

'When would this be, sir?'

'Oh, some years ago, maybe fifteen years ago. The doctor died, I think.'

'No, I'm talking about a man who died on Sunday night in a car accident. Two men in a car stopped suddenly on the road to London and caused a pile up. Both men were killed. We haven't been able to identify the driver. But the passenger was Daniel Bessel. He was carrying a file, with quite a lot of information about you, sir. Now why would that be?'

'What kind of information?'

'Let me ask the questions, sir. We'll finish more quickly that way. But I would like you to play detective for a moment. Why do you think that Mr. Bessel had all this information about you, sir?'

'Well, I can only imagine that he liked my books and was interested in me as a person,' replied Albert.

'What books are you referring to, sir?'

'Well,' said Albert. 'I've only written two. "Four and Twenty Blackbirds" and then "Life Makes You Weep". I'm working on a third. But it seems to be a non-starter.'

The detective put his hand in his pocket and took out a notebook in which he began to scribble.

'I see. And your books have been published?'

'Oh, yes and translated into other languages.'

The detective stared at him expressionlessly. He stood up.

'Well, sir. That may be the reason. I'm not a literary man, myself. So I know very little about published authors.'

He walked towards the door. Albert opened it.

'Good morning, Mrs. Blakeley, sorry to interrupt your morning.'

He turned to leave, then turned around again and faced Albert.

'Oh, one more thing, sir. What were you doing on Sunday afternoon?'

Albert paused.

'Sunday is the day Churchill died, isn't it? We were in Paris, just for the weekend. Sunday afternoon we were coming home. I couldn't say exactly. On the ferry. We drove home from Dover in a hired car. I have all the receipts.'

'Very good, sir. Thank you for your help.'

The detective seemed entirely convinced, much against his will.

Albert closed the door behind him, placed his finger on his lips.

'I'll make some more coffee.'

Frankie, who had remained almost motionless during the whole interview, suddenly breathed a gasp of relief.

'Oh, Albert, do you think he's gone?'

Albert went to the bay window.

'I don't think there's anybody about,' he said.

'I'm so glad he didn't ask me anything. I wouldn't have known what to say.'

'Well,' said Albert, 'he did have the element of surprise on his side. Luckily I was able to tell the truth. I don't know anything about this man. He asked me for a light once on the path down to the river and I spoke to him once in the pub. He never told me what his name was.'

'Well, he told me,' said Frankie, 'and he gave me his card.'

She opened her handbag and searched through it.

'Look, here it is.'

She handed it to Albert who looked at it closely.

'There's only a name and phone number here. Hold on a minute. I'll jot the number down in case we need it.'

He disappeared for a moment into his office. He came back with the card still in his hand. He took a cigarette, put it in his mouth, lit it and at the same time set the card alight and left it burning in the kitchen sink.

'That's an end to that. You don't know the man's name. If the detective comes back, as he may well do, he'll probably have a photograph. If he asks me I'll say we met him on the hill and he asked for a light. You say the same if he asks you. We don't know his name or anything else about him. We've nothing to worry about as long as we're natural.'

'You do realise,' said Frankie.' That this is Bernard's doing? He put the honey in the petrol tank making the engine stop suddenly, provoking an accident.'

'I think we owe it to Bernard to keep that to ourselves. Luckily, no one ever told Beryl.'

Frankie giggled.

'Oh, for goodness sake. He's well shot of her, isn't he? And, so are we.'

## Chapter Thirty-Four

They got up very early Thursday morning and reached Sheffield sooner than they had expected. They left the car in the university car park, not far from the barracks, and wandered around the streets until they found a café.

It was a cold, windy day. They passed a park with playing fields covered by a white frost, which gave everything a wintry look.

The café was warm and the waitress brought them very hot coffee, which they drank gratefully.

'My Uncle Bill used to come to Sheffield a lot. I think, at least once, he came with your father. You know it's funny. I used to see your parents, sometimes. They would be sitting on the bench at the end of their garden, looking down the hill at the river.'

'Yes, we did that a lot when I was a little girl,' replied Frankie.

'But,' went on Albert, 'we rarely spoke. Maybe, good evening or good morning. It's funny, in two years. I hardly exchanged more than half a dozen words with them. Well, it's also true, that they were away an awful lot. The house next door always seemed to be empty.'

'Yes. They did travel about a lot. But I think it was all because of work. I used to get postcards from so many different places, but almost always European countries. Mainly Germany. I think one month about two years ago I got a postcard first from Munich, Nuremberg, Düsseldorf and then Berlin. In just one week. That's when Chuck said he was convinced my Dad was a spy. We'd seen some movie about spies in Berlin and they'd followed the same route. Well, I suppose he was a kind of spy.'

'A pity though,' sighed Albert. 'I would like to have known them better now that I know you.'

She smiled at him. How handsome he looked in his blue suit. She had had to convince him to dress up for the ceremony.

He looked at her.

'Frankie,' he said, 'When we get to the end of this, when this is all behind us, will you marry me?'

She suddenly felt her body go weak. Her knees began to shake a little. She felt the tears well up in her eyes.

'Oh, Albert,' she said. 'I thought you'd never ask. Of course I will.'

'There's only one problem,' he said.

'What's that?' she gasped, suddenly alarmed.

'I haven't bought a ring. There's a shop across the road. Let's go in and choose one. I mean, if there's one we like. Otherwise, we can go somewhere else.'

An hour later found them struggling through the wind towards the red brick building which housed the army barracks. In spite of the cold, Frankie could not stop stretching her hand out in front of her to look at her new ring.

They opened the door and she gave her name to the smart young cadet in the entrance.

'And this is my fiancé, Albert Tucker,' she added, rather self-consciously.

The young man led them into a dining room with long tables, set for lunch. Most of the diners were already there and they were shown to two empty places between groups of middle aged, uniformed men.

The man sitting to her right, dressed in full uniform and sporting a white moustache, spoke to her immediately.

'I took the liberty of looking at the name card. You're Professor Cooper's daughter, aren't you?'

'That's right. My name's Frankie, and I've come with my fiancé Albert Tucker.'

'Captain Mark Ryder.'

'Oh,' said Frankie, 'I was told to ask for you. Actually your sitting next to me was no coincidence, was it?'

'No, it wasn't, of course. Who told you to ask for me?'

'My next door neighbour, or better said, my former, next door neighbour. He's now in an old folks' home. He told me to ask for you and tell you a code.'

'And what's that?'

Frankie laughed.

'You know, it's almost the end of January, isn't it? That means I've been back in England almost two months. Now, before then, I lived in Des Moines, Iowa. Unfortunately, I was widowed. So I came back.'

'Is that so? I'm so sorry to hear that. And you lost your parents, too. Bad show that,' the military man spoke in clipped tones. He then added, 'I did think you sounded American, actually.'

'Yes,' said Frankie. 'I've heard that before. Many consider Iowa a kind of backwater and most certainly, since I've been in Britain, something has happened to me almost every day. So I've become very wary.'

Frankie drank a little water and looked at her table companion.

'Captain Ryder, before I tell you what Uncle Willy told me, I think I would have to have your identity confirmed.'

The military man guffawed. A deep, contented laugh.

'Well yes, of course, Frankie. Don't you worry about it. Now, if you'll excuse me, I am Master of Ceremonies and have to introduce some speakers to the luncheon.'

He got up and walked to the presidential table, where he asked for and received the attention of the guests.

336

The lunch and speeches lasted well over an hour, but it left Frankie with no doubt as to the captain's identity.

When lunch was finished, another young cadet arrived to escort them to an auditorium for the commemoration ceremony.

It wasn't until five o'clock that Albert and Frankie were able to stand up and file out towards the exit of the hall.

Captain Ryder was waiting for them at the door.

'Sorry, I've been neglecting you, but I've had my plate rather full this afternoon. Would you like to come to my office and we'll have some tea?'

He led them down a corridor, opened a door to very large, plushly furnished sitting room. A desk and chairs under a window confirmed that it was indeed an office. The curtains had not been drawn and it was now completely dark outside.

'I did say tea, but may I offer you something stronger. Perhaps a sherry or maybe some Scotch.'

He did not wait for the reply but took some bottles and glasses out of a low cupboard next to his desk. He showed the bottles to Frankie who decided on the sherry. He poured a whisky for himself and offered one to Albert.

Captain Ryder remained on his feet behind the desk, drinking his whisky. Albert was sitting in a metallic chair on the other side of the desk and Frankie was sitting in another one.

Off the top of the desk, Ryder took some papers and handed them to Frankie.

'I think my identity is pretty much verified here. You are wise to take your precautions.'

Frankie glanced at the papers and put them on the desk.

'I was told to ask for you, but apparently you already knew I was coming. My neighbour told me I was to tell you the code words, Neptune, broomstick. He said you would understand the meaning.'

Captain Ryder looked at her somewhat amused.

'Yes, well this is very hush, hush, of course. He may be in a nursing home but he shouldn't've given out classified code words. Did he tell you anything else?'

'Nothing at all,' said Frankie. 'He said you would explain everything.'

'Oh, he did, did he?'

Captain Ryder finished his whisky, poured another one, and sat down on a swivel chair behind his desk. He sipped his drink slowly, squinting at Frankie through narrowed eyes.

Albert took out a packet of cigarettes, put one in his mouth and offered it to Frankie who took one. He offered the packet to Ryder.

'No, thanks. Don't smoke, never have.'

Frankie puffed on her cigarette and scrutinised his face. A lined forehead, jet black hair and dark brown eyes. Pale skin and a white bushy moustache.

The expression on his face revealed nothing.

He began speaking.

'Frankie, have you got the discs? Have you found them?'

'I haven't got the discs,' she answered, truthfully.

'But you know where they are, don't you?'

'For two months now different people have been asking me about the discs. I've lost count of how many. I was hoping you could explain something to us. But if this is just going to be another interrogation, I'm afraid this interview has finished.'

Frankie stood up and Albert followed.

'Sit down, damn it!' Captain Ryder, used to giving orders, snapped at them impatiently. 'I know you've been in contact with Gallagher and those wretched people in the US Commercial Office.'

'You know Christopher Gallagher?' asked Frankie.

'Well, he's no friend of mine, if that's what you mean, but we are aware of his activities. He's working for a German, Daniel Bessel, who in turn is an agent for a group of Nazis living in Argentina. Word's out they have a machine. It's the machine we thought we had. A large metallic disc. Your father brought it back from Germany, from Himmler's castle. But it wasn't the authentic one. Merely a replica. Took us years to work out it was a fake. At first we thought the real one was in South America, perhaps in Argentina, perhaps somewhere else. Now we think that the machine is in England.'

'In England?' exclaimed Frankie. 'Who has it?'

'Either Bessel or more likely Gallagher,' continued Ryder. 'Bessel may have brought it from South America. But my money is on Gallagher. He pinched it after the war when he was in the castle, brought it with him and has kept it all these years. Now he wants to sell it to the Nazis still dreaming about the revival of the Third Reich.'

Ryder paused, leaned back in his chair and took another sip of whisky.

'Doesn't matter,' he went on, 'if they don't have the little discs. Won't work without them. But if they find these little discs...'

'Why?' asked Albert. 'What does the machine do? What is it for?'

'Well, that's it, of course. As we've never had it we don't really know. But we understand it emits some kind of radio waves. These waves are able to control a power station, a broadcaster, the defence system of a country. In the hands of the wrong sort of government it is an invaluable weapon. By the time the war ended the Germans had perfected it, but by then it was too late for them.'

Albert sat down again. He picked up his drink, which he had hardly touched and took a sip.

'If the machine doesn't work without the discs, what is the problem? They haven't got the discs. Their machine is useless.'

'Well,' replied Ryder, 'sooner or later they are going to find them, if they haven't already found them.'

Frankie, who had been standing all this time, drained her glass and placed it on Ryder's desk.

'Captain Ryder, my life has been turned upside down by this affair. At first, I wanted to go to the police but was persuaded not to. Very wisely, because apparently this Gallagher has the police in his pay. I considered going back to the States but learned that this man has tentacles which reach wherever I may be. I have found over the last two months that I can trust no one. Is there any way that we can get to the end of this business?'

The officer opened the bottle of sherry, poured another glass and handed it to her.

'Please sit down, Frankie. We know your father had the discs and that they were hidden. Only two people knew where they were. One of those people was your father. And unfortunately for us, he had the authority to keep this information to himself. When his life was untimely ended late last year, we thought at first, that the secret had died with him. The discs would never be discovered.'

He finished his drink, took the bottle and poured himself another. He took a sip and continued talking.

'It was then that one of our agents in the States revealed that you, Frankie, had been programmed to find the discs should anything happen to Professor Cooper.'

'Look,' said Frankie. 'I was kidnapped in Paris, hypnotized by two horrible people and they apparently found nothing.'

Captain Ryder nodded.

'Yes, that was a mistake. Because it wasn't actually hypnosis. You had been simply programmed to find the discs. Quite another process.'

Frankie's eyes flashed angrily.

'You mean to say the incident in Paris was all your doing?'

341

'It was an operation directed by our agent there. The American woman who used to employ you. As I said, she didn't understand that simple hypnosis wasn't going to work here.'

'And did you have Mrs. Petersen murdered, too?' asked Frankie.

Captain Ryder took another sip of his drink and stared at her for a moment.

'We don't know how Ruth and Doris got themselves killed. They were following a lead and something went wrong. Bad show.'

'I was told that Mrs. Petersen was being investigated for tax fraud.'

Ryder snorted.

'Who told you that? One of those Americans you saw the other day when you went to the Commercial Office?

'Yes, a girl I used to go to school with who now works there. She told me the other woman was an FBI agent investigating Mrs. Petersen for tax fraud.'

'Yes, I know who that is. She's been keeping tabs on you since you got here. And on that Spanish chap from Madrid, nasty piece of work. And of course on the French boyfriend she picked up.'

'Oh,' said Albert. 'What's her connection with Gallagher? Because when we saw her she was with an American who was very friendly with Gallagher.'

'My dear chap, she works for Gallagher. As do the two men. We can't prove anything of course, but they've been feathering their own nest for years. He was a spiv years ago, used to sell stuff on the black market from the American base. Always had lots of Americans on the payroll.'

'Why do the Americans employ her if they know she's an informant?' asked Frankie.

Ryder poured himself another whisky and chuckled.

'Because, they don't know. You can't give the Yanks information. It'd be all over their embassy or whatever they call that wretched office. Ruth's cover would have been blown immediately. No, much better for us to keep a sharp eye on these people and say nothing.'

Frankie sat for a while without saying very much. Beryl had been spying on her all the time. And on Bernard. She stood up and walked over to where Albert was sitting and stood behind him, placing her hands on his shoulder and slightly caressing his neck.

'You know Captain, we got engaged this morning. Albert bought me this beautiful ring. I've had a pretty depressing past and I want a very different future. Tell me what I've got to do to put all this behind me.'

'I think,' said the officer, 'That first of all I'm going to need you to be straight with me. Could you just answer my questions? Do you think you can do that?'

Frankie nodded.

'Did Gallagher contact you directly?'

'No.'

'Who did then?'

'Albert Bessel. He came to my house.'

'What did you say?'

'I said I knew nothing about the discs which wasn't exactly true because we had come across a disc some two or three feet in diameter. But I hadn't realised that he was talking about much smaller discs. I thought he meant the machines. He gave me his card.'

'Did you know he was associated with Gallagher?'

'Yes.'

'How did you know?'

'Because I saw them in a restaurant having lunch together.'

'And how did you recognise Gallagher?' asked Ryder. 'Had you seen him before?'

'I was alone in the restaurant and Gallagher paid for my lunch. He told the waiter I was a friend of his daughter's. The waiter pointed him out to me as he was leaving with Bessel.'

Frankie went on.

'Bessel followed me about. Albert warned him off and Gallagher got in contact with Albert. He gave us an appointment and we went to see him. He offered us twenty five thousand pounds for the discs. I said I didn't have them.'

'And do you have them, or rather do you know how they can be found?'

Frankie hesitated. Albert turned around in his chair and their eyes met. She looked up and studied Ryder's face.

'Well Captain if I have to trust anyone I imagine it will have to be you. Yes, I found them and we have them.'

'Good show. Of course you have them. You were programmed to find them. Tell me would you be able to get into contact with Bessel again?'

Albert coughed.

'Daniel Bessel is dead. He had a car accident.'

Albert told him about the visit of the detective, the day before.

'And why didn't you tell this policeman that you did know Bessel?' asked Ryder.

Albert spoke slowly and softly.

'Well, he never asked Frankie, he only asked me. I'd only spoken to the man twice and really he had never told me his name. This policeman was not going to help us out of this situation and would probably only make matters worse. And possibly he was in Gallagher's pay.'

Ryder sat back in his swivel chair and studied Albert's face.

'I'd still say you were holding something back here. Something you know and you don't want to tell me.'

'What makes you say that?' asked Albert. 'I think we've been more than candid with you.'

Ryder chuckled, without smiling.

'Tell me, where did you do your national service?'

'I was in Malaya most of the time,' answered Albert.

'Quite so, special forces, I would wager. They teach you the techniques there. I can tell by your relaxed tone that there's rather more to your story. I'd like to hear all of it. Indeed if you want my help and collaboration you are going to have to put all your cards on the table.'

Frankie shrugged her shoulders.

'Rather a lot has happened to us over the last two months so it's not so much that we are holding anything back, it's very difficult to know what to put in and what to leave out. I think we've told you everything relevant.'

'I'd rather be the judge of that,' replied Ryder, 'You two know something about Bessel's accident. And I'd like to know what it is.'

Frankie picked up her coat.

'I think we're finished here Captain Ryder. I've told you all I know and really I'm sorry about that. We have the discs and we're hanging on to them for the moment. It's getting late and it's time for us to go.'

Captain Ryder moved out from behind his desk and placed his hand on Frankie's arm.

'Please, don't go. We still have so much to talk about. I'm afraid I get a little brusque at times. You mustn't mind my ways. I'll call for some coffee.'

## Chapter Thirty-Five

There was a knock on the door and a cadet brought in the coffee. Although it was still very hot Frankie drank it eagerly. The sherry had left her feeling a little drowsy and she wanted her wits about her.

Captain Ryder began speaking again.

'The last we heard was that Gallagher was looking to sell the machine and the three discs to the highest bidder. And I think the bids have reached a million pounds. Of course the machine is useless without the discs. Hence his interest in you, Frankie.'

'Why only now?' asked Frankie. 'He's had this machine for twenty years. Why didn't he pester my father for the discs?'

'He didn't know what it was until Bessel came from Argentina looking for it. Bessel had investigated several people, including your father, who had been at the castle at the end of the war when the machine disappeared. Or really when the three disc shaped machines disappeared. One of the large discs made its way to Madrid and was in the hands of the family of Salvador Jimenez. At first Bessel thought the other two large discs had crossed Spain and Portugal and made their way to South America along with all the German refugees. But he was wrong. Both of the discs had been taken to England. One of them, the replica, by your father and the other by Gallagher.

'Gallagher told us he was at this castle at the end of the war,' said Frankie. 'What was he doing there? I'd heard he never did National Service.'

Captain Ryder shook his head.

'You're wrong about that. He saw action in North Africa, spent some time in Italy and finished up at Wewelsburg Castle at the end of the war.'

Albert finished his coffee and and lit a cigarette.

'The question is what to do now. If Gallagher has the machine can't you just go in and arrest him and confiscate it?'

Captain Ryder shook his head.

'Gallagher is too well protected as you well know. And there is something else. If, the machine is confiscated who knows where it will end up. We, in my group, are just simple counter intelligence officers subject to orders. Once the machine and its three discs left our control it could be stolen again and the effects could be catastrophic.'

'Well?' asked Frankie, 'What do you suggest?'

'The machine must be destroyed,' said Ryder. 'There is an autodestruct mechanism. Professor Cooper was quite sure of that. The Germans were going to use it the night he took the machine and the discs and flew back to England. However it seems he got the wrong machine. It was Gallagher who managed to purloin the real machine. Fortunately, he didn't get the discs. I don't think he knew anything about them. Until Bessel arrived from Argentina.'

Albert looked at his watch. It was getting on for seven o'clock and he felt rather hungry.

Captain Ryder seemed to read his thoughts. He stood up and walked around his desk towards them.

'Anyway, why don't we call it a day, now? You must both be worn out and I think we've got to give this matter some thought. I'll pay you a visit maybe tomorrow or Saturday. Maybe we could meet for lunch. You're both on the phone aren't you? I'll jot down your numbers now. I'll consult with my colleague and see if there is anything to be done.'

It was cold and windy in the street when Frankie and Albert left the building. They turned the corner towards the university car park and a gust of wind nearly blew them over.

'Gosh, I'm hungry,' said Frankie. 'That lunch was so English, wasn't it. I'd forgotten how frugal meals can be here.'

'Well, why don't we have a Chinese dinner now. Look! Hong Kong Blues.'

Albert pointed to a sign over a Chinese restaurant at the side of the road. 'Do you like Chinese food?' he asked.

'I've only ever eaten it a few times in Des Moines,' replied Frankie. 'We used to go to Mexican restaurants when we wanted something a little exotic. Chuck really liked Mexican food. It was always a little too hot for me.'

They went into the restaurant. A small Chinese woman in traditional dress greeted them at the door and took them to a table. The walls were decorated in bright red and green colours. On one wall was painted a pianist with his piano and a jazz orchestra behind him.

They sat down at a table near the door. Frankie could hear soft, jazz music in the background.

The restaurant was not very busy and the food came quickly. They were both hungry and began eating without saying very much. The music seemed to get just a little louder. Tunes she recognised, had heard many times before and always tugged at her memory. She thought back to her life in America, going downtown at night in Des Moines with Chuck, mornings listening to Mrs. Petersen's stories, her parents visiting.

Another jazz melody, this time Glenn Miller she thought. The Little Man Who Wasn't There. Another rush of memory. Long before going to Iowa. Sitting on the bench at the end of the garden. The Man Who Wasn't There. What a haunting melody.

The music changed again, Benny Goodman and Peggy Lee, Get Me Some Money Too. Suddenly, she was dancing in a backyard, at a summer party in Des Moines.

Her reverie was interrupted by the waiter arriving to clear away their plates and bring menus for dessert. Frankie asked for an ice cream and Albert ordered a cup of coffee. The waiter left.

'What did you think of Captain Ryder?' asked Albert.

'Do you mean, did I like him? No, I didn't. Superior, upper class type. Snotty accent. Terribly condescending.'

'Typical army officer,' said Albert. 'I met a lot of his type while I was doing my National Service. And at first it seemed he had all the answers, but I'm afraid we're not going to get very much out of him.'

'I must say,' said Frankie. 'For one moment I thought he wasn't going to let us leave. And then he kept drinking and trying to ply us with booze.'

'I like this place, Albert,' Frankie went on. 'I think it's the music. I was so tense when I came in, didn't want to talk and I don't think you wanted to, either. But the food and the music have really made me feel so relaxed.'

Albert offered her a cigarette and lit one for himself.

'Do you want a cup of coffee? I'd like another one, I think. We've got to drive back and I want to have a clear head after that whisky he kept pouring down me.'

'OK.'

Albert found the waiter, ordered the coffee and asked for the bill.

'There's something at the back of my mind,' said Frankie. 'I think it's from the background music. I can't quite remember what it is.'

The door of the restaurant opened behind them and a gust of cold air made her shiver.

351

'Oh, Albert. Someone's just standing behind me with the door open.'

'Yes,' said Albert. 'You wouldn't believe it, but it's our Captain Ryder and another military chap. They're waiting for someone with the door open. Don't look. If they don't see us I'd like to get out as quickly as possible.'

'Yes,' he continued. 'Two other blokes dressed like generals or something and they're passing us, without looking in our direction. Either he hasn't seen us or he's not letting on.'

Frankie watched the four officers as they came into her line of vision. The Chinese lady accompanied them to a door, at the end of the restaurant.

'They must have a private room', said Frankie. 'Thank goodness for that. I don't think he saw us at all.'

'I wouldn't count on that,' replied Albert. 'People of that class will look right through you if they don't want to speak to you. Anyway, I'll pay and we'll go.'

He looked at the bill, took some money out and left it on the plate. Frankie stood up and put her coat on.

'Hallo again.'

Captain Ryder seemed to appear out of nowhere.

'I saw you when I came in, but couldn't say anything. Having a spot of supper with some guests from the ceremony. Look, I've checked my appointments for this week and I'll be over your way on Saturday. If it's not inconvenient perhaps we could manage lunch.'

'Yes, all right.' Frankie tried a smile.

'Any good places near you?'

'Yes,' replied Albert. 'The American Steak House in School Lane. I think it's Frankie's favourite and I certainly like it. Very discreet.'

Ryder took out a diary and wrote down the name.

'I'll have my secretary make a reservation for twelve thirty then.'

He shook hands and disappeared as quickly as he had arrived.

The cold wind bit into Frankie's face and legs as they walked to the car. A light fog was beginning to settle as they got into the car and drove out of the car park. The road out of Sheffield was almost empty. In fact, thought Albert, there was only one other car on the road.

The fog thickened as soon as they left the city behind and drove through the countryside. Luckily, there was little traffic except for the car behind them, which maintained its distance, never getting close enough to overtake them.

Albert pushed down the accelerator.

'Why are you driving so quickly?' asked Frankie. 'It's very foggy. Isn't that dangerous?'

'I think we're being followed,' he replied. 'In fact, I'm sure of it. Why, I don't know, as we're only driving back home. I mean they could just go home and wait for us there. There's no need to follow us.'

'Maybe they don't know that. Someone who saw us with Captain Ryder. And they want to know who we are.'

'Well, they are following us. They've started driving faster now. And now I'll slow down.'

'What are they doing?'

'They've slowed down too.'

Frankie sighed.

'Oh, for Pete's sake. I'm so fed up with this. Is there somewhere we can stop? A hotel? Spend the night there and continue in the morning. Look there, Albert, at the side of the road. Follow the indications. That's a hotel.'

Albert turned off the main road and followed a dark lane down to the car park of a brightly lit building advertising hotel vacancies.

The Chestnut Tree.

They parked and got out of the car.

'Have they followed us in?' asked Frankie.

Albert looked back towards the exit leading to the main road.

'No, but they may be waiting to see if we come out again. I don't think there is any other exit from this car park. We can only drive out onto the main road again.'

'So,' said Frankie, 'they either sleep in the car all night or get a room at our hotel.'

'Or go back to Sheffield,' added Albert.

'Look,' he continued, 'they seem to have some kind of café in the entrance. Let's have another cup of coffee and decide what we're going to do. What do you think Frankie?'

They went in and sat at a table overlooking the entrance to the car park. There were a few residents sitting at other tables, some of them drinking others just chatting, a few loners reading books or newspapers.

'That music from the restaurant is still haunting me,' said Frankie. 'There's a poem I remember now. My father used to repeat it.

"Last night I saw upon the stair,

A little man who wasn't there.

He wasn't there again today.

Oh, how I wish he'd go away".'

'Oh yes,' said Albert. 'It's very famous. American, I think.'

'That was the song in the restaurant. The little man who wasn't there. But my father would repeat it and then I would remember. The discs. And how to place them in the machine.'

Albert looked at her.

'What do you mean?'

'The discs have to be introduced in the correct order. If they aren't, not only will the machine not work, but it will auto destruct.'

'And what is the correct order?'

'Oh, it's quite straightforward. If you know. And if you don't well that's the machine knackered.'

'Could you do it?'

Frankie shrugged.

'I don't know. It came to me. Suddenly. But now I'm not sure.'

'Albert,' she said 'I don't want to stay here. Let's go home. To your house.'

'What about those people following us?'

'Oh,' said Frankie. 'They're bound to have gone by now. They haven't followed us into the car park. Unless they're waiting outside. And I bet they aren't. What I do know is I don't want to sleep here. Let's go!'

The main road was empty when they turned into it and they did not encounter another vehicle until they overtook a lorry about twenty minutes later. Another forty minutes saw them entering the road where they lived.

Albert pulled up some distance from their houses.

'You think they're waiting for us?' asked Frankie.

'I don't know what to think,' answered Albert. 'I just don't want to walk into a trap.'

They sat in the car for a while watching the street. There were a number of cars parked some of which Frankie recognized as belonging to neighbours. One or two, she would say, she had never seen before.

Suddenly the lights of a car appeared at the end of the road. A car pulled up in front of her house but on the opposite side. The driver turned off the lights, but no one got out of the car.

'That's what we were waiting for,' said Albert. 'I can't remember very well, but this could be the car that was following us. They knew where we lived and now they're waiting for us.'

'Do you think they found out we weren't staying in the hotel?' asked Frankie. 'What do you think they want?'

Albert snorted.

'Well, what do you think? Might be the discs? But who are they? Are these friends of Captain Ryder or of Gallagher or even Salvador Jimenez?'

The car door opened and a man who had been sitting in the passenger seat got out, crossed the road and stopped outside Frankie's house.

He walked to the front door. After a few minutes he went to the side of the house and disappeared from view.

Without a word, Albert slipped out of the car and crept along the pavement towards Frankie's house. He kept himself hidden in the shadows until he moved through the open side entrance.

He paused behind some bushes next to a neighbour's fence and listened until he heard the man's footsteps at the back of the house. He moved noiselessly towards the intruder who seemed to be trying the bay windows at the back of the house.

It was the work of a moment to slip his hands under the man's armpits and fold them around the back of his neck and at the same time push his knees into the small of his back. The man started with an agonizing howl.

'You're a dead man if you don't answer my questions very quickly,' whispered Albert, applying more pressure on the back of the man's neck.

'Albert, please, it's me Pailthorpe,' the man gasped. 'John Pailthorpe.'

'And in the car? Who's in the car?'

'My colleague, Mark Lang. You met him that day at the café with Beryl.'

'Why have you been following us?'

Albert pushed his hands into the back of his neck again. Pailthorpe whimpered slightly.

'You don't have to do that, Albert. We only wanted to know where you were going.'

'Why? Who wants to know?'

'You know who. Mr. Gallagher.'

Albert suddenly let go of Pailthorpe. The man turned round weakly and faced him. Albert punched him under the chin. Pailthorpe slumped to the ground. Albert reached under the man's jacket and pulled out his revolver.

Leaving the unconscious form, he slunk back along the side wall into Frankie's little front garden, over the low wall to the step leading to his front door. There he crouched behind a bush next to the step.

He watched the car on the other side of the road. The driver of the car got out of the car and walked to Albert's front gate, pushed it open and walked up to the front door.

'Hold it right there, buster.'

Albert pushed the butt of the revolver into his back. Lang raised his arms into the air and Albert frisked him, finding another pistol in a holster, under the lapel of his jacket.

He hit him on the back of his neck with the gun. Lang slumped to the ground.

'Albert, are you all right?' Frankie whispered.

'Frankie, where did you come from? You were supposed to stay in the car.'

'You didn't say anything to me. I came to warn you when the other guy got out of the car. But you seem to have managed very well. Where is the first man?'

'Oh, he's in your back garden, unconscious. They're the Americans who were with Beryl that time we were with Bernard in the café. They work for Gallagher. They've been following us all day.'

'Have you searched their car?' asked Frankie. 'There might be some kind of clue there.'

'Good idea,' said Albert.

He went into the house and came out with a torch. They went over to the car. In the glove compartment there was another pistol which Albert took.

Nothing in the boot nor in the back seat. Albert sat in the driver's seat a moment watching the road and what could be seen of their houses. On a sudden whim, he pulled down the sun shade. There was a pouch. He put his hand in and pulled out an Argentinian passport and a plane ticket.

He opened the passport. Adriano Pironti. Born 1935. Buenos Aires, Argentina. Photo Mark Lang.

He looked at the plane ticket. A flight to Buenos Aires the following week. He put both the passport and the ticket back in the pouch.

They walked back to the front door. Lang was still lying on the ground next to the front step, but Frankie could make out the figure of the other man wobbling out of her front garden, towards the parked car on the other side of the road.

Albert bent down and shook Lang. The man groaned and sat up.

'You'd better get a move on, or he'll go without you,' Albert chuckled.

He helped the man to his feet and pointed him in the direction of the gate. The man staggered down the path and crossed the road to the car.

Frankie and Albert stood until they heard the sound of the motor starting. The car drove off and they went into the house.

## Chapter Thirty-Six

'Do you remember the last time we were here?' asked Frankie. 'With Mrs. Petersen?'

They walked into the dark panelled lounge of the American Steak House at exactly half past twelve.

The waiter showed them to the table which had been reserved for them and they sat down. In the background they could hear the live music from the resident pianist. The restaurant was fairly full.

Captain Ryder was nowhere to be seen.

'I expected him to be punctual, being a military man,' said Frankie.

The drinks waiter took their order. Frankie asked for a Coke and Albert bourbon with ice. The drinks arrived and they drank and smoked while they waited.

'It seems ages since I was here with Mrs. Petersen, but it's only been a couple of weeks,' said Frankie. 'So much has happened since then.'

'And Mrs. Petersen is gone', explained Albert. 'Not to mention, Salvador Jimenez and Daniel Bessel.'

He looked at his watch.

'Do you know it's nearly one o'clock? I don't think Captain Ryder is coming,' said Albert.

A smart, middle aged waiter came up to their table.

'Excuse me, Miss Frances Cooper?'

Frankie looked up.

'Yes?'

'I have a message from Group Captain Ryder. He sends his apologies as he is unable to keep his appointment with you but was most insistent that both of you dine here as his guests. Shall I bring the menus?'

Frankie looked at Albert, who shrugged in agreement.

'Very well,' said Frankie. 'Did he leave any other message?'

'No, nothing else.'

A waiter brought the menus and took their order.

When he had gone, Frankie looked at Albert and said,

'You know, I've always liked this restaurant and as you told Captain Ryder, it's perhaps my favourite, but I must say I am quite disappointed. I was rather looking forward to seeing Ryder again especially after our little adventure with Beryl's henchmen. I thought he was going to clear everything up for us.'

'You're quite wrong, if you think he's going to do anything other than give us a free lunch,' replied Albert. 'I'm afraid this is something we're going to have to sort out for ourselves.'

The food began to arrive and they started eating. Frankie stayed very quiet, listening to the background music.

'There is something that I think we now know that he doesn't,' replied Frankie.

'What's that?' asked Albert.

'If the discs are not introduced in the proper order the machine will destroy itself. I know that now. And I am probably the only person who knows what that order is.'

'And how do you suddenly know that?' asked Albert.

They finished their dessert and the waiter brought coffee.

Albert lit a cigarette and offered one to Frankie. As she puffed on it she became very thoughtful.

'Albert. It's the music. Like in that restaurant in Sheffield. It's the song and the rhyme. He just played it. "The Little Man Who Wasn't There".'

'I didn't hear anything special.'

'When I hear it, I remember.'

'Each little disc has a symbol,' she went on. 'Each of the three slots also has a symbol. The logical thing would be to place each disc into the slot with the same symbol. But if you do the machine will explode.'

'What is the correct order then?' asked Albert.

'It doesn't matter. So long as you don't put them into the slot with the same symbol.'

'Frankie, how do you know this?'

'Because as everybody has been telling me since I got back to England I was programmed. I knew where the discs were. And I know what to do with them. Gosh, I could have solved all this mystery the day I arrived. All I had to do was listen to the music.'

'That's not true. You've never had the machine.'

'Yes, but Gallagher has it. And the moment he has the discs he'll put them in and destroy it.'

'What if he doesn't? What if he does it right? What if he simply sends the whole lot to Argentina? There must be people there who know how to manage it.'

Frankie looked at him.

'Well then, we call Ryder and tell him. But this is something we'll have to manage ourselves.'

'Excuse me, Mrs. Blakeley and Mr. Tucker.'

The two of them looked up. A waiter was standing next to them with a bottle of champagne in an ice bucket and two glasses on a tray.

'Compliments of Christopher Gallagher,' he smiled.

He uncorked the bottle and skillfully poured out two glasses of the bubbly liquid.

Albert picked up his glass.

'Frankie, a toast to the "Little Man Who Wasn't There".'

They clinked glasses and sipped their drinks.

It was after Albert had poured their second glasses of champagne that Gallagher seemed to slither up to them.

'Hello, you two,' he hissed. 'I hope you like the champagne.'

'This is,' he continued, 'an unexpected pleasure. I've been wanting us to have a little get together as I haven't seen you for quite some time. May I take the liberty of sitting down here with you for a few moments?'

Without waiting for permission, he sat down at the circular table on a chair between the two of them.

'I really have very little to say except that I am now able to offer you sixty thousand pounds for the discs. Thirty thousand when you deliver them and thirty thousand at a later date. You do have the discs?'

'No, I haven't,' replied Frankie.

'Excellent,' he laughed. 'Of course you haven't got them on your person, but by now you have located them and they are under your control. Shall we make an appointment at my hotel for tomorrow morning? That will give you time to get the discs and for me to withdraw funds. How about eleven o'clock?'

'OK.'

Frankie smiled encouragingly.

'It's a date then.'

The Scotsman stood up and bowed slightly.

'Until tomorrow, then.'

He walked off.

Albert took another sip and glanced at her.

'So you're decided?'

She nodded and finished her drink.

## Chapter Thirty-Seven

They left the car in the car park and walked up the steps into the Victorian mansion which was the Highland Village Hotel. Frankie had chosen a colourful combination of jacket and skirt whilst Albert wore a polo neck sweater and sports jacket.

They entered the foyer.

Standing to their right as they walked in, was a middle aged man, well dressed. To their left, was another man, much younger. Frankie looked at both of them with recognition.

They were the newspaper reporters who came to her house the day she arrived. The last thread was untangled.

The older man came forward and led them to Gallagher's apartment.

Gallagher was sitting at his desk at the far end of the room. He made no effort to get up or even look up at his visitors. He sat writing. The phone rang.

He picked it up and muttered in a low voice. He put it down and made another phone call, muttering once again in a low voice.

Frankie and Albert remained near the door. Frankie looked at Albert. He whispered not to move, just to wait.

Finally, Gallagher looked up.

'Well, are you coming in or not?'

Albert spoke raising his voice so as to be sure to be heard.

'Thank you very much. Yes, we will sit on the settee.'

They both went in and sat down.

Gallagher picked up the phone again and muttered into it.

The door opened and the young man they had seen previously walked in.

'If you would like to follow me?'

He led them to Gallagher's desk at the end of the room and showed them two small arm chairs, opposite the desk. They sat down.

The desk was enormous and the armchairs very small, leaving the visitor with the impression that he was a dwarf visiting a giant.

Frankie was sure this arrangement was intentional. The window faced east and the morning sun dazzled them.

'Well,' said Gallagher 'here we are again. Mrs. Blakeley and Mr. Tucker. And you've brought the discs?'

'No,' replied Albert. 'But the discs have been located and are in our possession. But, no, we haven't brought them with us.'

Gallagher snorted with annoyance.

'This is no good at all. I have the two machines, I have the money. But you have not got the discs.'

'The discs can be brought to us at any moment,' replied Frankie. 'That is not a problem. I would like to see the money.'

Gallagher stood up, opened a cupboard under his desk and brought out a small holdall.

'Here you are thirty thousand pounds.'

Frankie got on her feet and looked at him.

'I think we were talking about a larger sum of money than this.'

'Yes, Mrs. Blakeley. But, as I explained, once I have sold the machines to our friends in South America, much more money will be available. Thirty thousand is as much as I can raise at this moment. And this, Mrs. Blakeley, is cash in hand.'

'So the rest of the money you will give me later?'

'The other thirty thousand will be yours as soon as I am reimbursed by my friends abroad. Our arrangement always was half now, half later.'

He went to the desk, opened the holdhall, took out the money and counted it.

Gallagher opened the cupboard again and took out a metallic disc very similar to the one they found in the house near Fallowfield market, covered in strange markings with three very distinct slots each one identified by a symbol.

Gallagher laughed, Frankie thought diabolically.

'They all thought, the Americans, the British, your father, even that silly old spy who lived next door to you, that these were alien markings from a crashed space craft. There was, of course, no such accident, no alien space craft. These are the markings of black magic. Allied scientists spent years trying to penetrate the disc. They didn't realise there were three discs. One which I have kept all these years. And another, which I also have in my cupboard, an empty shell smuggled by a Nazi escaping across the Pyrenees and the other a clever decoy, taken by your father. Impenetrable, but able to baffle scientists for years, as they tried reverse technology to fathom its secrets. The only difference was that the decoy had no slots for the small discs that your father also took with him. He didn't know what do with them but knew they must be important. So he hid them. Only two people knew where they were. And you, Mrs. Blakeley, were one of them.'

'But what does it do?' asked Albert. He stood up and helped Frankie put the money back in the bag.

'What does it do, Mr. Tucker? It emits radio waves. These waves allow you to control a power station, a broadcaster, the defence system of a country. The Germans had it perfected when the end came. Too late for them to use. Himmler used it during his ceremonies in his castle adding to his mystique. Not surprising that the Spanish should want it or rather the little group represented by Salvador Jimenez.'

'This disc Salvador brought from Spain? The one you have in your cupboard. What is it?' asked Frankie.

'An empty shell. However the man who brought it to Madrid believed it to be valuable and so did Jimenez. So we let him believe that even offering him money for it. Jimenez, until he died, believed that he was an important part of the operation.'

'Why did you kill him?' asked Frankie.

'My dear, Mrs. Blakeley. I don't kill people. Jimenez died of natural causes just as reported in the newspapers.'

'A very convenient death,' remarked Albert.

Gallagher laughed again, diabolically.

'How right you are, Mr. Tucker.'

'And where's Bernard?' asked Frankie. 'Salvador was a nasty piece of work, but Bernard?'

'Well, the Frenchman was out of his depth in all this, wasn't he? But really we don't know where he is, do we? He simply disappeared. Anyway, enough of this small talk. Mr. Tucker, the discs.'

'Let me use your phone, privately.'

Gallagher moved to the other end of the room and poured himself a drink. Albert, in a low voice, spoke into the phone.

When he had finished Gallagher returned to the desk.

'Take your money.'

The telephone rang. Gallagher took the call.

'Yes, yes, show them up,' he turned to Albert. 'You've sent a lot of people to bring three discs.'

The door opened almost immediately and three men arrived from a well-known security firm carrying a small bag. Albert signed a receipt and the bag was given to Gallagher who checked the contents.

Albert looked at him.

'We'll be going then. Enjoy your new toy.'

Gallagher smiled, without any expression in his eyes.

'We will be in touch very soon. I see you will be able to see yourself out.'

Frankie, Albert and the three men made their way out of the hotel.

In the car park, Albert put the holdall into the boot of the car. He looked up at the hotel. In the picture window, where Gallagher's office was located he suddenly saw a flash of light. The fire alarm rang. People began leaving the hotel.

Albert and Frankie got into the car.

'Somehow, I don't think we're going to get any more money from Gallagher.'

'Very difficult,' laughed Frankie.

She kissed him. He started the car and they drove down past the landscaped gardens, through the double gates, into the main road.

## The End

Printed in Great Britain
by Amazon

84682204R00220